*Necrotrivia*
VS
SKULL

*to Shell Scott – Clown Prince of the LCD Private Dicks*

# Necrotrivia
## vs
## SKULL

*Jeremy Clarke*

*Fourth Estate* • *London*

First published in Great Britain in 1989 by
Fourth Estate Limited
113 Westbourne Grove
London W2 4UP

British Library Cataloguing in Publication Data

Clarke, Jeremy
    Necrotrivia vs. skull
    I. Title
    813'.54 [F]

    ISBN 0–947795–29–4

Phototypeset in Garamond by Input Typesetting Ltd, London
Printed and bound in Great Britain by
Richard Clay Ltd, Bungay, Suffolk

# Contents

# 1

## Shotgun Alien

One o'clock, deep-night-a.m., and no lift since I landed. On a beige highway where the dust is thick enough to hold, my breath is turning to pictograms in the sharp cold. Hands in pockets, my footfalls echo briefly and are then sucked up into the atmosphere.

A car approaches, I feel bright, white-light circles cut me like a cookie. I am a walking multi-dimensional being. You are a sleeping driver. I move into the lane slowly so your headlights illuminate my proto-proletarian everyman face. On the cue of your squealing tyres, I produce a shit-eating grin ear-to-ear. You pull up just parallel and I peer in at you, appreciative. The window rolls down completely.

'Cruel kidnapper?' I ask, smiling.

'Windproof. Rainproof. Lightly-lined.' You tap the roof and seats, inviting me in.

Why the back seat, you wonder, shifting into drive as I relax. Trivial conversation lends itself to boredom, then sleep.

Three a.m. Just you in the front and me in the back. Pretending sleep, I unwrap a handgun – you could call it a working model – and gently indent the trigger, release the safety. You unwrap a fresh deck of smokes. Don't mind if I do . . . The nicotine embroiders my brain. I'm pinned to the moon, Eskimo-bone-needle style, squinting pig-eyed into the midnight sun. Am I high? Man, *I'm high!* Exhale. Smell. Shiver. What could be wrong with a butt on the long ride to town? The drive is becoming an ordeal for you. The highway says: You are sleepy, very sleepy, your eyelids are heavy . . . I guzzle coffee from your thermos and draw deeply on the smoke: my heart is a stampede my pulse is on manoeuvres. What *is* this shit??

I open my window and watch filtered smoke evaporate in the wind. An explosion. A bursting roadside sign. The driver snaps back. He looks surprised.

'Zapped by lightning?'

'Fertiliser brew has a deadly kick,' I purr throatily, stroking the hidden gun-barrel. You're looking in the rear-view mirror at the teetering sign in our wake. I can do anything I put my mind to, but how would you know that? Tell you what, though. I could kill for more of that wild weed and a bucket of caffeine. I may have to. ESP is flying around inside the car, mine unhinged by this rendezvous with density, yours just flashing on mine. Looking as if you've caught a brainwave for the first time, you turn to me, insight cleaving your mediocrity cleanly in half.

'Buttered con slips away from prison?' Breaking the tension is your first mistake. My barrel presses the small of your back. 'Tragic end to driver's story?' you jest, with more hope than conviction.

'Talk with God,' I answer dryly. 'Double-bubble feature drive-in, next left, OK?'

You swerve into a sharp turn and we drive down a dark tube to the matchbox ticket kiosk. You pay and pull into a sparsely occupied lot. The Three Stooges beckon. Larry, Moe and Curly . . . 'Uh-oh,' our car speaker bellows harshly. 'Laugh riot!' you manage to squeeze out with the laboured squawk of an insect about to be dispatched by the bad side of a football cleet. Silencer time. The truth is here and you don't want it. I have no more time for your witless conversation. You turn to see me, a pleading expression sliding down your face. High beam it is. To the heart. Itching and jumping like a cat on fire, your soul is already out for trash when, shaking like a waxed leaf falling from a book, you slump against the wheel. I poke at the symmetrical wound through your barely soiled shirt. Now I am the main attraction. The door opens a crack. I climb over onto the front seat and you fall lifeless onto cold asphalt. Next to me two teenagers shriek in unison at the compass-point entry hole. Blood from your leaky faucet smears the littered pavement. I pull out my dog-eared *Dictionary of American Slang*. 'Eat Lead!'

You eat dust instead, as I power out of the lot. The snack kiosk draws me out of the car. I buy a wallet's worth of junk food and start my rotation diet then and there.

It's six a.m. I'm imagining pedestrians with targets on their chests, asking myself how much of this trippy tourism I can handle. Candy and cola is stacked up on the back seat – a 666-pack or *what*?

A local cop is tailing me. On this piece of Earth you think you're truly safe but you may be betrayed, officer. We're just animals. Anything is possible, you foolish man. You're bloated on beer and potato chips, the willing victim of too many afternoon sportscasts. I'd like to put an extra buttonhole on your shirt, asshole. You're in such a hurry you miss the passer-by until his snapped arm hits your windshield and cracked fingernails clutch the chrome. Your view blocked, you skid into the hard shoulder. I pull ahead, the wind whistling through my vehicle with a doggy whine.

I hear your accident on the wind, see the man rolling in glass, raking his face. How revolting. I'm low on gas. A Mars bar might help, too . . . Or make me homesick, ha ha ha . . . Or just sick.

At a gas station the pump jockey is wiping my windows. Back and forth go his hands, but small streaks of dirt remain. You smile and I mimic your waving hands. You look into my eyes, the second split by your decision. But it's too late for you to find a new life. One hand jerks signals to me across a void. How can I tell you?

3

Your time has run all out and don't look back because tomorrow is here and there is nothing to be afraid of any more.

You're on the ground. An oily rag draped across a leg is the flag on your grease-monkey coffin. Some kind of service is called for. I hold your hand, hold on to the Jello mould of broken consciousness, the squishy-squishy. All the stores are closing and the lights are being dimmed. You are travelling fast to the white light, flipping out. I watch your death instalment-style, feeling love for humanity kindled in my heart. I prop the body in my arms, watching with stilted sympathy as this human animal catches its final bouquet. You're quivering under the water of the one real baptism. 'Isn't this just how it should be?' I'm about to say, but then it's too late.

I go away a little lighter from everyone. I start walking. Standing still bugs me. Coffee has me tanked. Back on the road the sky is above me, plain grey. Love those jellybeans.

One ride later, without death, and I'm feeling really fucking weird. In a small town, rain falling around me, I'm dripping wet in a doorway, watching a puddle for my profile. I kick a magazine that turns to coal slush: 'The King *Is* Alive!' No kidding? I shuffle down a street where the prices are high. Hey, I'm just like you now – I want to be loved, I want to be something, too! This is the great mystery of life: what to do on a Saturday night? Time for some more food.

Inside a greasy spoon the customers acknowledge me by not acknowledging me. Taking a seat at the back, I appreciate the absurdity of my situation. Menu. I could get up and leave, but where would that get me?

A waitress inquires after my order. 'Yes, miss. Toast. Toasted . . . instead of plain.' She flinches. I feel my dictionary through my sodden pants. Oh well, who cares? The skinny kid hobbles away on heels high enough to give her an aerial view. Cosmic is just comic with an 's' thrown in. I've lost all interest in the secrets of the universe since I lost my marbles. It's all coffee-table-book fodder anyhow. Everything at our end of the galaxy is just a photo-spread to you. My toast hits the table, clatters and jars. This isn't nutrition where I come from. Its chemical compo-

4

sition taps out a story on my tongue: life strangled by cancerous tentacles. Hulks are hunched around the place. Old men drool over magazines with colour pictures that taunt them with the places and fun they never got to have. I wonder what all their toothless mewling is about. Who has time for the crap when the stopwatch is jammed in your face? In the tabletop I see myself – there is no person in a face like this. In my hands are lines, in my thoughts are gaps: Did I kill those people? I ask for the bill, trying to speak better. I have to try, although there's no shame in being a heathen here.

I need a bed. MOTEL. The 'In' door leads me to an ugly clerk. My feelings are on rewind while he fumbles in the cash register. The familiar pressure in my chest acts as the barometer of my peculiar intensity. Twenty-five bucks. I throw the bills to the bozo. I don't need this lousy toilet-dimension. Where is the road home? Bed feels like mush. My back and stomach hurt. I'm hungry for more sugar – that shit's *good*. Bright street-light circles of city sun throw shadows on the wall of my room. They crawl across to me. I get up and lean against the low sill. Watch: a skid, a blimp, a house, a lawn, a hearse. A door, a lamp, a rug, a couch. I hear a wine glass falling over. A toy bounces down a driveway. A window opens twice in the same place. This is my own book of my own movie. Hate it? I *love* it!

Back to the bed. I twist the sheets, wipe off the sweat. My experiences are transposing themselves onto each other like three or four recordings on the same cassette.

Everything I know about this bent piece of planet is wrong, and I'll admit it. Laid out on this crappy bed, pumped full of junk food, I wonder at the real extent of my potential debilitation. Living out my favourite fantasies of Earthbound existence is like lancing a boil with a compass. So far it's as gripping as watching leaves turn or a bathtub fill.

Your predeliction for meddling in abstract concepts of the future won't buy much mileage on the highways between Venus and Pluto. Down here you can meditate all you like, but up there it's

5

every vacuum for itself. You're all just so much Bazooka Joe to the Whore of Bubblegum, you sweet Betsy-Junes!

A joke I found at the back of a *Reader's Digest*: Two morons are sitting on the edge of a cliff, a big moron and a little moron. The big moron falls off. Why doesn't the little moron? Because he's a *little mor-on*! Yuk yuk. Earth: a nice planet to visit but can I *live* here?

Surreal is the only word to describe an episode of 'My Favourite Martian' I last saw worlds away. All the science fiction shows polish my apple. 'Star Trek' especially: Who *is* that long-eared asshole with the tickertape claptrap? If you all are waiting on a higher intelligence to rescue you then you best be laying in provisions. What self-respecting higher intelligence is going to sit still for having himself portrayed like a rabbit with a PhD? At school we used to hoot over this stuff!

'UFO' – now that show had some smarts! But 'The Jetsons'? What goes through your minds? Look, I *am* a being of higher intelligence, even if I am forking out my stolen pin money for a family bag of honeyed cashews. The closest thing you've got to reality is 'Bewitched' or 'I Dream Of Jeanie': I used to dream of Jeanie all the time, and getting her out of that stupid bottle ain't the better half of it! One day you're all going to have to jettison this fancy-pants cosmic consciousness schtick and get hip to the fact that higher intelligence isn't a passport to Plan 9. Friends, I spent two years watching your TV and rehearsing your slang, and to be perfectly honest I'd say you couldn't find cosmic consciousness if the gods themselves published a map in the classifieds of the *National Enquirer*. Spaced men and spacemen – ne'er the twain shall meet, and here's why: we've got better things to do with our time. I'm only here by default. So dig: the only genuine alien in this half of the galaxy is a psychopath! You thought we all walked around in jet-packs? Stow it, pilgrim!

I am just as bad as you – no, *superbad* – but with the advantages a cockeyed genius IQ confers.

Hang on! This is GREAT! Jeez – I'm on the local news. Now this is really what I call living. Only been on Earth a few days and

I'm a celebrity. Handy to see all my nefarious deeds reviewed – part of this food problem is memory lapses. Gee, I did *that*?

Well, it doesn't matter. I can seem any way I please and I've already been two people since I last dispatched a peon to the waiting room of The Twilight Zone. What's interesting is all this new TV. It took a while to click – everything I've ever seen is a good twenty years old! Aaargh! Twenty years of TV to catch up on. So many sitcoms and so little time! The cops are pulling out their hair trying to find the mystery killer and the mystery killer is pulling out his hair over the TV page. No wonder everything here seems so weird. Of course I've seen all the intelligence stuff back home, worked on it a lot, but I'm not half as prepared as I ought to be. It's going to be a fair old scramble not to look like the village idiot, and a time-warped one at that.

The news is putting the zap on my head. This planet is more screwy than I thought! Thinking about it, if I just lower my tone more and act as stupid as . . . *humanly* possible I might fit in and no one'll look twice. Worth a try. I didn't stake everything on getting here to let a little thing like a new host on 'The Tonight Show' throw me off. I've got to get ahold of a VCR and study up on this heavy development! I feel like sleeping, but why bother when nothing I can dream will beat this waking wonderland. The lines on the screen wave to me and I wave back. Here I am. Nothing to do but watch the square garbage compactor churn out flat-screen pet food. I rise every day like a cake-mix. Excuse my disordered energy. I'm a take-out person!

What does any of this bullshit accomplish or mean to you? Where I come from none of it is necessary. All I have to do is to wield the word-swords you all fall before so easily, little bits of origami. Where I come from the dustpan and brush of Creation is held steadier than you can possibly imagine.

I had a childhood. I may even have had a child, but to all intents and purposes I am the sonofabitch I never had. Witness my humble beginnings on that other ball of wax in a humble job, waiting to be blown out to this ball. Take me out to the ballgame! Three strikes and I was *out*. I'll never know what came over me, but it was big, black and round.

Yeah, so anyway, where was I? I happened to get off my planet. Out of jail, first, though.

In jail I was an 'A' student, I'll have you know: reading and writing, doing my homework until I lived and breathed your circus-zoo culture, you Western voodoo man, Mr United States of Nightmerica. My mission impossible? To boldly go where no humanoid has gone before, to infiltrate your forever backward world. I dreamed at night of this place, this shopping-centre parking-lot.

Against that backdrop paint my face any way you like, for I am the humanoid of a thousand faces. Gee, but I wish I'd brought my chemistry set! Whatever is happening inside my skin would need a seven-figure budget to put on the big screen. If you don't mind me being blunt – and right about now my mind feels like the rough end of a rubber eraser – this stuff you people eat sucks the big one! Nothing personal – if you're a person, that is. I'm more used to what you'd call low-cal, high-protein whatnots. Where has this heap of garbage been all my life?

The news rolls, and I with it, like a tin can off a conveyor belt from story to story. 'Dead nude found in cornfield'. 'Is ex-cop triple-killer?' Hell, what I pulled off to earn my stretch wouldn't make the kiddies' page down here. And every other minute it's 'Necrotrivia', 'SKULL', 'Necrotrivia', 'SKULL', whoever the heck *they* are. And wars, shit, you got them too! I am a refugee, a criminal of a sort you can't comprehend, but at least in my neck of the galaxy they don't split the long weekends between genocide, fratricide, matricide, patricide and picking sides. Were there ever people happier to die?

There's that pressure in the chest again, a greasy slick of sweat on my forehead and a sick stomach. All the effort and cultivation I put in is peeling like paint stripped off my soul. I'm raw and I know it. Blood pressure low; heartbeat regular; temperature normal; the body functions. Yeah, the TV is OK now but I'm sick of it. Let's see *action*.

8

Down the dark hallway, there he is: ugly boy, silhouetted in the TV glow. Romantic!

'Clean up your planet or perish!'

'Hunh?' Grunt.

'Is your poor English holding you back?' I drop my keys on the desk. He drags them away to their cubbyhole. Make the bill out to who?

'Nobody, sonny.'

'Yeah . . . but . . . who gets the bill? Who pays it?'

I love the suspense. And the question. What happens when he runs out of common sense? Human scribble with a bib for a brain. I want a camera so I can record the moment my patience explodes.

'Weak in math?' That *does* it. On the verge of giving you a bloody tattoo, my reality control locks in. I'm out of past tense and into pluperfect tension. My face less than an inch from yours I bark: 'In all this time no one has come back. Kind of makes you look dumb, Leroy, don't it? Your bargain is you and you can't send it back, jerk! Please hate me, *now*.' 'Leroy' is amused.

The door shuts after me. I'm outa there. I'm going to hitch-hike somewhere interesting. I may be an alien but now we are snapped together like the pieces of a novelty plastic Christmas tree.

A car pulls up. A hand pops out. Shake. A few candies crack when I lean against the door – my pockets are bulging with them. Traffic is light and I don't like to let you go.

Horizontal on the backseat, running my hands over my tranquil, hairless face, feeling the flesh as a tailor strokes velvet, looking for a crease to start on. Minute yet accurate pressure on a corner of my settled mouth eases the line of my lips into a different contour. Road noise interferes subtly with the work, massaging my temples with insistent rumbling. Against the seat the skin stretches, edges out and unrolls. Penetrating warmth surges steadily to nerve endings, distending some features'; muscle tissue contracts and bone shifts. Visualise; actualise.

My health is in my hands, my skin is reborn. Balling up the dead tissue like used bubblegum, I shove it into a crack between seat cushions and straighten up. In pale quarter-moonlight you spot me in the rear-view and see a person once removed from the one you picked up.

'Restore youthful appearance to your face without surgery!' I tell you, and shrug indifferently, with just enough arrogance to check your curiousity. 'The contrast is incredible!'

How do you explain cellular self-transformation to someone whose idea of rapid change is a slot machine? Outside, real rapid change is happening, from country to town. Looks pretty much as I expected: signs growing everywhere and gas on sale. I'm popping jellybeans again, colourful jellybeans. I'm giddy. Luckily, you couldn't read the *National Enquirer* in under an hour, let alone my mind, or you might recognise some popular fiction storyline getting too close for comfort. I wave my hand gaily, a cigarette winking at the end.

'Have you been near death?' he says, chatty.

Well, well, maybe that marshmallow of yours has a hard centre after all, sport! I suppress a giggle, Polyanna braids akimbo, and muster a degree of indignation.

'I don't ask questions. I'm twenty-six years old, very good to my mother, and would very much like to smash up your home. Time is closing in on you. Keep one foot on that pedal and the other clear o'your mouth, *amigo*,' I cajole. These punybrains bore me. What sort of dumbo intellect bugs the obvious until it bites? The temptation to end a life story almost milks me dry but I bite my new lip and serenely yawn, then ask, 'Why were you born?' just for the sake of it. I can't decide if this bozo is a clown or just likes make-up. As it stands I'm ready to gloss his lips twelve shades of red. No, it's too damn easy. I want to sightsee this big country, full of trees and types of lawns. I pause to inhale some carbon-dioxide, another cheap thrill.

'I don't want to be my own worst enemy,' you state with maud-lin bravado when the silence becomes oppressive, 'but how I'd love never to have met you today on this lonely road. I'm too young for this game.'

Who does this hysterical walking gland think I am? His mom? Worse still, his *conscience*? Before I can respond, or at least roll down the wall and free-form the highway with some part-digested potato chips, it starts again.

'I'm always suppressing my feelings to escape any sort of pain either way. My sister – my kid sister – always tells me to work on myself until each piece fits, even if it hurts. Would I like myself if I was a stranger? That's my starter for ten. Then, having come this far, *why* don't I like myself?'

I strain to choke down the laughter. Some people just get booked and put away for multiple murder, but I get stuck with a primal wet screamer. I'd heard about Californians but . . . If I wasn't so generally unsympathetic I would unwrap a fresh copy of *Jonathan Livingston Seagull* and practise some freelance Woolworths tarot psychology on this wretched specimen. Meanwhile, a whole state is zipping by.

'I think my personality is basically in a pretty rotten state, totally undermined by long moods of self-pity and bitterness. Oddly, my cure seems to be to drive myself crazy.'

Do you have to take me with you? I hate to think what this psycho would come up with if I really get threatening. Right, that's the last pine tree I miss! Afraid to be as caustic as impulse demands, I gently implore the driver to pull over at the next gas station, so I can *relieve* myself. I would just as soon trap his nose under the emergency brake and twist but one knows from long experience not to fuck with a fuck-up. I may be psychotic, but I'm not crazy! Oh, look, there's one now.

I dash around the back, key in hand. For a moment the key jams in the lock and I swear. Another ten miles of that sicko salad and I'll be spitting love-hearts. Rattle, battle. I'm in. Just loosen the window and the hinge before the unhinged one loosens me . . . Hoppity-hop and away. But . . . there he is! In front of me, in glorious wreck-nicolour. Aaargh. Understanding the inconsistenc-

11

ies of this world is easy looking at this mess. I smile wanly. He doesn't seem to notice that I have just tried to escape from him.

'A peaceful state of mind. Indeed, my mantra until a very . . .' He whines on. I look, listen and leap. And there he is, the world featherbrain champion, a trail of crimson goo forming a perfect dome on his pursed lips. Stopped the sucker in mid-analysis.

I walk way off.

# 2

## *Showbiz Almost*

After six days straight bingeing on shoplifted candy bars, my eyes, ears and frontal lobes were so crossed that optical illusions looked normal to me and two people walking abreast seemed terrifying. About a mile from the last hole-up, the details of which might turn your stomach around so fast you'd flip, I spotted some pay-by-the-hour flophouse called the Siesta Motel.

The Mexican theme went about as far as syphilis at a pharmacologists convention. This place was strictly from some ugly little pulp novel. Everyone in the place was overweight, except the owner. A TV sat in the 'lounge' with the hired man slumped over it, his rubber tyres piled up as Bob Barker did his carnival thang to millions. The slave loped languidly to reception after I made some scuffling and sniffing sounds. I might have been the outest-law in the West, but this cretin wouldn't have clocked Rambo VII at two yards. You wondered how generations of evolution could end up with people to whom a new fridge was more important than human suffering. Still, it wasn't my problem. Not being human myself, they could suffer all they wanted.

I paid the twenty clams with some purloined plastic and wandered down a narrow, Mactac corridor to one of many lousy rooms. A b&w TV, vintage 1968, glowed sullenly on the wall facing the bed. I threw my coat and shoes at the cheap table and checked out the mattress.

A real gem, this one, with enough support to sleep three bedbugs comfortably. In the event I found dozens. Not averse to company, I squashed a few for practice and let the less limber specimens snuggle down in the stuffing. Meet the conservationist in me! Hey, I have good qualities!

Some gameshow flickered (what else at three a.m. except some soap opera, and I couldn't consider those as other than documentary, to go by the semi-sentient slumber-party garbage I'd encountered since scamming this wicked world). I tried to get a decent picture, flipping the antennae around until I could at least see how fat the bitches in the front row were. The MC worked 'em like a masseur with a cattle prod, building up every prize into a dream of dreams.

The animated crud piped down and the show started: 'State the Obvious – With Your Host . . . Garth Glendale!' Well, give me a hernia and call me a dockworker! This little masterpiece revolved, in a crippled fashion, around the ultimate LCD plot, to wit(less): three MIT/Harvard profs are brought out, badly sedated on elephant and monkey tranks, and set before an audience of steelworkers' wives and roller-derby fans. Glendale dishes out LCD trivia questions about the price of Twinkies and how many pigs it takes to flavour twenty tons of gammon steaks. The trio of unwitting eggheads have to scramble and fry their hardboiled brains trying to guess the answers and appease the crowd. As the opening titles roll, buxom broads give the onlookers rotting fruit and vegetables for the losers. The prof who wins, if you could call it that, gets a grant for his pet research project. The government was so tight on anything that wouldn't kill that these poor highly-educated space cadets were being forced to spout wrestling facts for a living. Shit, where I ran away from these three'd be *loaded!* Well, this was Earth and what did I know?

'I'd make a g-g-great president!' boomed Glendale, decked out in enough plaid to grid a small city. The three big girls had the eggheads cradled in their cleavages just so, wobbling the suckers into a false sense of maternity.

'How do you spend *your* free time?' barked Glendale, waiting for one of the barely-conscious contestants to bite. One appeared to suck in some air but as he did so a bimbo plugged him with a big baby pacifier. The audience ate it up like pigs at sloptime, hooting and hollering as if there was no today, let alone tomorrow.

'Okey-dokey,' bellowed Glendale, swinging his ass from side to side just enough to get a few low-cut blouses in the balcony moving faster, 'Wrestling Round-Up! Who won the WWF title three years running, only to have his crown crushed by a six-ton truck later that same day?' Basically unintelligible, getting by on schmaltz, budget sensuality and car-salesman melodrama alone, Glendale bit on the question with dissonant doughnut diction. His post-Brooklyn accent flattened every syllable ruthlessly.

The three PhDs just shrugged, dribbled (wiped obligingly by the lovely models behind them) and moaned, their whimpers goading the audience into an orgy of produce-pelting. Covered in plant material best left on the shelf for a teenager to collect and dump, these once-dignified men of science might as well have hung up their mortarboards there and then. No Dean in his right mind would trust any of these narcoticised nobodies with getting a newspaper from a kiosk, let alone researching dickola.

Glendale hopped nimbly from question to question, from game to game, his ass on fire, pincers for eyes. The shouting, heaving mass were about to burst the stands, into the up-close downfall of the intellectual classes to the point of delirium. Glendale, apparently a closet NLP man, held them back with the odd Moses flourish and tonal variation.

Finally, the three lumpen contestants were released by the three bosomy babes and fell on the floor. Garth Glendale, effervescent, grinned happily at the Humpty Dumptys sprawled on the studio carpet and blew kisses to some homely housewives hovering perilously close to his aftershave. He leered at the front row, swelling his top lip noticeably to imprint his stinking saliva on a few unbelievably lucky cheeks.

15

'Wellllll, ladies and gents! Didn't we have fun?' Glendale asked, peaking with a violent final syllable that was sharp enough to cut through a chain-link fence. 'Life after Death? Scientists release new evidence!' he shouted, pointing gaily to the one egghead who hadn't entirely cracked as he rolled painfully out from behind the chairs, prodded by a pointy shoe. 'Ten dollars for your jokes!' heaved GG, and his slaves ran the length and breadth of the crowd madly doling out frogskins for every sick one-liner improvised at the expense of the scholarly slobs laid out there like so much soiled stationery.

The music arose, an MOR classic with muzak touches. Glendale flounced off set, trailing stuffed toys for the ladies in the audience.

I swallowed hard and kicked the set with my bare foot. Sleep came quickly and, in my dream, surrounded by Garth's ham-thighed hostesses, so did I.

# 3

## Sweet Dreams, Baby

I woke up two days later. *Spacelag*? At this rate holding down a job was going to be a killer. And, I began to think, I wasn't . . . going to be a killer, that is. Whatever happened to the soulless psycho I knew and loved? It definitely had a lot to do with what I was eating, but I couldn't help myself. Except for the fact that my gears seemed to be slipping badly, I didn't care. Being a murderer is OK for a day or two, but making it into a hobby was going to be more trouble than it was worth. Besides which, down here I wanted to be one of the boys; I hadn't spent months boring up Earth culture only to end up behind bars. The bars I wanted to be behind all had glasses on them . . .

The Siesta was wearing thin, so I set my sights on hitting the big city, which I knew to be one day's hitching away. But with my propensity for polishing off car-share enthusiasts, I chose public transport.

Back in reception the smiling owner took another twenty. 'Staying another night?' he asked pleasantly. The question was so assinine - I'd just handed in my keys – that I didn't deign to dignify it with even a grunt. I smirked ambiguously and skulked back down the Mactac.

In my room I donned shirt and socks and scanned the local rag. Nothing in there except grocery stores ads . . . I had to split this seedy barn. After finishing a box of Frosted Flakes I felt up to scratch and headed for the highway.

The open road beckoned, the wind was in my hair, the sun was up, and other stock road phrases, but the scenic route held little interest as the bus pulled into the express lane and I pulled into some timely reflection.

I'd made it to this dumb planet, finally, and it wasn't any worse or better than I'd expected. As for my psychotic episodes, they were over. Something inside had clicked and given way; I would just have to steer clear of certain inflammatory brand names, particularly anything with a creme centre. I was glad to be here. I'd never liked it at home and no one understood me . . . Maybe I sound like a teenager in some nickel-and-dime romantic photomag, but that was the long and short story of it. I had simply dropped out from one world into another, but here the stuff I did wasn't so much unprecedented as inevitable.

Maybe an hour later the skyline of Babylon sprouted on a hazy brown horizon. The fumes intoxicated me. I could see what they meant by a Clean Air Act – this was about the *worst* acting I'd ever seen. I felt like Kojak as the skyscrapers flew by and then slowed up as the traffic began its spidery crawl to the central station. Everyone looked miserable. I was going to be right at home!

Disorientation bottomed out and a fierce need to push my energy down every crack and corner of this zoo consumed me. Hands went to pockets, moved lumps of sugar mouthwards. Nose to the glass, I strained, rubbernecked, whooped, gawped and eyeballed. The bus hum soothed the savage in me. Here I was, a country mouse entering a fat trap, nothing to lose and everything to gain, a moth to the flame.

I looked back at a big blinking neon hologram: NECROTRAK II. Something in my clouded subconscious buzzed briefly. I registered subliminal input but then, like a fish leaving a circle of light, the impulse to pinpoint it flicked away. Necrotrivia: Just one more name on one more sign.

Just one more name *nothing!*

The city enwrapped me. I was alert and expectant as the haze around my head filled my lungs. I breathed laboriously, occasionally scraping out my nostrils, rubbing black snot 'twixt thumb and forefinger, and dropping the degraded strings of mucus in the aisles. My system didn't want any part of this, but I did. I was happy. With my sweeties, pocket money and guidebook, I'd be burning the banal at both ends by nightfall. I was kingpin in the alley of my choice.

Signs everywhere. I tried to read them all at once, my eyes going off at divergent angles, plastered willy-nilly to colourful consumer flypaper. There it was again: NECROTRAK II: TAKE A MONTH'S VACATION FROM SHAVING! with a picture of some hambone stroking his silken mug.

Skeletons sleeping in cardboard boxes; paraplegics parking cars. Dog eating dog food. An old house, still as death, with peeling doors and rusted locks. Streets burned, played and dealt out. A city sucking in worried men, chewing on life. These people were the fast food of the gods, hu-*manna* fried deep in the fat of a far-out fate.

Where to go? My skin was still tight. Every so often it wrenched my cheeks, stretching like a drumskin. It was distracting to suddenly have one cheek fall down. 'Have a nice day,' the busdriver remarked as I pushed the slack pouch into place again and clambered off the bus.

I got on the subway and boy was it ugly. No one looked at me but everyone was looking. Before I sat down I had to sweep a pile of old papers away, scattering them across the feet of flanking commuters.

Breathing in nervous silent puffs, the passengers' eyes flitted from one vacant area to another until all the unoccupied space was exhausted. Then their feet provided the essential diversion. Learning fast I fixed my gaze on the window across the aisle. The cement walls flew past. I looked at the reflections of others and their reflections looked back: more pockmarked concrete. The air was stifling. This bit was better on TV. The guy next to me tagged me, leaned over, pointed at the woman across the aisle and whispered:

'Attractive woman, fifty-four, five feet four. Looking for honest, sincere, well-mannered, financially secure gentleman who enjoys outdoors, dining out, movies, sports.' He raised his shaggy eyebrows suggestively. 'No perverts,' I finished, stopped for words.

On the platform a crowd peered in. I pushed through the herd. Did anyone notice my chin was off-centre for a moment? One woman admonished me and I looked at her so hard her false teeth rattled. I might have ruined her day. This ugly train had ruined mine.

A chunk of busy humanity shunted me aside as I paused to think. The busdriver had jotted down a few flophouse names and numbers for me and I got directions to the first. I was tired; the steady diet of crap was overtaxing my resources.

On the way a child walks up to me. What do I say? We might see things much the same, being retarded. Towering above him, I bend from the waist. He points a toy raygun at me and his tiny trigger-finger presses hard. Sparks spit out.

It's all going to be weirder than I'd imagined. I take the raygun and train it on a passerby, grimacing suitably to entertain the little feller. He's hep, waiting for his gun to really kill something. What sort of place is that? Look at the *name* of that movie: '76 Slices Killed Marie'.

'I'm six years old.'

'Bang!' Mommy appears from around a corner and jerks junior away. His screams are lost in the roar of traffic.

'Kid-haters form strange society,' I call after Mommy.


If I'd followed my nose I'd have ended up a tailpipe so I felt my way towards a slimy room above a tumbledown shoe store. There were other rooms, three I think. I didn't have any moving to do so I just paid the landlady, a fat old hag whose face was veined with forking capillaries like a close-up of some malignant virus. The room was habitable despite the dried-out Kleenex plugging the roach holes. The stake for the dump was hefty, considering its condition, and left me a little short. So what, I had sightseeing to do!

Time to go shopping. A window display magnetises my attention. The shelves buckle under tins of human food and tins of pet food which I can't tell apart. Instead I single out a bag of sugar, instant java and a jumbo cola. I've got to stop this wackiness, but accidents will happen. I grab a box of crackers smeared with goo and fill my hands with candy bars. Clinking and rustling I make my way to the cash register. In the line I have time to inspect the news-stand, racks full of sin-fodder, the Mayflower mentality to the max. My turn comes and I throw a heap of change to the friendly neighbourhood grocer and smile. And smile and smile and smile. The proprietor gets shifty, scratching his arms and biting his lip. The whole store is smiling at absolutely nothing. I shake my fuzzy head, chuckle and walk out, gnawing at the sticky core of a particularly spectacular chocolate phallus.

About a block later I'm already on my last bar, calories coursing through me. It's wonderful to peel back the wrapping and see all that waxy brown crud crackling and sliding and slipping between tooth and cheek – sometimes getting right down in the gums! Sweet muck and nuts on the roof of my mouth. Half-way down the next block I'm at the sugar, dissolving the granules on my tongue. It's delicious. It has to stop.

At the intersection I can't cross. Paralysed. From the ground up every single cell is shouting. I feel fantastic, in the truest sense. Black and white with a cherry on top, a Sara Lee Black Forest fire. I'm a Christmas tree about to peak. Legs trembling, melting into the sidewalk. Numb-Bo. I propel myself into an alley and slide down the wall, stupefied, on a pile of rotting mattresses, one hand palpitating in the sugar bag.

I confirmed, to my mild chagrin, that I *was* going retrograde. The constant carousel of fast food and junk food had turned my guts to fast junk, but a junk fast was out of the question. Where would

I be without my Instant Breakfast? Ugh! I was a native. Ugga-bugga . . .

Unforseeably, the food and other enviromental factors were rendering me incapable of meeting my genetic spec. My face had assumed a permanent expression, my muscles were atrophied and slack. The reality of it hung around me like a life sentence: my alien-contact high had hit a permanent plateau. Despite all this life was so damn *easy*. I had, as they say, actually *mellowed out* – roasted like coffee – since my arrival. Maybe I was becoming human, but how long could I take it? Gee . . . indefinitely. I was having big fun, lost in a crazy fog of do-easy. I was a cardboard cut-out ready to join the parade.

To mark this, I sought female company. One more scene to work into my ideal script, culled from numberless late shows relayed up the light-years. Now I could truly use those lessons to go to the front of the class. Meeting a girl was the next page, the next stage, in my programme.

The streets were jammed with late-night shoppers and habitual strollers. I could positively feel myself being changed, but into *what*? My theorising was just a wet dream in a sponge: wring it out tight and you'd see the holes in it.

I walked into the first bar I saw, a foul, dark cellar lined with old pinball machines, soggy beermats and people who needed more cosmetic surgery than they could afford just to look human again. Fragmentary conversation zipped around like deflating balloons, got caught in the cobwebs and bounced off the round, fluorescent lamps painted with various logos. 'Welcome to Prole City, USA,' I thought. 'Please turn out the beer signs when you leave.'

Surveying the castaways, I spotted one relatively attractive specimen, aged about thirty. She had a once-wholesome face, now slightly wrinkled at the edges, chapped hands and she wore squarish, tinted designer glasses that turned her head into twin TV screens. What channels could you tune in on that, I asked myself. Well, I sidled up to her and started to order. She'd noticed me; there weren't a lot of customers and what there was made her look like Miss America. The bartender, a worldly-wise and weary

22

working-class stiff, deftly dropped both my colas before me, silently mocking me for a soft drinker, obviously unaware that for me the glucose and additives permeating my sickly brew were more than enough to keep my inhibitions at bay. I was sipping gingerly and eyeing Miss America from the corner of my eagle eye, when she suddenly began speaking . . . to *me*. Not terribly surprising, but as the first real contact with the species, quite personally tantalising.

'I could have killed myself if I hadn't been afraid I'd botch that up, too,' she began placidly, 'I'm still licking my wounds after eleven years, but I've got that fighting spirit again.'

'Depressed man cuts off own head,' I said helpfully.

She continued looking at me. I wasn't uneasy but curious.

'Mom's ghost calls daughter to thank her for the funeral,' she came back.

This was getting moribund but I figured she was as good a haul as any and encouraged her to reel off her miserable list of misfortune.

I flattered her, she blushed. 'What's in a blush? Lots, say analysts!' She cheered up a bit. I put my hand on her leg – I'd seen it done in numerous TV movies and, wouldn't you know it, she didn't move. I took a good look at her up close – she was OK. Her rusty curls settled gently on rounded shoulders, dragged down by thirty-four inches that wasn't muscle. A skimpy skirt hugged fleshy, substantial thighs. I stroked her tentatively, feeling about the biggest heel in history but tempted to see how far I could push my luck, not to mention my pinky.

'Wife gets disease from her lover, then passes it on to her hubby, who gives it to his mistress,' she said matter-of-factly. I withdrew my hand, wiped it and laid it on the bar. The last thing I needed was running sores; I was already practically a leper without wearing a sandwich-board. I appreciated her tip-off, patted her thigh, or it could have been her ass, and made my way out. Phone sex seemed appealing but back at the apartment all the lines were busy. I was dog-tired and settled for the late movie, some caramel popcorn and about a pound of loose toffees. It was getting so I knew which junk took me up and which set me down, and right now I was taxiing in for a landing. After that I'd be ready to join Mary Poppins on the ceiling. Mary Poppins: now there was a real doll. I remembered her from some ancient broadcast and even then, surrounded by a vastly superior civilisation, her umbrella and garters got me panting. I don't know what was getting into me, but it sure was harder to digest than ingest. I toyed with taking an extended break from refined foods. Rolling a rogue toffee in one finger and stirring a coke float with the other, I considered the quite literally sticky state I was in. I couldn't cross the room without imitating a symphony in cellophane, the crunchy refrains resounding as my teeth bit off more than they could chew again. I really liked separating a cream sandwich cookie, licking off the icing like a cat and then stacking the biscuit for future reverence. Later on, when the pink popcorn and Red Hots were all gone, I'd go back to the biscuits and systematically eat them all.

For a while I distracted myself from snack-bar scoffing with snack-bar sculpture: a box of toothpicks, some Elmer's glue and a dozen choc-rods. My Eiffel Tower was a real show-stopper. As a hobby, dissecting confectionery would take some beating, but I had to penetrate the mystery of my insidious slavery to those tasty teething rings. And what I did to a donut . . .

I stopped a few trolleys when I left the all-night store with a box full of the shit – a glittering treasure trove of wrappers and cartons. From candy necklaces to Love Hearts to the promise of the Black Magic box, I researched the field devotedly, leaning over my trolley aisle after aisle, comparing prices, ingredients and packaging. I made goddamn lists! The car order boys were dumbfounded when I schlepped by with my twenty-pound haul. I winked, said 'Party!' and they shook their heads as the electric doors whispered behind my bent back. Half-way through that boxful, with my guts one big medicine ball, I contemplated abstention again. But come two a.m., with a hellish fever and an itch that wouldn't stop, I faltered and fell from grace into a family-pack of cupcakes, two boxes of choc-rolls, a six-pack of spicy beef flavour potato chips and a litre and a half of cream soda. I lit up a candy cigarette, sliced open a jawbreaker and got on down.

The next morning I started all over again. Crunchy peanut butter on Oreos and a Gatorade chaser with a spritzer of ready-made Kool-Aid got my gander up. A Pop-Tart or two, some Captain Crunch under banana milk and I was ready to break down the pyramids. The lunch menu would grow hair on a rock, so I won't make you suffer it. About that time I tried a microwaveburger but animal produce, in the main, I found vulgar. Ironically, however, I rivalled the world's finest zoos with my collection of diverse animal crackers and jelly teddy bears. The hardcore stuff – like five-cent false teeth made of 100 per cent confectioner's sugar – I saved conscientiously for emergencies.

Daily, the bag would be dragged in and deposited by the fridge. Ice-cold chocolate helped bring down my temperature. The days piled up with the papers and the pastries and the penny candies. I should have had a PhD but what I ended up with was bleeding gums, bloat and skin four shades of green. What, worry, me? I was now part of a sick society and, by God, if my brief didn't include being sick, what kind of crackpot chameleon was I? Eat, drink and be constipated: such was my motto as a mortal. If I'd brought shares in Rolaids the week I started on them I'd be a rich man by now.

Before long I was down to two bars, a forty-ounce Coke and half a deck of Popeye cigarettes. It was time to look for work. Paradoxically, perhaps, I was both over- and under-qualified. But I'd come to death grips with the irrefutable fact that, barring the intercession of ALFs – huh, that'd be rich! – I was here to stay. If I wasn't human now then I was going to have to start trying harder. This was like a dog trying to become a flea, but as far as I was concerned a flea fat on blood-sugar was better than a dog without a bone. I went job-hunting, foresworn to take the first job I found.

I hadn't been walking too long, bristling at every distasteful jostling from streams of piddling pedestrians, when I found a cleaning agency called Spic 'n' Span. My slang dictionary led me to assume it was operated by Hispanics but inside the small office was a matronly Jewish woman and her young daughter, looking miserable as only a teenager kept from heavy petting can. I joined the line of students and assorted nogoodniks snaking out the door and was eventually registered. The deal was ten green frogskins for two smelly hours and I arbitrarily selected two jobs, scrawled the directions on my palm and jauntily went off to meet my homemaker.

I arrived punctually for job one and was greeted by a stacked spinster wearing a tight red sweater and frayed black pumps. 'Man sells himself into slavery,' she mused, giving me the once over as if I was a prize heffer. She led me about the house, showed me the trouble spots. When we came across a photo of herself at about thirty, she sighed: 'I went from stout to stunning in fourteen days . . . and back.'

She handed me a mop and pail and other tools of the slave trade and left me to my own dirt-destabilising devices. 'When reality doesn't match your expectations . . .' I said out loud to none but an ancient rubber duck and Mr Clean, then started in with the circular sponge motions. I overheard my employer on the blower yakking to a friend: 'Thermal cellulite removal . . . not heavy, greasy, oily or perfumed . . . bosom beauty . . . a must for every household . . .' The mundane whining nearly overwhelmed the gritty emanations of my ministrations as I cracked the whip around the filthy bathroom and went on to vacuum at length, the hum and vacuous roar dulling my latent disgust for myself. What the hell did I think I was doing, selling myself short, being a loser!?

Over lunch Ms Yurthchuk bored me senseless. I gratefully wolfed milk and cookies before tackling the bedroom and living room, both incredibly uninteresting apart from a bubblegum-machine aquarium in the latter with a dead goldfish in it. The algae was so thick I had to scoop it up with a ladle.

I left half way through the third hour, feeling more liberated than Europe on VE Day. The prospect of another bout of scumscraping turned my turnip, but I went to job two like a lamb to the shearer. This time it was a house inhabited by a harried housewife. A little brat ran around hurling toys and food after me but I managed to stop myself strangling him by reciting some pop mantra I'd seen in an ad. 'Six-year-old boy gives birth,' remarked Mrs America as she showed me a toilet besmirched by a bad case of protracted potty training. Little Alf encamped himself at the threshold, mocking me as I wiped away the faeces. 'What a difference a day makes,' the pleased customer said, as if flattery might curb my desire to take her son and feed him into the Cuisinart feet first. Chop the legs, grate the hips, shred the torso, liquidise the head . . . Oh, well. I took my ten and left, really determined this time to break free, emancipate and otherwise rise above. A small ad in the back of my daily promised 'authentic' diplomas so I stopped at the PO and sent away for six assorted qualifications. No damn way I was going to be a cleaner too long. I had places to go, people to see, things to do . . . OK, *I didn't*, but at least I could not do it in style.


I got in about sunset carrying a few bags of crap and a pile of tabloids, ready to eat, drink, not-think and be merry. I'd found a budget clothing place down the street and invested in some ugly, cheap jeans and shirts, ten per cent cotton jobs that were drip-dry in case you got sick of them and tried to drown them. What did I care? I was taking minimum wage for a job a performing seal would turn its nose up at and right now, due to unseen but all-too tangible internal redecoration, I couldn't bark much or bite at all.

I flipped on the TV and scanned a few pages of the tabloids but couldn't fasten my interest. A bowl of Cheesies, a few diet colas and a self-heating slice of grease later I felt nearly human, in other words, sick. When in Rome do as the Romans do: gorge yourself until you puke. The news carried some items of passing note: some big operator called SKULL had got into a dungheap of trouble on a garbage haulage contract. They'd developed a 'superscow' that plied the sea lanes relocating trash, but finally one day ran out of space. SKULL pioneered a scheme whereby some dirt poor Third World series winner would cancel its horrendous debts by agreeing to let them relocate the population of some stack-a-jack shanty town in vacated barrios in east LA, mostly derelict since the gangs had moved to Silicon Valley. Then the 'superscow' would landfill the ex-hovels with trash. It was all going according to plan, the natives bought off with ghetto blasters, food processors and a good video trade-in allowance, when an untoward breeze blew millions of cubic feet of bellyaching poison right into the centre of the capital city somewhere south of the Equator. SKULL were going to get out of it all right, but the head of the company, Sandy Silence had to pop up for a public apology. You couldn't hear contrition in his voice, in fact I figured he was miming, but at least everyone knew where not to go for a vacation.

I was chomping Cheesies, getting that nice film of additives on my plaque, when I spotted a devilish roach making a beeline for some garbage I had stewing in a plastic bag. Immediately I put Plan A into operation, grabbing my disposable lighter and laying a trail of lighter fuel like a noose around the little beastie (we have bugs where I come from too, y'know). Seconds later the insect was pacing in consternation, encircled in a ring of fire. I slotted in my Johnny Cash tape (49¢!) to offer up a musical tribute. Then I picked up a big flat rock I'd brought in from the parking lot down the street and dropped it on the fucker from six feet. When I lifted up the rock, the roach just looked up as if to say 'Sounds big, jerk,' and leaned on his spindly legs. I stamped out the flames and let the little fella go back down a hole. Who was I to stand in the way of evolution?

Returning to my mangy La-Zee-Boy, feet up and mouth open to receive the salted sacrament, I watched the dancing images and went into a user-friendly coma. I really had dick to bitch about: I'd killed and not been caught, thanks to my face-saving; found lodging and employment; adjusted to this place as much as possible . . . Anyhow, there was no way I could go back now.

Feeling utterly self-satisfied, I leafed through a TV Guide. As I was zoning out, a sprightly ad for a fast-food chain came on – they were recruiting – and I decided to go for it. I was losing interest in cleaning. The fast-food joint didn't pay any better but at least I'd be able to minimise conversation and get free triple-thick shakes thrown in.

# 4

## Pie In The Sty

The edges of the blue blinds glowed eerily. It must be day. My stomach felt full of sponge marbles and a long read in the john didn't do much except get me through another chapter of the stupid detective novel I'd roped myself into finishing. The kitchen looked distinctly unappetising. I knocked some empty wrappers onto the floor for the bugs and flipped the lid off a jar of peanut butter, dipping chocolate into it, then washing down the wicked wedges with flat fizzy. Then I remembered, holy cow, I'm on the afternoon shift, *today*!

Mega-bummer! It's twelve-thirty already and I have to be on-line at two. Why-oh-why did I apply to that fry-sty? Pleased at my rhyme I pitched a ball of stale bread at some empties for a while, then dressed in my creaseless synthetic duds. I'm going to like being raped by this dumb planet, I tittered, high from the pb, burping contentedly, oblong bubbles of cola breath nearly visible in the dingy light. I threw a few clams in my pocket, checked for subway tokens and made ready to illuminate my bright new future.

One hour later to the half-minute I strode imperiously through the double-doors of the aforementioned spud'n'crud hangar and presented myself to the uniformed manager. He looked me up and down like a junior officer on a parade ground, deigned to shake my hand, and directed me to the 'Crew Room'. Whether I was supposed to feel like an air ace taking time off from the killing airfields I don't know, but on an upper level I found a bright box full of spotty teenagers wolfing down indigenous dregs. The inmates glanced up, pausing between chaws, and then slipped back into feeding time. I pulled up a moulded plastic ass-planter and watched these pubescent peons get down with some bad beef. Well, I thought bemusedly, at least I ain't knocking some pensioner's crap off my shorts!

Eventually the under-underling, about sixteen and obviously with the mental capacity of a child's thermos, advised me of my first malodorous tasks: sweeping, polishing, waxing, wiping. That really grilled my goat: I'd come all this way just to be repressed again. Fuck it, I thought, I'm going to plug this little sadsack and torch the pit. But then I decided to weather the storm a day. Nothing indentured, nothing ingrained, after all. Uniform rankling my delicate epidermis, I pushed up and shut up.

I had to watch a short video about the franchise's philosophy – two cutesy teens demonstrating the ropes and warning you not to take food out of turn – 'We always prosecute'. After that crashed course I was ready for anything and got nothing, just sweeping the floor behind industrious burger architects. I could overhear the assistant manager telling one hapless shmegege to 'make sure the pickle is in the centre of the ketchup and the ketchup is in the centre of the bun' as if instructing some neophyte in the ancient art of levitation. The smell of grease-sodden cow corpses permeated the air, the vents dragging out what they could but severely clogged and overworked. Lunchtime I could see the frontline troops facing ranks of drones six deep and eight tills wide, all clamouring for their dose of deGrade A beef and a shake.

By then they had me at the 'fry station' by the end till, dishing up French Fries, 'salting right to left at all times', in the face of three warming lamps that recreated high noon at the Equator. Sweat dripping, wrists aching, arms wooden joints and snapping sinew, legs seizing up, pulse falling down, I stood there for an hour and a half, busting my ass on both cheeks. Cripes, toilets and bathtubs were looking good, but I was determined to go the middle distance at least. Then the regional oberfuhrer showed up to inspect the troops and I had him breathing down my neck for a millisecond, saying to the intimidated but secretly thrilled Asst. Man., '. . . hot, crispy, fresh, delicious, nutritious . . .' as he brandished the julienne blade like a Samurai with a prized sword and put one of my potato coffin-nails into his gaping maw. I wanted to do a half-nelson and dump him in the tray, then salt him left to right, and exhaustion alone prevented me. A moment later *his* lieutenant, a comely, buxom Indian woman, passed by and I smiled at her and said something about arteriosclerosis. She looked horrified and rushed on.

After the noon surge had abated and I was standing aground like a gunner on Iwo Jima some assinine supervisor collared me and said, 'If you have time to lean you have time to clean,' and pushed a broom at me. I took it up sullenly, cursing to myself. What a rotten plum this was!

Later on I thought I was getting a break. I'd had my free lunch ('two dollars maximum worth of food, please') and was attempting to digest it without medical help when I was urged to refill the thick shake supply. A stumble, a fumble and the flaky slop was floor-bound, much to the derision of my overseer, who pulled me off it like an ambulance man discouraging a do-gooder passer-by from giving first-aid. I just about belted the wimp, but again, stupidly, let it wing itself onto the heap of ignominious belittlement that was my current lot.

I was steered bodily to the dreaded deep-friers, where racks of proto-pies were lifted and lowered and lacquered until 'done'. The supervisor carefully showed me how, when and where to do, undo and don't, and left me to it. Now, if it had been a twelve-digit prime number he was after I would have wrapped it up in under a second but this elephantine, sizzling machine had me in schtuck. I lowered in one rackful of apple pouches, gently. The foaming fry came to the brim and receded and I laid the poor suckers out to dry. I quickly slotted in a second load when, horribly, half of them plopped lopsidedly into the vicious vat. A massive head of devouring oil gathered typhoon-like at one edge and had just topped the brim when it started seething up the other side as well. The supervisor, his sixth sense working double overtime, swooped in for the admonition, crying out, 'What the . . . *heck* . . .', and went to saving the drowning apple soldiers. Eek! The remains floated up, disembodied, charred, wholly inedible. 'Stupid robber,' he hissed at me in a womanish voice and then returned to beaching the gutless pies. I felt vindicated in a childish way as I watched this automaton and reflected on the acned putzes I'd seen in the 'Crew Room' earlier that day debating their chances of making manager by twenty. I figured my little mishap had undoubtedly sealed my fate, but was very much mistaken. The church loves a sinner and my fluorocarbon congregation was no diff, taking me back with tears, fisticuffs and fondness.

'Tragic beauty takes suicide swim,' said my supervisor, tongs holding up one particularly paraplegic pie. And he looked at me in a way that made my belly flop. I was out of that place in record time, grabbing one last freebie and a box of straws. At the door the supervisor waved me off, smiling sadly, stroking the pie with genuine compassion.

Back home I knew time had come for drastic, radical, final action.

# 5

## *Beware! Office Furniture Can Make You Sick*

A car alarm woke me up early. Rolling from bed I was poverty in motion, a few blankets fighting for the privilege of getting off me first. I tried the TV and got 'The Bad News of Jesus', a faintly reverent God squaddie's cross-walk that featured Brad Botz, whose ubiquitous motto – 'the Devil Finds Work for Idol Hands' – decorated more billboards than I had Smarties. After a cryin' shave I interpolated myself into the shower and let the steaming water hyperventilate my pores.

Food was a fridge too far so I settled for Botz, whose casual separates crippled my vision. He was extolling the virtue of hard work, but his lilywhite silken pinkies betrayed his avowed love of the blue collar. He got some miner from Virginia to repent. 'My past sins blight my life,' crowed the confessional lung-cancer candidate as Botz, the conning tower to end all, held him close. 'A failed failure,' he said tragically, and had two melancholy midgets meekly take away the purified one.

Botz's wife, a fairweather frump named Betty, began the obligatory hymn, 'People Won't Talk'. Betty's tonality bore an unflattering resemblance to a bull moose with a hernia and the woman herself wasn't far off some kind of hoofed herbivore.

Brad swayed arrhythmically to the hymn, his eyes slits, as Betty straightened her blouse compulsively, braying the mournful lyric.

The bouncing ball that followed each sacred phrase on a sub-title strip looked ready to bolt and you felt embarrassed for it.

Finally the hymn passed, as all trials and tribulations are wont to do, and Brad returned to the luminous lectern.

'Y'know friends,' he began, the laugh wrinkles around his eyes and mouth gathering into a web like glass in a broken windshield, 'huddling in the cities, you Christians, you students of God, in search of answers in the face of prolonged and disastrous wars, the greenhouse effect, longtime drought, famine . . . Yes! Let me tell you something I've been wanting to tell you. Shall I tell you?

'I . . . I . . .' He grips the lectern, stricken by revelation and his prostate. 'I . . . I called God last night. Yes, I did! I *called* God . . . I had to *speak* to Him. I called God! I called God . . . but he wasn't there, but..he left me a message . . .'

At this point I was forced to leave Brad to his celestial answerphone to visit the local couch-potato ammo dump. Popping sugar cubes while pawing the products got me all het up, but nothing could beat the beautiful feeling of simply piling high the horrible purchases that would shortly shore up my savaged soul. As I waltzed down the narrow aisles wherein the treats were tightly stacked, a voice like wet liquorice announced the specials, and I ran to them with open arms.

I burst through my front door like a Red Army colonel on the Berlin city limits circa 1945 and arrayed my purchases around the couch. I'd missed Brad but the news was revving up as I re-read the recruitment ad I'd now set my fat heart on. The deal was basically a trial period dotting 'i's and crossing 't's for Cro-Mag-Non, the copywriting side of this Necrotrivia joint I'd been bored silly with on the newscasts. Synchronicity being what it is, just as I was peering at the embossed NT logo on the ass-end of my pie carton, an item bounced off the screen about the place. The girl who dealt with legal stories was badgering some stoic spokesman concerning rumours that Necrotrivia was involved in undermining SKULL Systems by poisoning their water supply. A heavy-handed ruse, to yours truly at least, but the guy who ran Necrotrivia came across like someone who might have attended nursery school with

Don Corleone. Although you never saw or heard him, this guy's minions acted as if Ivan the Terrible was stuffing their dispatch box. 'I'd rather kill myself than say he's bad!' said one. 'Secret rat-eating group not so secret any more!' And with that she held up a photograph of SKULL's board of directors. The embarrassed newscaster hastily ushered in a commercial. Intrigued by all this hooplah, I finished my application, excited and pleased to be clear of cooking and cleaning for good.

Searching a back-issue of the daily paper, I found a photo of Necrotrivia's HQ. What a classy anthill! A massive opaque glass cube, at least twenty storeys high, with no identification bar one, deep-red NT logo above the central set of double-doors. The forecourt was dotted with the usual lame landscaping-and-asphalt, but a weird marble monstrosity took pride of place amidst the standard issue eye-sorcery – a reproduction of Louis XIV pissing into a pond of live tropical fish. A small circle of stunted trees surrounding the old codger, commemorating the first forest defoliated by NT in South America. Contented employees sat on miniature gargoyles shaped as stools and benches while they snacked out over lunch. My hands fairly shook as I stamped my envelope.

An odd note was attached to the appointment card that was biked round next day. It told me how to find the appropriate department, then went into small print to the effect that there would be no formal interview. A hand-written addendum explained that the man whose job I was to fill had died at short notice and had already been replaced. However, another more important vacancy had come up and, in view of my 'excellent' credentials and a shortage of decent copywriters, NT was willing to give me a crack at a heavier duty job than sense dictated my attempting. I thought over all this on the subway, reading the note over and over.

Off the subway, on the way up to the street, a drawn and gaunt bum stumbled up, begging for redemption. 'Spare me a dime?' he inquired with the deference of the desperate. 'Write a song, pal,

I'm a credit man,' I quipped. It was a lie, of course: I wasn't rich, I had no reason to expect to be, but I felt sure that soon every catalogue in America would have my name on their mailing list.

Was I *right*.

After the usual security bullshit at reception I was called into a narrow, airless strip of space, locked doors at each end, with a red and black table down the middle. At one end my interrogator sat, tightly erect, his big, bony, pink hands clasped solemnly in a lap of gaberdine creases. I wondered what the real score could be: was I going to get a formal interview after all?

My eyes met his like a thread going for a needle, colliding awkwardly a few times before finally interpenetrating with smooth suspicion. We both breathed lightly – it was like being interviewed by a Moonie. His hand reached across to shake mine and then retracted like a switchblade, an oversized silver wedding ring on his right hand emphasising his precision gesture with a dangerous flash. Quickly he skimmed my paltry submission, mostly pirated from ads I fancied all dressed up in autobiographical profile constructed from true-life success stories in a positive thinker's almanac that was chock-full of absurd rags-to-riches ballyhoo.

He was definitely not a talker. You could tell by the way he didn't talk. He shrugged to signify whatever point he had reached in his silent deliberations, and then hid again in his cloak of stilted officiousness.

I eyed him curiously, wondering just who they thought I was and why they'd picked me to begin with. On the far wall hung a dartboard with Stalin's picture pinned onto it, dozens of pinpricks perforating his nose and mouth. These people weren't red-under-the-bed types. They'd shifted all the beds and skewered anything that moved. The man disdainfully studied some part of my messy application. I felt acutely self-conscious. He looked at me, lingering on my eyes, and handed me a folded piece of paper with a black and red embossed letterhead. I read it carefully, toilet-trained for the workaday world, eager to please myself and anyone else with surplus green to shoot my way. At this point a lock clicked and a guy walked in behind me. He gave me a friendly punch on the back of the neck and introduced himself.

Ice Hell, a man of about thirty with steel-grey skin, green eyes and the mannerisms of a prudish schoolteacher. Hell had in fact been a schoolteacher, and he later confided with unnerving readiness that he had been booted off the staff for distributing White Power propaganda. His smiles were all licked stamps, wet and sticky on the back, dry and smooth on the front. He referred to Necrotrivia as 'The Operation' as if he were talking about a lobotomy, portentous in a driven sort of way. His eyes were glassy, one-way, and I felt that if I'd picked them out they would have rolled easily into the palm of my hand and reflected me perfectly. As Hell led me through a maze of stuffy offices, I noticed that no one was particularly busy, yet no one was idle. It was as if they all knew that to betray their fundamental lack of interest would result in a heads-on-sticks firing line. And I got the feeling that at this outfit severance pay meant losing an arm. 'Need new ID? Privacy?' Hell asked, steering me graciously to a small, greasy cubicle between two peons. Both were bent to tasks too important to look up from. One had dandruff, one didn't. Hell lightly dusted the desktop like a baby beating on a dandelion puff and then gestured for me to try out my own swivel chair as though he'd just bought me a free ride on the roller-coaster at Marineland. I worked the chair around a bit to appease his evident excitement and then stood up. 'The higher you go, the lower it gets,' Hell said, and although I'm sure I heard him wrong, that *was* it. What the, uh, *hell* was that supposed to signify? Hell didn't look like the sort of queer fish who'd ever spawn upstream enough to encounter Zen so I put on the brakes and just looked at him quizzically, which had an instant and odd effect. He excused himself nervously and departed for a pre-emptory piss.

'Mere work.' Pardon? My neighbour had craned his bull neck around the sharp corner and was observing me. I looked like the new boy, OK, but I felt like a new species the way this hosehead was watering my plot. OK so I *was* a new species, but this lummox wasn't to know it. I smiled beatifically, like a saint in those medieval triptychs that kept the peasantry nailed down for three Cs, but this fellow-worker (ugh!) just looked at me. And looked at me. And . . . You fill it in! I was starting to look for a window to fall through when Hell returned. I was embarrassed to be relieved to see him, but next to Mr Happy, Hell was positively heaven.

'This funny life,' remarked Hell, back in the saddle after his inexplicable bladder call. 'This here is Van W. Workman,' he added, patting Weirdsworth on his shoulders. Workman smiled at Hell, so broadly and so long that I thought his lips and teeth were siezing up. Shit, I was starting to realise Necrotrivia wasn't exactly your average Forbes 500 company. Workman let his lower lip slacken and Hell, returning the smile tooth for tooth, suddenly shut his trap. Then, unforseeably, he handed me a *chocolate bar*. I took it, ate it, swallowed too fast, coughed, and thanked my sinister benefactor. Hell shook my hand, saying in that matter-of-fact voice one normally reserves for dishwasher repairmen, 'Honesty is a thankless job.'

I gestured in the direction of an anonymous door at the other end of the room – smudged and warped, it stood in stark contrast to the relatively civilised areas I took to be my new habitat. Hell raised his eyes skywards, chuckled deeply and, boyishly thrusting his hands down his pockets, fidgeted and said, 'World-famous professor says he took a ride in an alien spaceship.' I did a double-take, as you can imagine, unruffled my plumage and waited for Hell to elucidate. 'A picture of courage,' Hell said reverently, polishing his diction on each belaboured syllable, 'Mr *Rock*.' And he gave me a double-whammy that could have segmented an orange at fifty paces. So that's where the legendary Rock is, I thought. Hell, seeming to read my thoughts, tapped my shoulder, and when I looked at him said, 'The one key that can make you rich before your next birthday! But: you'll see spots with his tricks . . .' Workman, overhearing us, snickered perniciously. Hell whistled long and low, physically screwed my head around, and bantered about anything but Rock. Taking a different tack, I innocently asked about SKULL. It was if I'd insulted his mother. Hell stiffened and creaked, his features screwing up bizarrely. 'Religion versus booze!'

I was trying to unclue this crypticism when Hell, taking a scale model skull from his coat pocket, dropped said object on the floor and stamped on it violently. 'A lot of gall,' was the end of his demonstrative set-piece. Workman winked at me; that worried me even more.

Hell, apparently miffed, turned on his heel, sneered into the middle distance and left me to avoid Workman. I'd just about refloated my credulity when Van reached behind me and grabbed the guy on the other side. Mr Exe, he was called, and he looked like a tooth-fairy fresh from the Gulag. 'Introducing the new rascal!' Workman exclaimed like a regular guy, thrusting me at Exe, and went back to work.

Exe shook his head comically and shook my hand. We exchanged few words, but I did manage to wheedle some straight info from him about all this Necrotrivia-versus-SKULL guff. Rock was obsessed by SKULL; he'd been running NT a lot longer, but SKULL had been neck-and-neck with them for a few years now. Exe was obviously in fear of Rock, too. He said that Rock was committed to returning Necrotrivia to its pre-eminence, by fair means or foul. He didn't want to say too much about SKULL, though, suddenly stopping in mid-sentence and going back to work.

If I'd known then what a wet-rag Exe was I'd have had him promise in writing never to pester me. But what *did* I know? I'd be paying taxes soon. I was stuck in a place a mother-in-law's convention wouldn't disturb. My ultimate boss – Mr Rock – exercised a mysterious power over all he employed, be it fear, fierce adoration or cynical obeisance.

I ate more sugar, stamped my foot like Mr Ed and slumped in my swivel chair. I'd already had one of those days and I hadn't even been there two hours.


'Of course, I expect you'll have your own ideas when you move in,' Hell rambled, 'but the last place you'll need to touch is the bathroom. We put lots of work into it and it's very cheerful.' Was

I trainee to a brush'n'bowl fetishist? No matter what I did I always ended up a puppet on a flush chain . . . I yea'd and nay'd as expected, looking over my plain black tubular desk, conscious that as I did so a small aperture in the wall flickered in time. It must be a camera, I thought, and was tempted to model.

'The best and latest product ideas from around the world,' Hell chuckled, positively gloating. 'I wish we'd invented this twenty years ago.' He pointed at a computer screen that showed a grid on which threads of material were being woven into a model's coat that, when read diagonally, said 'Buy before you die'. Underlaying the actual composition of the coat was a complex mosaic depicting a severed head, bleeding. 'Gadgets we love to hate,' grinned the creep, like a little kid enacting petty revenge on an unwitting victim. 'Savage thrill, jungle shades, perma-colour indellibility,' he waxed on, wringing his hands red and sore. I detected the omnipresent sniff of a heavy cocaine user about this person. 'The story is clicking into place,' he continued. 'Take a fresh look at living.' I was.

'God Is Love – Get It In Writing.' The flame-red neon sign swung above my head, its sub-legend – 'There Is No Honour Among Thieves' – nearly parting my hair as I followed Hell into the typing pool. I held myself well, carriage upright, intimidated somewhat by the functional layout of the room. Several rows of WPC temps exchanged printouts and, occasionally, words. Across the room, like chaperones at a high-school prom, sat their over-seers, decked out like hero sandwiches. If you'd mistaken them for Christmas trees you wouldn't have been too wide of the mark. I saw one girl furtively sniff some correction fluid at the side of her desk. Groggily she raised her head and set to work again. 'Many neglected children come from wealthy homes,' Hell smirked, gesturing obscenely at a girl adjusting her laddered pantyhose. 'Strange beauty customs!' he went on, seeking sycophantic agreement. 'The best part of your next dinner party is just coming out of the oven,' I replied, nudging Hell playfully while the object of his desire tugged her dress back over gangling gams.

The room felt silent, despite the murmer of conversation. Employees spoke stealthily, their laughter guiltily ill-concealed.

Hell moved out of the pool and over to a block of screens. 'Come over here,' he insisted, staring into my eyes with apparently psychic intent. Maybe he was Rasputin's long-lost stepson – with a beard he could have passed for his brother. I had to stop myself saying, 'Ivan, your borscht is ready!' purely in jest. By now I had realised that for all Hell's intimations of a free-reining, back-slapping sense of humour he had absolutely none whatsoever.

My eyes wandered around the strip-lit office to where a few like-attired juniors were proofreading the copy of some hapless joe, tutting and wrist-slapping whenever possible. 'It can't be healthy, it tastes too good!' said one to the other reprovingly. 'If you don't like the first pattern I can show you forty-nine thousand others,' his colleague said, ersatz etiquette straining. 'The quality is remembered long after the price is forgotten,' interjected a third party, for all the world looking like Donald Duck suffering withdrawal symptoms. 'Don't get caught with your pants down,' admonished the one apparently in control, bending a plastic ruler just in reach of a loud snap, then flexing it back on itself, watching the plastic distort with satisfaction. 'It is dangerous to you and harmful to us', was the final word, at which point the trio dispersed quickly back to their desks tucked away in glaring alcoves.

I fidgeted, aware with a start that I was meant to be paying attention to Hell. He was pointing down the open-plan aisle to some guy, saying 'He's sized up twenty-one tobacco crops,' and waiting for me to be impressed. My guide obviously hadn't noticed that we were in utterly different worlds as we spoke. It was then that I realised that what I'd taken to be an air-vent was seeping a mild sedative gas, not strong enough to visibly affect us, just enough to dull the edge. In a bewitching moment of mind-reading Hell nodded to himself, sniffing the air like a groundhog coming out of a fallout shelter.

'I'm still having trouble. Can I speak to the floor manager?' A servile cipher stood in front of us, clutching a tiny radiopager and hopping from foot to foot like a man waiting for service in a bad restaurant. After a second or two, the floor manager arrived, exhibiting an underlying tension that pinched back his lips like

41

invisible stitches. 'It's come to the crunch? Sit down and press the buttons,' he said icily. The screen flashed and, with a little neck-craning, I glimpsed the readout:

'Advertising rates as published are at the absolute discretion of the Company. All goods, services and contracts will be deemed to be subject to the provisions of the Company and the Company will accept no liability arising from delay or for any reason whatsoever unless this number can be quoted in full.'

# 6

## Portrait Of A Mad Man

Hell had to get me started on the road to ruin so, at precisely nine o'clock the next day, moments after we'd both arrived, he sidled over to me.

'I can teach you anything you want to know,' he said, straight-faced.

'Wow!' I rejoined, wondering how long we could go on before I slammed his fingers in a drawer. Sensing my hostility, he got down to crass tacks and placed before me a shortlist of projects I would be expected to see through. It was quite nightmarish. Nothing I'd monitored back home ever seemed quite so bent, but here I was, the boy with his finger in the Grand Coulee Dam, primed for action. I surveyed the briefs imperiously, hoping Hell would leave me alone. I wonder why I don't like Hell so much, I thought, then realised he was one of those queer birds you don't need a reason to dislike. He was sent here by powers unseen to be the sticking post for other people's disdain and rejection. The way he soaked up and spotlessly digested anyone's repulsion convinced me I was right.

'Your formula for success?' Hell asked circumspectly as I came to grips with the ideas before me: 'E-Go-Go', a game all the family can role-play; 'What's My Bag?', a series about the lives, loves, and leftovers of bag people; 'Hide 'n' Swastika', a mini-series dramatising the wacky lives, loves and medical experiments of a team of Nazi expats down on the health farm in Uruguay; finally, 'Salute The Morning', an aftershave packaged in red-and-black boxes with funny little squarish symbols all over it, an illusionist's swastika Rubik cube.

Well, firstly, I'd like to say that I noticed NT was into the Third Reich like nobody's business (but their own). Secondly, I couldn't have cared less. Thirdly, I didn't know where to start. Hell still hovered behind me annoyingly, waiting for a sign of action.

'Now you can benefit from fifty years research,' a WASP woman from across the office said to me as I leafed through again. When she saw I was puzzled she went on, 'Some strange advertising type came up with the line,' pointing covertly at Hell's back. 'We've put a bit of colour in our briefs,' she noted, brandishing a colour xerox mock-up for 'Salute The Morning'. I didn't really need the reception committee hand-me-down new-boy treatment, but I suffered it. Something about this greying, garrulous bimbo confused. Face front she could have been the guy who parked my car every morning; from behind she affected a wiggle somewhere between crates rattling on a forklift and a jellyfish with lumbago.

'I want to be alone,' I said in a sultry way, hoping she'd appreciate my filmic allusion.

'What could be more natural,' she said pleasantly, and I noticed how deep her voice was, sort of effeminate Charlton Heston.

I watched the wiggle recede up the aisle and shrugged. No sooner had I done so than Hell darted over, cuffed me playfully, gestured at the broad and said, 'Right disease. Wrong animal.' He winked at me so exaggeratedly that he had to catch his contact lense and then, executing a martial turn on his squeaky heel, he returned to his incredibly tidy desk.

It wasn't until much later that I discovered Barb's – for that was her name – secret. According to Bikinidold – you'll meet that prize soon – Barb was a male nurse who went through an identity crisis just past forty-five and, when his wife died shortly afterwards, invested the life insurance money in a sex-change. Now she temped out of the Chain Gang agency for NT, collecting a widow's pension and chasing unattached hard-up bachelors at Atlantic City when long weekends would permit. She actually snagged one, some Jewish businessman who wouldn't consummate the marriage until the honeymoon. Imagine his surprise when . . . Well, *imagine* his surprise!

Lunch delivered me from this ordeal by mundanity and I left the building, sure someone was following me. Every time I turned around someone would just be *missing*. I can't explain it but the upshot was that when I got to the local eaterie, Contains Real Juice, one of the NT fellows materialised next to me.

'A simply fabulous free offer,' he smiled, offering his manicured hand, and a menu. Free lunch? What the . . . uh, hell. (Already that word was beginning to bug me.) I ordered the special, 'The Diet For People Who Hate To Diet', wondering when my host would introduce himself. Suddenly the hand shot out all over again. 'Hank Bikinidold! Meet some interesting new individuals!' And he straightened his tie ingratiatingly. 'Meat with the goodness frozen in,' he said, slapping his thigh. I laughed. Well, I didn't laugh, it was more like a backward death rattle, but it made a benign impression. I already had HB pegged as the gumby he turned out to be.

Hank chitchatted, I listened. 'Burger surprise,' he commented, cheekily lifting the corner of his bun to see the grotesque sauce leaking over his cow pattie. 'Perfect partners!' He bit into it neatly, swallowed quietly, wiped his lips tidily and then did it all again. I managed to restrain my incredulity by tucking into my skimpy din-dins with concentration befitting a chess Grand Master.

'Necrotrivia: The generation of innovation,' Hank boldly proclaimed and I nodded dumbly, hoping we were on either side of a fault line about to default. Alas, no, the gods were with HB. ('Everyone calls me that because of my name.' No kidding, I felt like saying, I thought it was because you're straight and filled with lead.) He chirped like a sparrow in springtime, Necrotrivia this, Necrotrivia that. By the end of it I wished I was still a bowl 'n' brush technician. He got the bill so I could almost forgive him. Greater love hath no man than this, to lay down a crappy lunch for a friend.

'Can it be relied on to fill a 38b?' Hank chuckled, eyeballing a receptionist as we entered the hallowed lobby of Necrotrivia Inc. I wanted to sew up the jerk's eyelids by now. Hell watched us come in and scribbled something in his Psion. I heard a strange banging and crying from that small, dark, windowless office at the far end of the floor and thought nothing of it. Everyone else heaved a sigh like galley slaves on group therapy and pushed their pens and pencils, italic nibs and stencils, rub-ons and lift-offs. I sat there like a pig in a poke, snout aloft, trying to sniff out the future. It didn't smell so good.

I went into work early because I thought I wanted to work. When I got there I didn't. I didn't want to work, I didn't want to think about my not working. I think I wanted to go back to sleep. Fresh memos littered my trays and I got a spike to order and stab them. Words crawled across paper like limp spaghetti dyed bright blue, and black and red. There was enough work to bury Hitchcock and the idea of actually tackling it made me fit for the lead in *Psycho*. Yes, they like workers here, I thought wistfully, secretly flattered to be entrusted with substantial tasks. Take someone like Volmer downstairs, for example, he was such a chronic turtle that the company had paid to instal a toilet in his cubicle to save him making the return trek to the little executive's room.

I had before me the financial report for the previous quarter which boasted gloatingly in bold type on four packed pages that we were all of us '31 percent richer' than the same time last year. I flashbacked to my fast-food fiasco and the day the floor manager was striding about proclaiming that day's lunch-hour turnover the highest yet, while I was crouched next to a milkshake machine, head low like some godforsaken grunt down a foxhole at Verdun, knees soiled with fluorescent milkshake powder, wondering to myself, 'So fucking what for two bucks an hour, pops?'

The report heading was supported by a slogan in bold red capitals: 'Triple-digit profits relieves double-digit inflation'. You really felt like shaking your own hand. On the back was the photograph of some retarded lackey in the filing section grinning with gapped, poorly retouched teeth, and sporting a think-bubble that read: 'Get your smile developed!' negating the possibility that a regulation human face might grin spontaneously. Necrotrivia posited that you were born frowning, not crying – that was weak.

I stared into a grubby ashtray, counted the butts and guessed at which one would take me over the line and into cancer country. I waited in vain for a phonecall – even a heavy-breather would do. I just wanted an excuse to leave my desk, and a stroll was unthinkable. Rarely did I need to leave the NT building – Rock dealt with the clients himself after vetting our work. Anyhow, as a new-bug I was visible. If I made a habit of going AWOL I'd get my walking papers at a run. So I scuffed my shoe listlessly against the desk and doodled. My mind took a holiday and left no forwarding address. I was thirsty but the cooler was on the blink – Rock had pissed in it on April Fool's Day and something in his urine had poleaxed it. The man from the cooler rentals came around, tinkered, shook his head and left with a test-tube full of stale $H_2O$. He never came back.

Rock really was in a class by himself, possibly because no one else would be in it with him. I'd had contact with my liege lord only erratically so far, and while I was wondering when I might be granted an audience his P.A. slunk over and beckoned to me.

I straightened my tie and brushed my trousers. Although I knew Rock to be an inveterate pig, the rituals of meeting the boss had to be acted out. The P.A. stood by and toyed with her hair. She was carrying a beat-up copy of Spillane's *One Deadly Night* in one hand and an unwieldy pint-glass cocktail in the other, with the miniature parasol seemingly bitten off midway down the spindly handle. Bikinidold had told me that Laurieanne – that was her name – routinely read Rock pulps. Spillane was his favourite author; he'd had *The Body Lovers* read to him no less than twenty times.

Laurieanne indicated that I should go right in, so I did. A figure was slouched behind the anachronistic metal desk painted crimson red. A small framed photograph of Joseph Goebbels at Nuremberg decorated otherwise once-white walls. What I saw was far more worrisome than the volumes of covert office gossip about Rock had led me to imagine. I'd never seen Rock properly before. Outside his office he was difficult to see frontally, apparently existing in peripheral vision only, a black light darting past. A series of beer cans and a pitcher of Kool-Aid stood empty along the desk; dust and disenfranchised hair, facial and pubic, had settled on some like dead insects. Under the desk were six stacks of pornography, dog-eared from abuse, neatly divided according to perversion: animal, vegetable, mineral, etc. The dim, windowless room was clammy, in contrast to the regulated dryness of the other offices, and an air-conditioner in the ceiling, spilling unruly micro-organic fur, hummed hardly at all while droplets of dead water spattered Rock's warped in-tray.

Nothing moved.

Rock looked at me piercingly. He didn't speak right away. He smirked. He was pulling my spinal chord like an epileptic at a funfair. I reclined as comfortably as possible in the hardback chair and braced myself. Was I to be chastised, encouraged, discarded? Meeting the boss I could handle, but this was more like meeting my maker.

I waited for a hint. It didn't come. Ten minutes I waited. Rock had me solidly, sordidly cornered, and he was looking ready to bite like a cobra after a hunger strike. For lack of confidence I smiled weakly, knowing how snivelling I appeared. He seemed mildly placated, but remained silent, gloating. The smile became a grimace as I nervously re-chewed my cheeks, the cud already perforated and seeping blood. I implored time to accelerate and get me over with. No luck. We were digging in for a few hours, I knew that, but why?

He continued to glare at me, exercising an elusive control over my mood, synchronising each twitch precisely for effect. A psychology major would put him in an exhibition, so crushingly definitive were the opaque machinations of Rock's greasy allotment of grey matter. Ughsville! I shivered and quivered, trying to while away the showdown in acquiescent deference to my tormentor. By now even our breathing – mine thin and crispy, Rock's thick and chewy – was distracting. I almost stopped mine altogether, but I figured self-induced asphyxiation at work a trifle gauche. So I flapped my pig-iron foot, the pins and needles intense, tapping and savouring the molecular dance of staunched blood-flow. Long did I tap. Tap, tap, fucking tap.

I was bored, apprehensive and still. Nothing moved. A goat could've eaten my clothes off me. When you're facing a predator, play dead – hey, I've seen those nature films, too. But he saw through me – I was just a transparent anatomical model to him, my brain cells on slides. His twitching was contagious. I gave in. All the way. I had those funny little pops and grunts your body gives utterance to below the surface when you want to explode. Rock spoke gently: 'Study shows how you use up your lifetime. The future is coming. Are you ready?'

'What's the future of carbon copying?' I was fidgeting badly, picking the lint from my pockets and chewing my lower lip.

'A thirst for living – a task for fine scotch.' A drawer creaked open like a crypt and Rock prised free some firewater two-star bourbon, probably battery acid with a few trips left to go. He dung-beetled his brows, thin and wispy bristles forming a perfect elongated V. Beady, olive eyes, like a prairie dog's at sunrise, flashed messages I couldn't psi out. A low belch emitted from his compressed lips. For no apparent reason, Rock picked up a pair of tinted glasses off his graffiti'd and pen-knifed desktop and donned them ceremoniously. 'The way society's going these days, I decided it was time to adopt a low profile.' I puzzled over that. What Rock had said was a considerable understatement. In fact, he'd been seen only three times in our section since the onset of the last campaign: once to borrow money; once to harangue Hell for the hell of it; once to feel up a new temp. I was about to smile, relieved, but opted for the failsafe NT frown. Why Rock wanted to see me I didn't know and I hated being kept dangling, though God knows I couldn't afford to let him see it. Once bitten, twice sly.

Ugh. Those Stalin eyes, enough to give the working class a

complex. Although I never touched liquor or beer, a fact Rock was distinctly unimpressed by, I felt hungover, as if thousands of Santa's elves trained by mercenaries had trodden my brain, stamping my thinking-cap into a swiss cheese pancake with enough relish to cover a quarter-pounder.

Rock sent out Laurieanne for a cola and chips for me, a grand gesture after over an hour of psychotherapy. Then something jerked in my line of vision and I fell off my chair. I fall down all the time, I hate standing up. The only time I want to be standing up is to hail a cab and that's only so I can sit down, but Rock had *done* something to me to precipitate my physical fumble. I got back on the chair with a minimum of fuss, ate my treats like a browbeaten budgie and averted my eyes *anywhere*. If this wasn't a blasting in disguise, I don't know what is. But like I said, I *didn't* know what Rock was. To get his measure you'd need a yardstick, an attack dog and a whole lot of positive thinking, none of which I had access to as he glowered at me over the bottle he was casually draining. When it was empty, he popped it into the wastepaper basket before withdrawing another from the drawer.

A knock at the door and who should appear but Miss Shunk from Rock's secretarial diving pool. 'Come in and sit on the lap of the great dictator, come in here and sit on my nice warm lap!' he moaned. The temp looked at me. I walked out, shutting the door behind me – a great escape. Across the flexidisc files the girls looked at me with expressions of bemused concern or repressed fear. I had thrown their sister to the sharks. Their oh-oh faces crinkled like cold cling-film. That was one tomato sandwich who was about to join a new club.

I stretched full-length in my dinky chair and watched the VDU. I could hear the walking, talking pneumatic tube struggling, her protests drowned out by the low hum of first-gear perversion. You could feel the ouch of tight heels and toes advancing helplessly to the jaws of the waxpaper tiger, the great uncle of small girls and buyer of lollipops for a new generation of soon-to-be-arrested adolescents. Ah, the flower of youth, so sad to see it dried, pressed and then shredded by the Fu Manchu of 5th Avenue. Pain, pleas-

50

ure, potted plants and pizzas. I plunged a thumbtack into my palm, Crowleyesque. Next door the continent was listing heavily; the scrape of rubberised furniture coasters on cold tiles.

There is, they say, a good side to everyone. Which possibly explains why in all the time I knew Rock I never once saw him in profile.

Life: be in it. I went out to lunch.


When I got back, restored by slabs of fudge and some hardcore espresso, Laurieanne summoned me again. Rock welcomed me back with an eldritch grin. Is he going to promote me or what? It was a classic no-win situation, as that guy had said. I buttoned and stiffened lip and collar, wiped my perfectly shined shoes from nerves and trotted in, perhaps too gamely.

'Africa on the phone.' Rock had the receiver precariously balanced on his index fingertip, deliberately ignoring the disembodied voice above him. 'Comes from a place where men have never seen a Big Mac.'

'Yep?' I prepared for whatever contingencies might arise. Rock regarded me with a sporting antagonism. If he fired me I'd demand my wages, insult him and stamp out. If he promoted me I'd just insult him – he liked that and I liked to please him. For the moment I froze; I might need a blowtorch later to get mobile but I wouldn't risk saying something wrong. Not that I had a clue what it might take to offend Rock.

'All right, Edmund,' Rock said, 'get off your high-horse or high-zebra or whatever and tell me what this campaign can cost you. Think of a figure and double it.' Rock used his palm to do an imitation of jungle drums. The voice raised and lowered. 'Twenty? Forty? *Eighty?*' Rock was enjoying himself, thinking of all that embezzled UNICEF. You could picture him in a tiny village, daintily torching each thatched roof, his jaundiced eye recording and storing images. 'OK.' He looked at me meaningfully and my

51

anus contracted. 'I have my numero uno ideas man dying to get to his desk and go mental!'

What had I been dumped into? Reading minds wasn't my MA. Come to think of it, I didn't have an MA.

Rock slammed the receiver down and slapped his knee, the reflex action throwing his drink over his lap. 'Phew, nothing is going to ruin your morning,' he said to himself, wringing the drink back into the glass, adjusting his braces and sipping his bourbon on the rocks with a twist of rayon houndstooth. It turned out that Rock's dark continental client needed me to advertise the fact that he was about to attack the country next door, this after having concluded a truce. 'These guys pull my pud,' Rock wheezed. He ran out of breath giggling and jammed an inhaler up one nostril, pivoting on the back legs of his chair. I smiled with what was intended to be self-confidence. 'Sounds big,' I added, for effect.

'Lucky devil-worshipper you!' Rock enthused. 'Just wrap up that copy and fire it off to the SOB. You'll be wearing the cartridge-belt in the family from now on – a superb free gift!'

My anxiety subsided and I flooded with self-image at high pride. Despicable? Yes! Rock was becoming my Big Brother, my foster-father and surrogate motherfucker. The whole thing smelled worse than week-old burger but I cared nothing for ethics.

'God love those wacky barbarians!' I exclaimed. 'Trust ol' Eddy to start a bush war, the card!'

'Yeah! Whittle your lighter flints into spearheads! I curse them but I keep on, it's in my blood! The reds are cashing in.' At this juvenile juncture we both had laughing fits, Rock's sounding like a nervous breakdown in reverse. I shot an elastic band past his bobbing head and hooted, 'Give me a bongo and call me Mammy, let's get non-aligned!'

So it went, another day another dollar, or from what my intelligence could gather, lots of dollars.

I opened my throat to carbonated barrage as Rock got out a new bottle of bourbon. We whiled away the afternoon groping his porno collection and arm-wrestling.

I lost every time.

Back home I slit open my first full paycheck: I'd made more moolah for forty hours' work than most people on the planet see in a year and I felt like celebrating.

I went to the landlady and demanded the finest apartment in the house. As luck would have it, the guy in it had just been 'slashed' by a female serial killer and it was free. I moved my meagre possessions and acclimatised myself to new rooms and 'roaches. I didn't need to live in a glorified dogbowl now, but I'd kinda got used to canine containerism.

With my TV on a crate, plastic bowl, plate and glass in the cupboard and a spoon and fork laid out by the stove I felt like royalty. I dragged my bed into the appropriate space and plunked down the clock-radio, stacking tabloids daintily by. An ice bucket sat in the corner, ready to receive pop and choc; my Roach Motels were cunningly distributed. I propped my stalks up and had the ol' bulbs scanning the TV guide. Work from home? Who, me?

I pulled up *Human Plunger*, a dorky comic I liked, especially Dr Ben Gay, Plungey's MD sidekick. The ads killed me, all the ways to get kiddies refined, sliced and wrapped into nice square breadheads. The news was coming on, and it usually stung me into motion. Today I'd have needed a wasp up my rectum to get me motorvated.

'Burgers beat cancer!' was the featured lead. I, the putz who came in from the cold, watched aghast. How could I be on the same planet with such philistines? *Get outa my cave!* For a race that prides itself on its evolution you'll have to run pretty fast to catch a toilet freshener in the next galaxy.

I switched impatiently to 'Is This The Living Endtime?', a show I followed, um . . . religiously. It revolved around predictions of the day to expect Armageddon, and each crackpot cult had a shot at making their case. Tonight it was the Episcopalian Women's Bowling Club laying their butts on the line for the week after next. Then I noticed that this was a repeat! Is nothing sacred?

The mail was in the box and I was delighted to find my shiny new Necrex card. I fingered it and dreamed of catalogues, junk mail and monthly statements, to say nothing of bonus gifts and

53

limited free offers. I felt pleased to be a young exec with a future. Boy, this is going to be fun, I reckoned as I munched on a Danish pastry the size of a football. After cleaning and the fry-sty it was time for yours truly to do a little living!

How little I couldn't have possibly imagined.

# 7

## *How To Go Shopping*

Outside the grey clouds sifted the sun like Sani-Flush. I saluted the dawn with a packet of chocolate raisins as fellow pedestrians rushed past. The smack of pavement on shoeleather filled my ears; my feet transmitted the subway rumble below. Rednecks with red necks comingled with diverse dickheads; herds of heads bobbed and weaved. Dusty air, thick with the aroma of decaying diner specials, induced a sneezing attack. Alongside one crossing folk leaned on a burnt-out customised van, its murals flaking pathetically. Shoppers peered inside, hoping for a sight of the sordid.

I arrived and stepped into the reverberating elevator. It was like any other day at NT – already building sluggishly to an anticlimax. Yet we at NT shared an indulged indifference that made us peerless in our pursuit of company goals. 'Better living through adversary relationships,' was how Mr Rock put it.

Ah, you had to *be* there.

'Face it: stress shows.'

Hell had come to my outhouse, right into my partition. Open-plan offices were made for moments like this.

Divining Hell's innuendos could make a good hobby – if I had the time for one. 'No picture could do it justice,' I rejoined lamely, playing my hand with all the enthusiasm of a busboy pocketing a lousy tip.

'Introducing tropical tanning,' he continued, utterly into his prefab physique. His tan, which had probably expended enough UVA tubes to make the Black Hole of Calcutta a dayglo heaven, gleamed in the strip-lights. 'Strict and stylish,' he added, fondling a muscular forearm not long off the Nautilus.

'Look, Hell – ' I began and then, realising how dumb I sounded, returned my mutilated attention to the task at hand. Hell hung around, a debonaire vulture on a lino branch. His beetling brows sent invisible symmetrical rays to my face and I blinked involuntarily. Forget the 'hate-him-so-much-I-love-him' crap – I *hated* this Benetton Bozo. But I hated a lot of people and drawing up an itemised, prioritised list might cut into my Christmas bonus points drive. I ignored the putz but he interjected, 'Ecology and elegance combined in a new and eccentric baroque,' referring to his greenish, custom-tailored outfit. 'Look, Hell. Tear a leaf off your sleeve and go wipe your ass!' I snapped.

'Not all people who think, think alike.' Hell smiled understandingly and dropped a recent report on SKULL onto my desk. It was subtitled 'Where Profit Is Not a Dirty Word'. I fingered the thick wad of photocopies, speculating about the Jolly Rogers - and not for the first time. After all, what really separated us from those hamsters besides the specification for the wheels we ran on? Either way, the metal rattled.

SKULL's attitude bore the same stamp of generic neo-fascism as ours did, but it wasn't as paganistic and had a philosophical bent permeated by post-grad liberalism. We were strictly pragmatists; SKULL were in love with their juxtapositioning of fact and fiction. We were Druidic lumber merchants while they went in for Judaeo-Christian icon-pornography. NT and SKULL had a secret, scrap-book sort of love affair with each other, a limited liaison. Employees would meet up late at night and then disappear down the sewers from whence they had hailed their taxis, carefully covering up for the theoretically taboo encounters. Right now we were experiencing a truce of a kind – HQ was full of flowers sent to make amends for misunderstandings and we reciprocated. The added expense bugged Rock – his idea of a sentimental expenditure was the inscription for a tombstone. As far as he was concerned, the flowers would show up next spring anyhow. Sick leave? That was permission to puke.

'Prize Draw Guarantee' ran the SKULL mail-order blurb, above a photo of a happy couple with the man telling his other half to 'whip some SKULL on me baby' as the posed amid stacks of products. The report dealt with two new SKULL launches, a new life-extension drug called MORELIFE, and a new range of Vatican-approved rubbers. The latter were designed for clergymen. Lately they'd been cut loose from confessional fondling by an edict from the Pope instructing them to stow their frocks at weekends and let it all hang out. Too many lawsuits, too many unwanted congregation pregnancies, too many choirboys having psychotic episodes – all traceable to God's own. There was to be no more private Sunday School tutoring, either. The old boys missed their sins, though, the best part of a beatific blow job being secrecy, apparently. To these eternal choirboys old time religion was synonymous with donning a hair-shirt and going to the barber for a short and burning backsides.

The condoms had great names – 'Temptation', 'Revelations', 'Promised Land' – and were sold in threes, natch – the Father, the Son and the Horny Ghost. It was an auspicious break with tradition, but only weeks later SKULL dumped the account, fed up with Mafia interference and dubious cults asking for professional advice. Everything comes down to money. Intellectuals love it . . .

Overleaf a shoutline announced: 'THIRTY FREE DAYS – Live Thirty Twenty-Four-Hour Days More Or Your Money Refunded To Your Estate!' Some big Swiss cheese had invented a 'foolproof' life-extension drug to coax bonus breath out of gray mares everywhere. Just pop for four figures and you could put off the Last Rites for a month. This was classic SKULL, always on the winning side of humanity, whoever *they* are. 'In a major medical breakthrough our Life-Lab team has finally produced a proof-positive

Extension Treatment! Easy-to-take capsules regenerate dead tissue, unclog blocked arteries, restore brain vitality! Your miracle will become part of a bestselling videobook entitled *Stay Sweet and Live Longer*. Join Mr R.S. who says:"Since MORELIFE I have already lived an extra twenty-three days and the doctors tell me another forty to seventy hours is possible!" So cling to life with MORELIFE.'

What a world.

All very diverting, but I had work to do, too. About a dozen identical manucripts in front of me needed different titles. I'd turned over a few: *Convicts Turn Sharks; Elvis Presley as God; Cops on Skates; Herbal Muffins* (oh those New Age noodniks!); *Price For A Bride*.

These 'Modern Popular Library' pulps had started a few years ago when Rock's secretary at the time realised two of her romantic schlepics were virtually identical and cued her boss. He put six hacks on it the same day. So far NT had pumped the bums for around three hundred titles, the stories drawn from hats and cut up over and over. I'd read *Born Pregnant* and the plot really wasn't any worse than half the *New York Times* Bestseller List. Some jailbait is born and bred in a backwater, gets raped, goes AWOL and JD, gets knocked up, etc. The soft-core was a little heavy-handed but at ten-for-a-buck mail-order the white trash were eating it up.

My concentration faltered and I thought better of it. The sunlight – even filtered through ten tons of peel-off ozone – laid on my desk invitingly, and with Hell moving around the far end of the room clicking his insectile heels I was restless and more. Hell. Ugh! For a human being he sure was *sub*. Anyhow, it being nearly chowdown time, I winged it through a few ideas and landed by the exit. Mr Exe was just edging out, too, brownbagging it, the poor nebbish, and averting his downtrodden gaze. For a sardine in a shark pool, Exe was a hard swimmer, head above water and clear of the fish-hooks Rock cast at him for kicks. Exe had been with NT over ten years. 'On the three thousand six hundred and fifty-first day we rested,' he would sometimes say with enough worldweariness to have you grabbing the nearest noose and flexing it. I'd gotten as far as standing on a stool once, but looking down at the floor noticed a pattern in the tiles I'd previously missed. Five seconds later I was nose to the linoleum, checking out a bastardised swastika. Trust Rock!

Mr Exe walked out with me, practically arm-in-arm. Maybe he's a faggot, I thought. 'Don't make fun of sex-change guys,' he blurted. Jesus, I was on the same plane as a psi-dyke, like the least desirable place on Earth after any famine zone at feeding time. I felt a heavy Father Flannegan session impending, with me in the cloth and this marshmallow on the clerical couch.

'The doctors cut off my breasts by mistake,' Mr Exe continued. Knowing what to expect, I led him to the rear cubicle at the local hash-slinging microwave gunge-hut. Shit, I thought, who the hell's going to work up a lunch-hour hunger with some weird, chromosome-crossed fellow employee spilling his guts and petticoats?

I ordered my usual – some burnt bacon, peanut butter, two generic chocolate bars and three Cokes, one iced, one no ice, one lukewarm. Mr Exe unloaded his sorry sandwiches and felt inside them, using a tactile test to upturn the latest obscenity his life partner had inflicted. 'Buffalo ranch,' he rumbled, and bit into the first half like a little wind-up false teeth toy pulling on gum. I was about to puke when the three Cokes arrived and, having ingested them anteater-like with slurping to match, I felt as sick as he looked. With this parity prevailing, I let the inverted slime pour out his story. There was a few volumes' worth, punctuated by my crunching cordite bacon and pb sticking noises – the roof of my mouth becoming a salt and sugar stalactite gallery - and by the time an incidental intermission rolled around with the blessed benediction of my customary Cream Pie Supreme, the feeble fuckwit seemed to have drawn his most pressing puss my way and took a breather.

Feeling a profound need to change the subject, possibly destroy it, I casually reeled off the day's front-page headline – 'Six Hundred Hitlers cloned by Russians'. As mortal fate would have it, this only got him railing in repressed tones about how Stalin was a woman and Hitler wasn't exactly one hundred per cent he-man either. Now, I never figured the two big moustaches could give a pet rock an orgasm between them, but knowing Rock's fondness for the Great Dictators, I didn't want to draw fire and flood upon myself by aligning with some crinoline-craving covert catwoman. 'When a woman-hater gets larceny in his heart, the last person he should ever trust, is a girl,' I told him, but it wasn't enough to staunch the muddied flow of this basket case's wanton weaving.

Exe wrung his blotchy hands and, setting down his sandwich, looked at me levelly, with great gravity, and whispered, 'Rock.' Before I could say ' 'n Roll' or some other evasive tidbit, he'd gripped my forearm and begun reeling off a sizeable, albeit disjointed list of accusations about Rock, of whom he was plainly terrified: 'Three dead for a couple of bucks . . . They didn't have a chance . . . They could throw the book at him, and he'd still walk. As a boy he hunted grizzly bears by the light of the moon. When he became a man he tracked women in much the same way.' Exe paused, trying to get a rise out of me, his grip still firm. 'He kept a macabre "treasure" underneath his mattress . . . The trail ended on Lover's Lane, grim and bloody. The fiend kissed and fondled his virgin prize, then threw her out so he could drive a few times over her body with his car.' I was getting interested, but Exe was so overwrought at this stage that I just exclaimed 'Oh?' as naturally and neutrally as possible and, feeling as if Lee Strasberg was on my case, asked, 'Is it time to go back *already*?'

'Special promptness bonus,' Exe said, slotting back into routine. NT was visible out of the corner of one eye . . . Or maybe I just had some dirt in it.

I never asked Mr Rock about his past but, drawing on yesterday's papers and covert office gossip, I managed a fair scissor'n'paste reconstruction. It kicked him out of 'Who's Who?' and squarely into 'Who's *What*?'

From what I could scavenge, it seemed Rock had served in the Special K – Korea, to you – and seen his share of firefights. I often pictured him putting a hole the size of a designer donut in the base of some superior's skull, one of those legendary battlefield 'accidents'. That was his idea of promotion now, so why not? Anyhow, fantasies apart, the facts pointed to a childhood spent in some unrelievedly mundane burg called Thriftown, located smack dab in the geographical centre of the US, Kansas, in the centrifuge suck of middling America.

Nothing much distinguished his school days. He was an avid teenage operator and even got a few hookers off a drugs rap in his high-school years by rearranging the local cop shop's files. I don't know if he had any parents – hell, he may have been hatched, aren't all reptiles? – but he had an uncle who influenced him a great deal, a scrap metal merchant who patented a trash compactor design and got, uh, *filthy* rich. So, there it is in a soggy, sundered peanut shell on a pillow of discarded cereal cartons and banana skins: Rock's role model was a glorified garbageman. The effect this had on his embryonic psyche can not be underestimated. Proximity to a fortune founded on waste, (trash = cash etc) fucked with a head likely to have been inherently aberrant to begin with. It's in the genes, see!

'Unc' – who favoured the pint-sized, petulant tyke – bestowed on the boy a strange sense of values. To imagine Rock in his prime, diverting himself by feeding goldfish into a stapling machine or putting firecrackers in a paraplegic's colostomy bag, made you feel that whatever gene pool this crafty cretin derived from only had a deep, dark end – Rock was doing front crawl before he could walk. No high-school records were available for him, although I sent for some out of curiosity. In fact, the school he went to didn't acknowledge the fact. A horrified clerk, when he heard my inquiry down a submarine phone line, merely broke the connection with a severe slam. I guess he wasn't terribly popular.

Rock didn't make it to college or university, probably not deigning to suffer the company of normal mortals, but he did send off one of those matchbook cover correspondence school forms and proceeded to take all forty-two courses and graduate in all of them. With this great knowledge he established a successful phone sex racket using copies of *Hustler* and some broke girlfriends. Out on

61

his ass after the police busted him, characteristically he turned the other cheek and got into mail order. This was where Rock started to shine: the Rock of slave wages, the mastermind of Necrotrivia Inc. The hard facts on the growth of his insidious first empire are now lost in the back pages of back issues of a hundred LCD rags, but I do know – 'cause Exe passed me a sample once – that he was heavily into 'novelties' at one point, and later on pioneered a peculiar line in bestiality disaster flicks – *Flaming Fur*, *Virgin Wool*, *Dog Eat Dog* (you get the idea!) – that fit like a love glove. If ever there was a man born to crossbreeding the whoopie cushion with copulating pigs, X-ray specs with sheep, it was himself.

Having amassed a large cash sum and run out of stock, Rock split Thriftown with his childhood sweetheart and a new car, and went to the big city. I don't know which one, but that's immaterial. His wife – he met her after sending his girlfriend off to secretarial school one morning and changing the locks – was a former roller-derby queen named Lynette. This six-foot plus bruising bitch, who towered over her hubby, cashed in her chips whizzing around wooden tracks the length and breadth of Smallville, USA, eventually abdicating her tin crown after a major hip joint replacement job necessitated by a particularly nasty collision with a rail. She never was the same, it seems, and Rock divorced her because of her unsightly limp, relegating her to zero alimony in some fleabag motel hell with a pockmarked neon sign and a <u>female concierge</u> who got through a disposable blade a week fending off her meno-pausal peach fuzz. Eventually, luckless Lynette wound up in a crappy private sanitarium where, come nightfall, they would hear her literally bouncing off the walls reliving the highlights of name-less, forgotten roller derby title fights. Life's a circle, all right! She died when a Christmas tree fell into her bathtub, electrocuting her horribly, pine needles and burst fairy lights flying.

I guess Rock got away with it because they never had any offspring. Rock, the eternal adolescent supreme, hated kids and damn near killed one under the pretence of a fun boxing lesson. He had the kid's jaw reset which was big of him, and I think he had to cough up some major green to save an eye, too. A Big Brother he *wasn't*!

That was it, basically. The stacks of dough Rock made selling sneeze powder, Swedish aids and cut dope he invested in sculpting Necrotrivia. Unlike a lot of big operations that dote on their corporate history, Necrotrivia remained mysteriously silent. Rock had been in league with a lot of dirtbags building up the business, reputedly scoring heavily in gunrunning, illicit biotech and artificial intelligence en route to penultimate glory as a CIA operative. Necrotrivia, the name registered years before, finally emerged one day behind seventeen different fronts, consolidated in a sweep. No shareholders, no board members, just Rock and his galley slaves. Every morning he'd pull up in his Rent-a-Wreck Caddy and park it in his special space with a screeching and squealing of brakes befitting the death rattle of some huge metal dinosaur with emphysema.

That's what I found out. There's plenty more, of course, but I'd be getting ahead of myself. Then I might trip and, hey, you wouldn't want that to happen, would you? Well, *would* you?

After work I felt that shopaholic itch and, checking for my virgin Nectrex card, I cabbed it to the nearest mall. Walking in was like stepping the wrong way through a two-way mirror. Every dollar-hungry corporation could see me and feel up my credit rating but I, the unwitting consumer fit to be consumed, knew nothing but an insatiable appetite for *stuff*.

Swarming over purchasable properties, coupons and cards rustling like grass snakes, peons sated themselves on goods. Money changed hands, changed lives, changed and changed, recharged, charged, stayed the same – on sale. I put my mug in the trough and slurped up the Good Lord's bounty. The cornucopia of crap tilted over me, a numbing shower. Twenty-two TVs winked at me knowingly, each on a different channel, some on the *shopping* channel. Wow, was that surreal! What could those TVs possibly know about me to be winking so? Nothing and everything! I wanted to embrace a game show host, spin a wheel, play pretend roulette. Two hundred assholes dressed up for the Mad Hatter's tea party on 'Let's Make A Deal' – I wanted to imbibe the collective unconscious, the great filthy, unmasked Jung ones, whose whiter-than-white washing, virginal folded towels and panties, cleansed of the blood of baseball games and menstruation, skinned shins and elbows, held a nation of detergent-heads in thrall. Rinse cycle is tough, tight but hot and wet. Numb-numb.

Hands on plastic like a showdown at the mediocre corral, I faced the windows and shelves, the mannequins and rails: one day all this will be yours in a million no-interest payments, but I kept one finger on the trigger and the other on my dick. I wanted so badly to break my credit cherry that it was like my Nectrex card, sensing it was feeding time, was stretching down my pant leg and out into the stores like an unheralded hard-on. 'No Limit' – that's the epitaph of these lamb-eyed, bug-eyed bozos, I thought conde-scendingly: No Limit! But, like, who ever said there would be one in the first place? Hell, even Moses left a disclaimer on the Commandment about coveting your neighbour's wife's ass.

For now, for then, for always, I needed to own some shit to throw against my internal vacuum – upright, cannister, industrial, or otherwise. Ah, now what should it *be* today? Cheese, chicken ice cream, chocolate, chips (salt'n'vinegar, ketchup, tomato, BBQ, roast ox)? Walk on, walk on, sonny boy, urged the twinkling hundred-watt stars above me and walk on I did, under a cacoph-onous canopy of muzak. I loved this stinking place, all of it! The wall-to-wall mirrors, enough of them to induce self-consciousness in a Zen master, edited my life into slices, pressed up to each other like hostile relatives at a shotgun wedding. I passed myself walking backwards again and again, at right angles, half and whole, drawn and quartered. Clerks flew into my reflection: shapely shop assist-ants and matronly mother-in-laws absorbed and absolved my image. This was dreamy, this was creamy, this was almost too good for words. But in this label-crazy loop, nothing is that.

Another thing I noticed as I was being gaily exploited: fat people

64

everywhere. Fat, badly-dressed cattle, penned in by their own force-fed blubber, all trying to eat the sacred cow that hatches the golden credit card – but not enough holiness between them to launch a spaceshot to the Vatican. These heaps of sweaty, cash-registered lard burped and bumped and ground together, jostling freely, enjoying their degraded status, making themselves do it again and again and again: Buy, Buy, Buy before you Die, Die, Die. Before your valves seize up and, like an engine sucked dry, your heart surrenders its sludge to the autopsy man. I envied their tabloid-toting innocence, virtuous vacuity, venerable fucking lopsided stupidity. Make yourselves as little praying dolls and come unto me, all ye who are weary and heavy-laden with shopping, and I will give you . . . credit? Come, come, again I say *come*, unto my motherlode of mindsucking scum, O ye faithful down-payment chumps dreaming a dream as pertinent as a pimple on God's patoot. The minutiae of their mental gearshifting riveted me as, one after the other, they lined up and listened spellbound to the chattering registers. (I did, too, and loved it.)

I felt needed, *wanted*, for the first time since I'd arrived. I realised that this buying was at the molten core of my host civilisation. I, the parasite, could graze at will, a tiny tic on the back of one screwy beast, along with all the rest of the tranked up slugs and speedoes high on bad cola and cheap chocolate and splatter videos. To be a somebody, even to be a goddam nobody, you had to *buy*. Legitimise, verify, sanctify your existence, link arms with Maya, shoot the duck and win a prize. Seventy billion people have walked this Earth since time immaterial, all lining up in one way or another for this fucking sale. My cheeks positively went convex just whistling Dixie over the whole dirtbag. Somewhere in a distant galaxy, eating potato chips, some little green man is saying, *Get a load of those fucks, they wanna eat out just to feel fed!* I was as bad as the rest, now, for sure.

Two thousand years of Revelations can't be wrong! What St John saw projected on his ol' cave wall was definitely in colour, on all channels at once and not unlike our own nine o'clock news. This is – I flattered myself – my poetic sense surfacing like a curd of crud (ain't that a dandy anagram?). I held up a blue jellybean like a philosopher's stone, polishing it with saliva, seeing my reflection in granules of refined sugar. No one ever learns, I knew in a microsecond flash, no one knows if they're here, there, or over there somewhere: it's one big, scummy fishbowl. Just you consider this, friend, while your wife hangs out the laundry: in sixty million years none of this will matter. Cockroaches will inherit the Earth and wear Ray-Bans. What's better still to contemplate – because that last observation is about as new as a Beverly Hillbillies reunion – it doesn't matter anyhow! So let yourself go, to where I can't say. Me? For the first time I could see the silver lining in each cloud, and a little tag in each silver corner: *100% Manmade Fibre*.

# 8

## Lovers' Leap

Ice Hell had invited me to dinner with two 'couples' he knew and I, the ineligible bachelor, accepted, being at a very loose end and baited by a curiosity too far launched to be staunched. So I selected my best drip dries and caught the express out to the furthest neck of the 'burbs. Square rows of long, low, double-garaged split-levels lay before me and I counted up to 10,001, Hell's number. No, not 666, get serious!

Hell greeted me with a facsimile of style learned piecemeal from correspondence courses on etiquette and being popular. He took my hat and coat, and led me down, down, down to the sunken living room/dining area to introduce me to the couples that lay in wait there.

Benjamin and Elaine and Paul and Tracy were seated, one couple per maroon love-seat, pulled up to matched inflatable hassocks. Hell seated me in an ornate repro Louis XIV that looked out on carpeting straight from Escher. He lorded over his mediocre semi-circle of friends with a zealot's glee, conveying drinks and canapés ceaselessly, having first gathered in one place every variety of brand-name snack cracker and mixer known to man. By eating and drinking a filthy amount I just about avoided conversation, thereby indulging myself freely in observing Hell's interior decorations. He put the 'ass' in aesthetic, all right: quite unbelievable. On one bookshelf stood a proud rank of the first volumes from mail-order sets in leather-look, leather-feel, leather-smell leatherette. On the wall facing me were three 'stuffed' girls' heads – a blonde, a brunette and a redhead – realistic likenesses moulded of skin-textured pliable plastic. 'One of their nicest qualities is they don't talk back,' jested Hell, catching me off-guard and practically off my trolley with additives. Mahogany plaques shone dully in the dimmer-lit alcoves where Hell exhibited high-school trophies and trinkets picked up on business trips to Midwestern hellholes, including a six-foot cob of corn with a neon 'IOWA' flashing at strobed intervals, making the radiant hair on the girls' heads glow unnaturally every third second. I diverted my derelict gaze with difficulty and had only just refocused when I spotted another certifiable aberration: a personalised home bar set into the wall, topped by a collection of little model cars. 'Forty American and foreign cars, only five dollars,' Hell remarked proudly, sucking the juice out of a rind. I sipped a cola and lime and noticed a dog-eared, rebound proof of Rock's book, *The Theory of Intellectual Violence*, behind the glasses. 'The best book you'll ever read about relationships,' Hell sagely advised. I scrutinised my drink to avoid cackling.

Entwined like toy monkeys on the love-seats were the couple of couples. They were chatting quite amicably, not seeing me really. Benjamin was telling Paul about his lawnmower sharpener; Tracy and Elaine earnestly discussed the timing and location of their respective upcoming vacations. Shit, I thought, I could take a vacation in your head, bitch! These simple folk, regular black holes-in-one, were a living documentary on 'burb bores of the budget Bacchanalian binge epoch.

Ben (I *can* call him *Ben*, can't I, ha ha ha!?) and Paul wore much the same clothing – perm-pressed pants and pocketless designer shirts, their burgeoning rubber tyres kept deflated by twenty-minute workouts and chasing secretaries at the Christmas party. Paul's shoes – black loafers with precocious buckles – gave way at his spindly ankles to those dumb Scottish-type socks professors wear to hook jailbait. His fingers wore rings; his hands were thick

68

and meaty. Ben, a more urbane type, wore a company tie and a gauche green and mauve cardigan. Out stuck a gold Amex.

'Pass your drug test?' Paul asked conversationally, provoked by my conversational paucity. I nodded, shifted and studied my drink . . .

Benjamin stroked his shiny pate and said to Tracy, the faintest innuendo evident, 'Some areas of my body are no-grow areas.' She gave his crotch a sidelong glance and said, 'I believe in magic.' The wife-swapping ingredients settled into the bottom of the conversation snugly. Hell played host, hilariously, by turning on 'Ignoring the News', his fave NTV production. The girls talked complexions. 'Slackening skin? Hey, be firm with your face,' Elaine said, pinching her pal's embryonic double chin until the flesh went white.

Paul, who had a booming business bronzing baby shoes, and Ben, who counselled juvies, were studying the show. An item involving a fellow who lived entirely in shopping plazas had caught their four eyes. This man literally never went out. He lived in a hotel built onto a plaza, ate at its restaurant, went to the in-house theatre, travelled only where the subway would take him, holidayed at other plazas and bought all he wanted and needed at a few chainstores. He made it sound pretty fine, actually, although he was white as an aphid. 'This is where the fun is!' he exclaimed to the camera, gesturing out of his apartment at the helicopter pad of the building across the way.

Hell served dinner on individual TV trays square on eight. It consisted of various TV dinners mixed and matched and mulched. We guzzled the guck merrily and by now, six colas in, I was participating ably. I even pinched Elaine's round, firm bum when she went for a powder (I'd like to be that puff! I thought) and she giggled in spite of herself, checking to see if hubby was watching – but no, the meat-oaf was still jawing to Paul about the shopping-centre man and prices of cars, beer, death, taxes and whatever else their brains contained. Hell joined in at odd intervals but mostly enjoyed seeing his plan come off: people being nice and normal in his condo. 'Another year of increased profits,' I heard him boast to the boys as he rolled up his sleeve to reveal the latest Watchman with special holographic enhancement feature and optional 3D. I was suitably impressed. Suppressing my contempt, I exerted myself to go to the john before my bladder had an out-of-body experience.

Elaine, she of the rounded rear, was just leaving from powdering platform number one. I was tempted to grab her wrist and take her with me to be seduced in style by the medicine cabinet overlooking the toilet and matching radio-cum-bum wad dispenser, but thought better of it. I slipped her my number on a piece of toilet paper, slapped her left cheek, and brushed past meaningfully. 'A performance you won't forget,' she whispered, tweaking my forearm. I grinned as lasciviously as possible. On the pot I read *1001 Elephant Jokes* while savouring Elaine's limited free offer. I think I'm going to like this planet, I said to myself with more than a little lust. Outside the door high-pitched laughter and lower pitched chuckles melded. When I came out the lights were almost down and Hell was loading the VCR with 'Coming to Town', some terrible NT skinflick about a horny hayseed who hitches across America serving her country. I caught Elaine's roving eye a few times but didn't want to push it. Just as the girl on a swing was blazing a trail to Minnesota I nodded off, to wake up much later with a blanket over me and my shoes neatly tucked under the chair. I found a triangular folded note under the cushion. It read: 'Tired of being turned down?' I was more amused than insulted and drifted in and out of sleep, imagining hitching across America with Elaine in one hand and a six-pack of cola in the other, just the two of us, and a dog . . . and a cat . . . maybe a goat and a chicken . . . find a little place . . . settle up and settle down . . . raise a few kids, raise hairs on my neck, raise her dress . . . Like that.

I bundled myself into the office, and Laurieanne bundled me into Rock's. There he was squatting on his desk, remote control in one hand and a jumbo bag of BBQ chips in the other. He acknowledged my entry by belching and then went back to his creaky swivel chair to enjoy the show he was rewinding on the video.

'Idols Of Flesh', an NTV production, didn't lower the tone so much as deep six it with a piano, two safes and enough concrete to sink the foundations of a major office development. Experts in the art of scriptwriting had devised this soap concerning the day-to-day lives of six AIDS sufferers. Sounds big, right? It might have worked but two of the actors were TVs to begin with, and one, who *really* had AIDS, looked too bad to be pretending to be sick and rather damaged the show's cred. Anyhow, Rock ate it up, along with the crap cluttered on his in-tray – chips, Cheesies, left-over pizza and half a Hero, plus sundry pop, booze, pills and some deep-green weed that stank worse than high tide off Long Island.

'Idols Of Flesh' rolled along, with Ricky getting a blood change and his lover having problems getting his test results. 'So effective it sets the standards for all others,' Rock happily opined, and I bobbed my head. 'Law officer learns about Satanism,' Rock called out with glee, dangling the next twist in the plot before me. After the reg twenty mins (minus hard-sell space), Rock switched to the news. Even I was laughing now. SKULL had fouled up big this time. Their new cybernetics system had defrosted ten thousand preserved people, swamping six city blocks in rotten ice and formaldehyde. Rock hooted and hollered as the talking heads exposed SKULL's no-no blow-by-blow before millions.

Sandy Silence came on, lips compressed and eyes heavy-lidded, to explain. 'My researchers have left me eating dust,' he said, then parried an inopportune question with, 'Don't fence me in! Our dream is shattered. It's all down to medical science now.' He pointed haplessly at ten body-bags laid end-to-end on the forecourt of CYBERSKULL. The melting mummies steamed in the sun.

'Victim covered by thousands of stings,' Rock commented, shaking his head sternly at Silence's soaking. I scoffed cheese puffs, crammed crap cola and read Rock's stack of Danish pastries. Seeing SKULL pussywhipped buoyed up the boss like nothing else. A while later two piping hot pizzas arrived, fresh from Enrico's enchanted oven, and we tucked into the deep-dish joke-puke. Wo, this *is* the life, I reflected as I pitted an olive: pizzas with the boss; free cola; unlimited job opportunity.

Rock's mood was so merry that I dared to ask the one question that had been so far unanswered: What is SKULL's story? Rock bit his lip and gripped a slice of pizza ferociously. Saying nothing, he yanked out a slim folder from under one hazardously high pile on the corner of his desk and threw it onto my lap. A pale label read 'SKULL'. Handwritten notes were stuffed into the margins of neatly-typed pages, and I set to deciphering it all. The facts were as succulent as I'd anticipated.

SKULL Systems Inc. (Motto: The Great Protector) had been founded by Sandy Silence, Harvard/MIT yuppie smoothie extra-ordinaire, eight years previous. Sandy was the second – and favorite – son of Professor Steven Silence II, a weapons systems analyst and former pro 'ball player. Sandy graduated first in everything, *cum-lauda* etc, and at the age of twenty-seven spent a five-figure inheritance setting up SKULL. Originally SKULL was a mere consult-ancy, advising bigwheel Hawks on how to get their talons on megadeath hardware and software fast, and creaming a cool twenty per cent off the average hundred million transaction. Within ten years Silence had more billions than limbs and had reinvested it in arms, stockpiling them fastidiously, pioneering his unique 'arms library'. He put a lot of the Third World into the Fourth World that way and never looked back, just kept pyramiding his capital, expanding SKULL until it bit at Rock's athletes' feet.

Silence prided himself on neatness and punctuality and lots of other Emily Postisms, but that couldn't prevent most SKULLduggers looking like ex-cons. SKULL scouts handpicked likely A-students from campuses across America, looking for amateur human beings whose swagger could be easily moulded.

SKULL was Silence's exclusive preserve – the only other person remotely close to his power and influence in the company was Crypto Peerless, Silence's childhood bosom buddy. Silence and Peerless went around with each other, faces set in Scrooge McDuck shapes, shedding capitalist blessings on the little people, quacking triumphantly whenever an exemplary scam paid off. They were genuine and committed, beautiful in their devotion.

Silence deferred to Peerless as Jekyll would to his Hyde, the latter laughing with mannered cruelty. These two, interlocked, co-operated mental machinery to rival the post-'real gone' machinations of the CIA at their coolest. A menacing ambience surrounded the duo, and SKULL's subversive, pervasive assault ensnared millions, its lurid sheen illuminating the asphalt jungle and burying many a lesser mogul. A lot of people saw danger in SKULL's imperial aspirations; what I saw was a textbook exercise in pushing the extreme. It hurts, but like a splinter it eventually works itself out. SKULL breezed past all save NT, skirting an abyss filled with proto-K-Tel recreations into which farm teams feared to glimpse.

Rock and Rock alone, who got there first and was forever hell-bent on kicking away SKULL's omnipresent gauntlet, could deal with Silence and Peerless' demented duality of play and earnest. Rock had the ugly, muscular control to occasionally puncture their monstrous miasma. Rock, at heart, was an old-fashioned huckster who treated his environment like the peeled, bummed-out wallpaper it was, while Silence had some facetious faith in death culture, in keeping the Promised Land, in building a better world - even if he totally fucked it up in the process. After all, Silence and Peerless were processed themselves, individually wrapped slices; Rock was crusty cheddar, smelling bad and looking worse, but one whiff and you were floored. SKULL's quest was tireless; NT's tiresome.

Unlike Rock, Silence was a family man. He had three sons, whom he referred to as 'My Three Sons' – after the famous sitcom trio. His wife, also named Sandy, role-played the woman behind the man, but every scandal sheet enumerated her extra-marital suitors. What she did behind her husband's back was enough to give him curvature of the spine.

'Looks good after years of horseplay!' Rock once said of Mrs S, pawing a poster of her in the latest *Inside*. Never one to resist temptation other than for the sake of a bet, he smirked lasciviously and said *Inside* with such a degraded inflection that my buttocks literally clenched in derision. Rock tore out the poster and did something with it: I recall seeing it a day or two later in his tray, half-open and held together by . . . Well, what shall we call it – organic glue?

My intrigue with the SKULL file beginning to trouble him, Rock dragged me from my orbit and drily admonished me: 'Careful . . . hidden cameras may be watching you as you try on clothes in stores.' What the hell was he trying to tell me? I eased the topping off another slice and bowed my head in silent contemplation.

What was happening to me? Where was I going? Why did I like this idiotic life of mine? Who am I? *Who cares?* I finished my pizza.


Necrotrivia was becoming a bit of a habit, as in needle and spoon. I was forsworn not to touch the hard stuff; my idea of a profound fix was a strawberry sundae, coke float, two-pound bag of Oreos and two cups of coffee lightened liberally with an ounce or two of creamer, the sickly shiny type that makes the inside of your mouth taste like wallpaper paste.

No problem. But the people at Necrotrivia seemed to be inundated with drugs and alcohol. Hell, that straightest of straights, even he wouldn't turn down reefer, preferring a blend he called Mega-Hopi Mindfuck that some wacky Yaqui he'd met on a camper holiday in Arizona would send him in the mail. Exe was into mixing and matching downers and hormone pills and didn't mind describing in gender-threatening detail how he could watch his protuberant proto-breasts inflating and deflating depending on which formula he was improvising that week. Barb, who was as appealing in fishnet stockings as Godzilla in a negligée, wouldn't have protested at a funnel being fastened to her chin and upper lip, so freely did she imbibe sour-mash, gin slings and zombies, often in the same glass. Bikinidold, who boasted of his 'nose for making friends', was all ready to start tunnelling for a third nostril – his first two had caved in when the freebasing had hit a home run. Laurieanne, she was high on Rock, and *he* was so permanently basted that prolonged exposure to him guaranteed a paramount contact-high.

And there was I, the pop-up picture of innocence with my coagulated cocoa and double-deckered Danishes and popsicle stashes. I may have been as ornery and oligarchical as the rest of the white-collar reprobates hewing wood and carrying water, but when it came to good, old-fashioned chemical self-abuse, I was a pussy. Surprisingly, no one bugged me overly about it once I'd established my preferences. I did try a tiny toke of the Mindfuck but nothing happened other than an atom-splitting headache, so I gave it back to offended Hell saying, 'Of every hundred Americans, three are mentally retarded.' Hell, fried to a crisp and having trouble with his diction, giggled, 'Suitable for a museum,' and cuffed my ear. Oh brother.

Rock was indifferent to my lack of enthusiasm for his shortcuts to Nirvana. Additionally he knew, as we all did, that he was just the type who'd damage himself totally and still croak at a hundred-plus, a timeless wreck submerged in himself. You have to know your limits and, physically, Rock had none – his molecules were set so wide apart that the junk fell through. His mind? Now that was something else. It filtered the stuff unevenly and his retention of a million substances, many unlisted, was probably the only thing that could conceivably topple his tenuous tightwire act.

I'd find Rock in his office alone, frequently, tripping on tequila and scrumpy – he hated LSD, associating it with flower power and other positive imagery – eyes closed, screening phantasmagoric nightmares on both lids in 3-D. 'Small turnout for visions,' he'd say; or, 'A very reliable source, I can assure you,' and wait for me to exit tactfully and leave him to delve into the cobwebbed caverns of his subconscious. Around his chair would be forgotten take-outs: 'Exterminator' chilli; Elvisburgers; 'Decadent' brand chocolate-chip cookies.

Back at my desk I'd look at the others beavering away and sigh contentedly. You'd hear Rock singing *Stop the world I want to get off . . .* tunelessly, the oldie he always incanted when he was fixing with ease. Hell and Bikinidold would turn to each other and, on a count of three, harmonise on *Everybody needs some bloody sometime*, and then fall into each other's waiting arms, incapacitated by their public buffoonery. Laurieanne would shake her head reprovingly. Exe, the stick-in-the-mud incarnate, would groan derisively and work harder. Barb would slap her beefy cellulite and watch the flab ripple inside her hose. And me? I'd laugh, by God, and why not? It was fun . . . Yeah, sure it was.

Anyhow, what did it matter to me? I'm only here for the food . . .


The phone rang. I salivated. She purred. I growled.

I'd been hoping that the dizzy dame who'd bumped and ground me at Hell's soiree would use my number. For once, just once, I wanted to see everything in its place. Like her at mine. That picayune party may have been an open-and-shut case of the blind drunk leading the blind drunk but there was no mistaking fantasy for reality now. Elaine was at the other end of the blower and her breathing sounded heavy to me – maybe because my ear was glued to the receiver with beads of perspiration.

'Find out what your dreams mean,' came the velveteen voice, disembodied contact floating on a double bed of warm air. I cradled the receiver in my hands, said a silent prayer, followed by *Thank you, God*, out loud, and prepared myself for the best.

'How women's bodies tell men: I like you,' I replied. I could tell she liked it because the glue around my ear started tickling. I loosened my collar, and other items of clothing too.

'Friend in need? Don't look a gift horse in the mouth.'

I was thinking of looking in her mouth with my tongue. This was all happening a little too fast for me, but if the horse wanted a race I was game. Bets were down and odds favoured the longshot for the ride of his life. Elaine was whispering now, a throaty, no *husky*, party invitation that had WILD printed all over it. If this wasn't my lucky day, then I wasn't likely to have one. A flash detonated in my brain and I recalled the name and address of a lowdown motel not far from NT that might be ideal for illicit sex. She took the *bon mots* and other bait like a shark served a salmon platter. A date, no less. I put down the phone, wiped my damp palm against the wall and started looking for some clean clothes.

The Nozone Motel was a dingy, three-storey pink'n'blue sandwich that stuck out from the offices and automats like a sore slum. As I made my way there my conscience was at bay, despite the knowledge that in a scant few minutes I'd be in the company of a woman who wasn't strictly single. Knowing Hell knew the couple involved was creepy, but his head was so far up his rear end that even two wing-mirrors, a periscope and an Indian scout wouldn't help him see more than what was right in front of him. And to say I'd formed a low opinion of 'Benjamin' was a considerable understatement. So with these justifications in mind I sallied forth to meet my Waterlulu.

Elaine, however, did have reservations. Under another name. I didn't see her at first because I was preoccupied with a piece of gum adhered to my sole. Chipping and pinching at it, I was oblivious to the five-feet-plus of potential pillowfights observing my sticky undoings. She cleared her throat once, meaningfully, and when I looked up she smiled. I had to narrow my eyes. She was really much more than I had remembered, wearing much less. It was hot outside but not half as hot as under my collar. I thought I could smell the tabs burning.

'Here's licking at you kid,' she chirped. 'Volunteer patients are needed to help test promising treatments.'

'I volunteer,' I said. I was more than dazzled, I was practically incapacitated.

Elaine looked stunning. I was stunned. Her close-fitting two-piece hugged curves that should have needed a permit. Sandals revealed squarish, perfect toes and ankles; legs hewn of silken marble filled simple net stockings. Past that, I'm afraid, my hands might not be steady enough to reliably commit to paper. She could see my appreciation and repaid in kind, squeezing my free hand in a happy-go-lucky way. The diffident receptionist tried not to sweat when Elaine seated herself beside me, her bottom depressing the cushions just so.

'Quick quiz: Do you give or take in relationships?'

'I give what I got and take the rest,' I parried, and she laughed, a full-bodied laugh. What else? A body any fuller than hers would need two skins! I tried to take my eyes off her cleavage but my eyes had a mind of their own.

'How to accept a compliment gracefully,' she cooed and walked over to the desk, booked us in, and scooped the key casually as you please. I pleased.

Down the hall to our right was Room 109, a humble double with a broken lampshade and a bedspread best left unspread. Once inside completely I stood back to regard my discovery. Mouth of a maneater, mane of a Madonna. Hair of a Harlow, lips of a harlot. I drank her in and was giddy.

Elaine took me to the bed and we sat down. To alleviate my overworked imagination she provided the distraction of polite conversation. I was in no mood for etiquette but played along, paralysed by lust and an incomprehensible foreboding. We were close together now, hand in hand, her feet nuzzling my calf. She talked about this and that . . . her husband mostly. Oddly, I didn't care; I was hardly listening anyways, just luxuriating in our furtive foreplay.

Ben, it seemed, was the son of a Senator with two left feet, whose Commie sympathies had gotten him dumped when McCarthy was on the rampage. Ben, therefore, was not able to pick his jobs too carefully and wound up a counsellor entirely by default. But his misfortune had tainted him and when he started dredging up all sorts of previously sublimated bitterness, Elaine, generally an ebullient type, had gotten fed up and gone fishing. I wasn't her first catch, she freely confessed, just the latest, and she enjoyed rubbing in how truly trivial our time together would be. That was OK, I didn't want anything else. But obviously she needed to get some hostility towards men out of her system before she let them into hers. What did I care?

Once her thirst for confession was slaked, Elaine deftly removed her top. The black brassiere made a gorgeous silhouette in the dim light and I let it stay on a while longer. Call me romantic . . . it's your life.

'I don't *have* to look back. I spend plenty of time enjoying today,' Elaine murmured as she lay across the spongy bed.

She talked some more, to exonerate her absent spouse before committing the cardinal sins. He wasn't the sort of guy to feel sorry for himself, she said, other people did it for him. It all got to be too much; he'd played by his own rules and lost and she couldn't respect that. His attitude to women now left a lot to be desired.

The bed bounced as Elaine sat up abruptly and rolled down her hose. At intervals she'd stroke my back and sigh contentedly before continuing her cross-examination of herself.

'. . . and they're *off*!' I exclaimed foolishly as my socks hit the floor. It knocked Elaine out of her introverted orbit and, apologetically, she said 'Lipstick is a red giveaway of things to come,' planting her pout on my pucker with sudden, passionate intent. I hit the lights, she hit the jackpot.

Adultery? Did someone say *adultery*? 1. Shut up. 2. I'm an adult. And furthermore . . .

# 9

## *Wacky Witch-Doctor's Dirty Trick*

The daylight scared the shit out of me. It's a bad attitude you got there, son, I thought wistfully, counting washing-machine lint under my blanket. I felt trapped. I didn't want to get up and go out but I knew I would eventually succumb. I wasn't particularly hungry, so instinct failed me. I knew I couldn't face a shower so that temptation was no-go . . . The only drawback to my escapist thought progression lay with the realisation that at NT one law above all was sacrosanct: punch in or be punched out. Never having been a fight fan I flipped my polyester lid and made tracks. I stepped out and into a glass of water. On a mental alertness test at NT one morning I'd gotten such a low score the examiner snapped his fingers to check I was awake. I wasn't then and I still wasn't now. The big sleep of the big creep, you might say – if I hadn't said it first.

Wiped foot. Wiped floor. Got a grip on myself and the bedstead, whipped my spine into position, and scanned for a razor.

You know, some mornings aren't meant for shaves, and today I faced it like a woman with a hormone imbalance. Cowering like a troop carrier off Ohmaha Beach I grabbed the blade, absconding with it to the little men's room. I didn't bother with mirrors or any other aids. I ran some hot, brandished the weapon and felt lather part and skin cringe. The first cut was trophy material, a quarter inch long and about as deep. Blood went everywhere. My puss looked like a Red Cross transfusion pitched into a bowl of cornflakes. I quivered and steadied my hand, reaching for a corner of toilet paper to cover the crater and dribbling like a basketball player. It's a messy business, shaving.

Slowly I dragged the twin blades back and forth grumbling that this Earthly life could stick me with so cruel a test. Suffering may build character but in my case it stopped strictly at 'Ouch, ah shit!' etc. One by one additional pinpricks of blood surfaced, forming a join the dots I was convinced spelled GIVE UP, ASSHOLE! The battlefield at Ypres looked better than I did, festooned gaily with tissues of many colours. Finally I finished, casting the blade into the blood like some sort of medieval priest performing a freaky fertility rite and relaxed those parts of my face not rinsed away.

Aftershave stifled the cuts brutally, forcing the cells together into an unholy alliance. I ran my palm over my throat, felt the damp, sticky blotches and, satisfied a tank tread with snowchains couldn't do a worse job, leaned on the sink and wished I'd stayed in bed. Wished badly.

Rock had arranged some entertainment for us. Polishing his name plaque with some oil from his nose, he informed me that no less a personage than Dales Jr, patriarch of Spiritual Hedonism (US) Inc, was dropping in on his private astral plane to let us in on a few 'mysteries'. Rock and Dales were wheeler-dealing over the concession rights for the Eastern seaboard, a slice of apple pie worth a mill-a-month at least, and that was excluding the Junior Spiritual Hedonists proceeds and dayglo pentagram royalties.

Now, life's no bowl of cherries but Rock positively cherished the pits. His saying, 'If at first you don't succeed, plant a stool pigeon', had paid off again and I was in his lair to find out how. Having piqued my curiosity about Dales Jr, Rock told me the star distraction was circling the airport as we spoke. In the meantime, he had some 'things' to tell me . . . Great, I thought, *another* mindfuck! Clearing his desk with a pimply forearm, Rock pulled up his chair and explained the *raison d'etre* for this *tête à tête*.

War was about to break out in a Middle Eastern fossil-fuelled fiefdom. SKULL and NT were the beneficiaries, in that the only way the combatants could have all the funds *and* all of the mess, officers' or otherwise, was to get TV involved. Instead of giving it away skirmish by skirmish to the nightly news, the antagonists were agreed that the entire war should be sold to the highest bidder, with the idea of making the ultimate *verité* war picture.

Rock, with his nose for carnage, had gotten there first with a splendid offer and had his best poison Ivy Leaguers jetting to the Gulf and back daily with the papers. Just when the purse strings were nearly sewn up, in steps Sandy Silence and his starchy crowd, and tries to cut himself in with one side, creating all sorts of divisive problems for Rock.

Of course, Rock and Silence knew a good/bad thing when they saw one and could suffer each other's camera crews on the frontline. But there was protocol involved, as well as greed and more than a little pride. Covering the war would be a TV landmark, prestigious, profitable, the docu-drama to beat all docu-dramas. Rock and Silence had been stepping on each other's toes lately to the extent that a corns exchange was plausible. Rock wanted the whole war – or nothing. He would never settle for nothing, and Silence felt the same.

I was beginning to understand my boss's uncharacteristic fondness for Dales Jr. Silence and Dales were bosom buddies: Silence's pretty pubescent daughter went to a Dales Jr camp in the summer and their wives were distantly related. But Silence shied away from doing business with Dales, whose cockamamie Eastern promise disagreed with his own Founding Fathers cant. Rock figured that if he could get Dales' ear and a common hand in the till he could second-guess Silence if the going got rough over the war rights set-to. Rock or Silence might need some leverage somewhere and Dales, despite his love-thy-neighbour lines, had all the connections you'd want in a crisis. Rock's only hope of balancing Silence's advantage was to put aside his own reservations about Dales' millenial *modus operandi* and come to an arrangement.

The situation with the war rights was deadlocked, stalemated, a standoff (one of your own . . . ) Rock's pigeons had flown home bearing rifts, messages about bum deals at the front and not such hot stuff at the back, either. So Rock, the fiend-in-need, had on top of the Dales deal assented to (Are you sitting down? If you're not, don't blame me when your head bounces!) – *a summit meeting with Silence!*

In all the years Rock and Silence had been in competition they'd never met and now they were squaring off for a face-to-face, toe-to-toe, dick-to-dick high level hoedown. Rock was going to meet his neatnik nemesis, the great SKULLmeister, Mr 'What-Makes-Smiley-Run?' Silence. What a day! A man who burned the canteloupe at both ends peering over a stretch Caddy bar at King Worm. Jee-*sus*, I thought as Rock filled me in, the facts solidifying like quick-drying concrete: Quit while you've still got a head!

Only such an auspicious occasion as this could get Rock to crawl out from under himself, but it seemed a dead cert that the old man of the bottlecap mountain would briefly eschew the discomforts of his office and greet the day personally. Rock ran down the details and they flattened me like a Mack truck. Stunned, I almost got up to crawl off and *do*, when Rock pushed me back in my chair, reminding me of our imminent visitor.

A headache starting on the temple rims, I relaxed a little and waited. Rock was merry, and I couldn't figure it. He hated Silence with a passion, always had, and I'd heard him swear repeatedly that nothing on Earth would get him in the same room. And now, at a moment's notice, he was preparing to stake NTV's reputation on fleeting minutes of glad-rap. Rock saw my incredulity and luxuriated in it, humming sweetly as he thumbed through a back number of *National Geographic* – he loved the ones with those great pix of buxom young native girls doing handicrafts outside their huts – periodically smiling at me and winking exaggeratedly.

I asked Rock about Dales and he obliged with a lengthy and admiring summation of his mortal spoils. Dales Jr was something of a whizzkid and right up Rock's back alley. His dad, Dales Sr, had made a pile trance-channelling for Elvis in football stadiums, touring repeatedly as the 'Elvis Church', rigging faith healings and speaking in forked tongues coast to coast for credulous cretins of all colours, creeds and credit ratings. The day the old man croaked, midway through a rendition of 'Suspicious Minds' in Rio, Dales Jr inherited more money than I'll ever spend and set to work redirecting his father's ministry. Already, at seventeen, a crochet-kit tycoon, Junior went to India, Japan and Mexico (or said he did – Rock claimed he'd bought a penthouse in St Louis and had a six-month orgy, sending a stand-in to every mystical nook and cranny on offer) and then came back with the greatest yuppie religion of them all, Spiritual Hedonism, a godless amalgam of forty-seven faiths, arcane schools, theological positions and assorted commercial precepts. Now, all over the world, greedy yuppies were chanting some Jap gibberish as they sashayed around their apartments in sandals, waving stinky sandalwood incense and intoning the sacred mantra and other assorted hits of India c. 500 BC.

Dales turned up incredibly late. Rock and I had just about forgotten about the holy cash cow when a deferential tap was heard at the door and in crept a shaven five-footer with a wordless smile on his lips and a basket on his arm, a regular truth fairy – sabre-toothed variety. Rock grimaced at me and then bowed low to the Great One while I, petrified by all the schtick, stayed put and suppressed a hoot of derision. Dales gave me a flower, which I stuck in my pants pocket, and a little booklet entitled *Black Triplex Tranquility!*. Rock waved his hand at me, telling me to grin and bear it. I did. Then the nervy jumped-up little profit sat cross-legged on Rock's desk before greeting us sonorously with: 'Yes! I want.'

'Martians will land this fall,' Dales told us deadpan, and as if to illustrate his 'point', pulled an infrared photo of Mars out of his basket. Rock and I looked at each other knowingly.

Dales composed himself, adjusted the folds of his robes, which were a rich paisley, and, like a great teacher directing his automatic transmission, spoke to us seriously.

'Who amongst us hasn't stared with despair into a bowl of soup and asked themselves "ultimate" questions? Why am I here and not somewhere else? If I were somewhere else, where would I *be*? Would I like it there? Is there a dry cleaner there who knows how to treat suede properly? Is there suede there *at all*? And so forth.'

Dales paused and shut his eyes tight, hummed a lilting tune and then, staring into the filing cabinet, resumed his routine.

'Of course, we all want to know the answers, particularly the one concerning quality suede care. But, try as we might, through existential rain, shine, sturm und drang, and other sundry metaphysical mishegoss, the answers elude us. Why? Are they the *right* questions? Who knows?'

By now Rock and I were rapt, believe it or don't, due to Dales' practised master hypnotism. I realised, semi-lucidly, that his robe was doing something to my head and the way he stroked his striped love beads was kissing off my conscious volition . . .

'Take your average Zen neophyte, f'r'instance. Here is a nun or monk so determined to reach as near to 'vana as possible that they will solemnly try to answer questions that any normal, logical guy or girl will realise are utterly silly and detestable. After straining themselves for weeks or more, going to the Moonies and back, they discover when they stub their toe one day that the answer is, 'Your mother-in-law has new earrings', or 'Take out the garbage.' Greatest of the so-called "koans" is that timeless query: "Why did the Zen Buddhist cross the road?"

Now the accepted "direct transmission", as these wacky poverty-loving mellow-yellow robers call them, is "To get to other side." Nevertheless, if the master who has posed the question had a busy night before your interview or is given to hyperbole, the answers can be as varied as the leaves on the trees and about as slippery.'

Dales sipped some herbal tincture while Rock and I ribbed our eyes mechanically, drowsily regarded each other under heavy lids and felt eight miles high. Dales surveyed his conquests and, once again tinkering with the beads, resumed his rap.

'Interestingly, there has been no competent wedding of Zen and Judaism, despite the plain fact that a Yiddish Mama is a natural

Zen master with a mean koan few can match. The common YM koan runs: "Isn't the soup all right?" The acceptable enlightened response is: "How should it be?" Yet Zen has not approached the challenge of this great tradition. Imagine the progress that could be made! Upon the Zen master asking the Jewish lad: "What is the sound of one hand clapping?" The boy cannily replies with: "Who claps with one hand?" Before which clear answer the Zen master has to bow in veneration of a superior mind. After all, friends, who *does* clap with one hand . . . apart from amputees? But, though Zennies will profess humility they avoid such encounters!'

Rock shook himself violently, disgusted at his own lack of vigilance. Dales watched impassively, putting on his compassion face, looking at me with the same contrivance before continuing.

'Still, I digress. The fundamental question before us is: "Am I here?" Let's, for a moment at least, ignore the Jewish answer – "Where should I be?" – and really grapple with this fine fragment of realisation-in-the-raw!

'Are you there?'

Rock and I nodded dumbly.

'If you are hearing this in the office then you could say: "I am in the office!" But, and you must follow the gist of what I am driving at closely, if you are in the office, is it an office or only a metaphor? But, let's be frank, an office is not a metaphor for much . . . Except maybe *another* office.'

'And there it is: suddenly! The hundred-watt bulb of creation has been lit! Indeed, the office *is* a metaphor for an office! And so it jolly well goes! The seasoned metaphysicist can take such a philosophical position and drive his materialistic friends up a wonderwall. In the launderette at the precise moment when his friend produces a lone sock from the drier and clutches it mournfully you say, imperiously: "Are we not *all* sock separated from our matching metaphor of mixed fibres?" The friend, anxietised by this presumptuous, idiotic, aggravating arrogance, shrugs. The wise-guy-one sees his chance to counter-attack! "How can you shrug at this sock? This sock has been here before time itself began. Maybe before the rinse cycle began! If this sock is the Universe and we are the molecules that make up this blend of fibres then our entire yang has been a void and at any moment existence will itself implode!"

'The friend, spying the missing sock, produces it in triumph, and is about to speak sharply in his own defence when the initiate grabs it jealously and, brandishing it high, emits an inhuman yell, collapsing in a heap and sweating profusely. "To cut a long satori short" he bellows, transported at his liberation. "What the hell is going on?" asks his terrified pal. "Everything and nothing," laughs the freeman. "Sounds like an episode of 'Happy Days'." "It is!" yells the being of light.

'And so we see where we are.'


Rock and I came to some time later; Dales was gone. Rock was very embarrassed at being duped at his own game. What was worse, he hadn't even got verbal agreement on a deal, let alone closed it. But that would come later. Dales had left behind a pink and blue embroidered folder embossed with the Spiritual Hedonism logo: a lamb lying down with a stock certificate. The organisation's motto, *2000 Years Of Civilisation Can't be Wrong*, was fluorescent and glowed unappetisingly in the near-darkness of the room. Rock opened it carelessly, skimming page one. 'Listen to the message,' Rock sneered and slid across a tape to me, a subliminal financial fix entitled 'How To Be a TV Preacher and make Big $$$!'. Rock had moved on to a prototype prayer credit card that would spirit away your plastic tithe automatically into SH Inc's Swiss account, the other ninety percent to be immediately converted into guaranteed high-interest bonds underwritten by Spiritual Hedonism Investments (US). This boy Dales was no cartoon chipmunk and the nuts he was gathering were strictly unshelled. The know-it-all goofy guru had even included a section on legal advice, featuring lawyers educated comprehensively in Egyptian and Babylonian esoterica whom Dales referred to throughout, cutely, as 'Perry Masons'. As if all this mumbo-jumbo wasn't more than enough, there was a proposal for six hundred 'Blessing' auto-parks, where your vehicle could be washed in Lourdes water before a tune-up overseen by clerical mechanics! Rock was stunned by the array of temptations here, particularly page five where the caption 'Living further out may not be so bad after all' was followed by a plan for franchised astral projection retreats. 'Wisdom is part of our tradition' read the gothic blurb on fake parchment, not unlike the presentation employed by the Rosicrucians and their ilk.

By now Rock, fully awake and breathing tight Scrooge McDuck breaths between puffs on a cheap menthol, was excitable. Look at it this way, he had only been expecting a modest cut of some buttons, balloons and souvenir programmes and here Dales was handing at least a quarter of net on the biggest Godscam going. Now, Dales may have given us some post-hypnotic autosuggestion or otherwise tampered with us – a possibility Rock acknowledged when he suddenly realised he was saying 'OK, kid, this is your lucky break' to himself each time he finished a page – but he was digging being in the hands of a master and didn't mind the squeeze if it ended up making his dough rise high enough.

I leafed through the proposals, diagrams, indexed earnings projections – and had to admit that Dales Jr was probably the best I'd been used by. Rock started getting philosophical, even metaphysical – unusual for a man to whom intuition is smelling your own fart before it happens – and then began waxing lyrical on his 'beliefs', the biggest load of ballyhoo he'd yet lowered around my ears. Without any prompting he got around to saying how he wished he'd had a kid to pass on Necrotrivia to. This may sound like a deeply moving flaw in his façade, but to hear him you would swear he was talking about passing on leprosy. Anyhow, he ended up describing in repellent detail how, as a child, he would electrify his gerbil's cage and then prod it into an escape attempt, watching it writhe on the wire to the accompaniment of war picture soundtracks. As he drifted in his retrogressed reverie, I wondered what would they do with him in Hell. Rock looked at me momentarily, sensing my curiousity and, cocking his finger to his temple like a gun, said 'Ugly marks disappear.' He held my eyes in his developed

88

vice-grip, exerting invisible pressure on my psyche. It was like having an icebox over my head. It stopped. Rock splashed some horrible aftershave in my face and I fell off my chair.

Rock got up and left the office, stepping over me and laughing brazenly at my incapacitation. 'The nasty truth behind those rumours,' he said, clearly, as if at an elocution lesson. Which led me to believe, lying there in a puddle of rancid cola, that I had just been elocuted. On my elbows, rubbing my eyes and feeling my pulse, I got up and sat in the office alone, feeling like an interloper in the treasure rooms of the Pharoahs. But there was nothing of value there, not a goddamn stinking, useless thing. You'd love me to say right now, just like some wetrag gimp, that I broke down and cried and became a missionary and did my own washing forever after. Well, wrong again, and fuck you to the max: I knew where I was and where I was going – I was nowhere and going nowhere else. Rock owned me, picked lock, rifle stock and pickle barrel, a hostage to Fortune who was going so fast on his treadmill that I felt like that gerbil on the Wall of Death at a county fair. I was disoriented, drinking to calm my adrenalin, not sure if Dales or Rock had fucked with my head. Probably both had. I sat in *his* chair, put the light back on and thought the thought you think when you think you have be thoughtful. My problem, I reflected, is I don't take life seriously enough. Having thought which, I watched 'Virgin on the Ridiculous', a particularly sick NTV softcore spoof, and ate my body weight in pretzels. Remember back about two hundred words where you thought I would cry? Funny, I don't.


It never rains but it pours, they say, and I was knee-deep. What with organising the Rock/Silence summit meeting, carrying the usual stack of accounts and trying to lead a private life on weekends and public holidays, I hadn't seen Elaine for days, or maybe weeks. Since I was duty bound to say next to nothing about everything I did, doubly so because of Rock's escalating security around the war-rights altercations, this was probably just as well. But if you get a stocking in the mail one day and a brassiere the next, you have to ask yourself some searching questions! Damn, though, wasn't I Rock's pet rock? The non-man with no name had found room at the top, I was a regular guy. I loved the pace, too, while hating it passionately, and delivered as never before. The summit was coming together like a grilled cheese sandwich, its key ingredients melting inexorably towards the rendezvous with animosity.

And, what should happen but the Fourth of July is pulling up fast and it's an election year, no less. So to top off all the other crap, I get roped into helping Exe and Barb cut and trim one of the candidate's campaign features. Ah, yes, the days of gruelling hands-on stumping are over for good. Now each candidate fields his features the statutory six weeks before polling day and lets the box office determine the outcome.

Our man, John Smith – the Republican, natch – had a dandy ultra-right game plan, promoted by Exe's ingenious 'Dance like a butterfly, sting like a WASP.' Smith was ahead in the polls and looked certain to scrape the bottom of the ballot-box. Dales Jr had made a fair old impression on me and I stirred elements of two of his best sellers, *Money Can Buy Everything* and *If I Were You I'd Be Somebody Else*, into Smith's chunky sound-bite soup. Dales was a precocious pain in the Acts but I wasn't averse to diving into his drivel for a few bright baubles to adorn Smith's bull neck.

What peeved me was that just as I was getting a manhandle on the presidential ratrace, the news of Rock and Silence's forthcoming kibbitz burned up the industry bush telegraph fast enough to give holy Moses a hotfoot. So it was time to roll out the red parapet – spikes, boiling oil and all – and put the pit-bullshitters down. The media, to whom Rock was a spectral curio and Silence a necessarily evil newsmaker, shuddered with anticipation at the prospect of pinning both prize butterflies at once. Which wasn't a chorus line of jumping beans to me until I discovered that Rock needed me as minutes-man. Rock and Silence were each to bring one p.a. and Hell – the obvious choice – had cancelled out at the last mo' to attend his Alma Mater's reunion. I was duly deputised and sent home to make ready.

I entertained brave thoughts of a mutinous desertion, sensing that now it was going to get very ugly indeed. I summoned up my best Robinson Crusoe scenario, with Girl Elaine and I on the deserted beach and just a ghetto-blaster, butler and subscription to *Penthouse Letters* for company.

I saw myself throwing Rock's dirty door wide, standing there in the half-light, hands on hips gunfighter-style, and firing my best W.C. Fields raspberry at the little big man. Then, arms folded, I'd sit on the desk and say, quite matter-of-factly, 'I don't like your planet, I don't like your company, I don't like your species and *I don't like you!*' It would be the triumphant end of an error, my finest hour. But, predictably, I never got further than furtive hamming in the full-length mirror, striking Napoleon poses and mouthing Machiavellian catchphrases.

By the end of the evening news I was tucking into a wildly shaded layered sponge gateau when a messenger of doom arrived. The cold hard fax of the matter were on my lap and I buckled in mentally. Date, time and place: it was all there in grainy b & w. There could be no backing out now, not without tripping. Rock didn't get out of the wrong side of the bed, he got up in the wrong room, and I didn't want to be the one on the cutting edge when his fold-up cot jackknifed . . . Damn it, damn it, damn it, – I was committed . . . Or, at least, I ought to have been.

# 10

## Cadillac Of Lemons

The day of the summit dawned, in itself a disappointment. It would have been preferable to just wake up the far side of the whole ill-omened shebang. But, oh no, my alarm sounded at seven as planned; and as my eyes opened I felt the fickle finger of fate tickling me. Rock and I were to be collected at ten a.m. from NT HQ and spirited away to the Minute Carwash on the Kennedy Overpass. Silence would be waiting in his own custom Turbo with Peerless the Pitiless. My palms were sweating before I got out of bed and standing wasn't easy. Don't ask me why a formidable fellow such as myself was so shaken and stirred by the day to come undone. I just had a gut feeling so strong that all I could feel was guts in knots, tighter than a scoutmaster could master. There was a B-western on the box and I watched the wagon's circling as I downed a bowl of Cheerios, finding irony in everything – from the name of the cereal to the ridiculous hokum on the range. Why me? I asked a dozen times.

I triple-checked the spy stuff Rock had me buy the day before, saying: 'Your word against theirs. Now have proof with recording systems designed to keep you in control.' Fine, but even the air traffic towers at LAX couldn't control me now. I had everything: a luxurious briefcase recorder, secret pen recorder and, in the bottom of my own case, an electronic memory telecorder.

A cab took me downtown and, humbled by trepidation, I shook security-man Reiner's hand and sort of smiled at him. Horrified and disconcerted, he saluted and went back to his video monitors gratefully. The elevator to the third floor was empty, luckily, so my pacing went unseen. You know, you can't pace much in an elevator over three floors, but by making small concentric circles I maximised the experience, stepping out giddily and letting the momentum of my dizziness propel me to my desk. There, on a weatherbeaten memo-pad, Rock had scrawled: 'Put yourself to the test!' Underneath he had drawn a little mushroom cloud with me on its curly cap. Ha ha ha.

Laurieanne conducted me into Rock's office dramatically and, pointing at her charge like a mother proudly sending off a favoured offspring on its first school day, she sighed contentedly as I recoiled slightly at the incongruous sight. Rock: (a) shaved; (b) wearing fresh clothes; (c) and shined shoes; (d) had brushed his teeth so that in places they were white; (e) had on matching, albeit chipped, vintage NT cufflinks; (f) wore a tie; (g) had on an ironed, nearly tasteful cotton casual shirt with all its buttons and an intact pocket; (h) had had a trim; (i) didn't have the shakes, bad breath or dandruff. I was immobilised. Rock looked *human*. I clung to the spare seat, regaining my composure but unable to break my gaze. Rock, drinking in my incredulity, stood up and modelled his new look. Laurieanne, overcome with pride, seated herself and wept in a dignified, maternal fashion. On Rock's *tidy* desk was another little drawing he'd done of a tombstone with his own name on it and the epitaph, 'BEATS WORKIN''. I nodded at it and let out a strangled laugh, then moved back to the wall to take in the boss resurrected. He offered me a cola in a clean glass and poured himself a mineral water – yes, you read that correctly, pilgrim – and actually downed it, smacking his lips afterwards as if he'd enjoyed it. I searched the desk area for a concealed mickey of gin or vodka or scotch but there wasn't a whiff of perdition anywhere. Laurieanne crept out, sniffling.

'Mine when I need it, theirs when I don't,' Rock explained blandly, executing a perfect catwalk twirl to show off his cut and drip-dry. I was flabbergasted to say the very least, awed by this warrior-warlock-witch-doctor-wacko-will-of-iron-windbag. This was the man who, only twenty-four hours earlier, had been seen in the lobby celebrating Independence Day with a bottle of Sterno and a jar of olives, throwing ladyfingers at the clients and giving away party hats.

I accepted the turnaround and faced Rock respectfully, readied for anything. Rock stooped towards me and said loudly in my ear: 'You may consider me a God!' I nodded, looked away and hoped a UFO would take me away. Nope.

Rock circled the office, sipping mineral water, flexing his muscles and reading a copy of *Sports Illustrated*. What he hoped to gain I wasn't sure; I guess he wanted to give Silence and Peerless no advantages. I felt inadequate but excited as we set off in our plush hired limo, the uniformed driver chitchatting about the forth-coming election. He was a right-wing Buddhist who'd just been on a weekend study retreat on 'Death' and, let me tell you, by the time he'd pulled up to the carwash I wished I could garrot him and let him get the facts first-hand. I was edgier than a razor coming off a strop and not much for conversation. Rock was deep-breathing, entirely confident, his small, monogrammed, *new* briefcase in hand. I don't know how or why he let Laurieanne engineer his look but it was great and I was proud to follow two paces behind like a Chinese concubine. It was a short walk to the anonymous Minute Carwash and as soon as we crested the drive-way I spotted Silence's straightbacked silhouette in the backseat of his gleaming Turbo. A huge stretch Caddy was parked in the middle of the main washing bay, two uniformed butlers at either door, waiting on the men. Silence was talking to Peerless and Rock trained his eyes on their profiles avidly.

The items up for discussion were many and madly complex, ranging from the election to the war to the weather and how best to control them all. Rock took measured strides and we got into the Caddy seated on late-model leather, the bar open for business. I let my eyes dart but was careful to keep my body still as, sud-denly, Silence and Peerless walked purposefully over and got in, lowering their six-foot-pluses of tight muscle and broad bone decorously to do so. Rock ignored them but I couldn't help gasping at the dynamic duo in the flesh.

Silence was strikingly handsome, as they say. His jaw was cut glass, his hands suitable for modelling, his eyes intense behind prescription RayBans. The creases in his trousers could have been ironed by Pythagoras; his handkerchief, pink with blue flecks on a field of light silver, was folded like prize origami. He laid his hands in his lap gently, breathed invisibly and deferred to Peerless with almost imperceptible signals: a crooked forefinger or minutely inclined foot. Rock drank it all in, equally mannered and malign. Meanwhile Silence lived up to his peculiar moniker, waiting for us to break the soundbarrier. The air in the Caddy, air-conditioned to perfection, cooled our jests to a whisper. Silence pulled up his trousers a bit and Peerless, responding precisely to the signal, unfolded a print-out brief for his own reference. Silence grimaced at Rock, the latter acknowledging the starting pistol by elbowing me to bring out our goods. What a pumped-up potlatch! I quivered and handed Rock the essential pages.

Just as Silence was about to say something, Rock pre-empted him by politely pulling out of his pressed pocket a stack of incredibly rare baseball cards and handing them to his rival. Silence was aghast at Rock's acuity. I reeled at my superior's superiority. What intelligence had geared for him the fact that – as he told me later – Silence craved this set of 1954 World Series cards to complete his world-class collection, that these very cards had eluded him a full ten years. How the hell did Rock even know he collected them? I'd never seen it in the papers. But there they were, good as new, all eighty, prettily shrinkwrapped in a flawless cardboard box.

Silence was dumbfounded, appreciative and on guard. He shook hands with Rock, then inspected his hands and fingers for dirt. Rock smiled with satisfaction and gave Peerless a souvenir NT gold fountain pen that played a popular song when you refilled it. Peerless took it somewhat resentfully and pocketed it, leaving the top to protrude from his breast pocket. Silence packed away his cards and wanted to get down to business. Rock believed in great chiefs exchanging gifts before talking cold turkey, but Silence, thoroughly modern, had brought no trinkets or token of respect for Rock. Clearly embarrassed and annoyed at Peerless for skipping so important a detail, he had to let his huff subside before making ready to broach the first topic on the agenda, the Gulf TV rights.

'Designer cannibalism,' he began, handing Rock a proposal on the split and splat of the deal. Rock read it quickly, and handed it back, nonplussed. 'Pick up someone your own size,' he blurted out, surprised by Silence's shoddy offer. Peerless shifted, his hostility now horribly visible. I just sat and watched the two master butchers carving and counter-carving, selling men and materials, laughing seldom but often grunting sardonically as they agreed to differ, or differed too much even for that. Peerless and I conveyed paper and pens and pencils, stowed contracts and made drinks. Silence and Rock hated each other vehemently, but in the greatest traditions of greed they overlooked such petty concerns in pursuit of higher profits.

'The corporate brochure,' Peerless said, handing me SKULL's prospectus, a lovely little white vellum number embossed and bordered with deep blue.

'Key elections are shaping our world,' Rock was saying, discussing the big day with Silence, who contemplated his remarks over a freshly-squeezed Orange Julius. 'Another medium, the television version,' Rock went on, and gave Silence the dirt on his end of the presidential pantomime. 'Spectre of communism . . . never too young to subscribe . . . turning point for America . . .' The words tripped off Rock's tongue effortlessly and Silence took it all in with interest, returning in kind. I couldn't believe how well it was all going. Then Rock, en route to a précis of his views on religion, started dropping weighted slights about Silence's old-time devotion, and the mood changed mercurially.

Everyone looked at everyone else. I stared out of the window. The drivers were at the doors to the washing bay, smoking and kibbitzing. Four bodyguards were at the other end, doing likewise. For the first time I wondered why we were in a carwash at all. After all, Silence or Rock could afford any penthouse in town, and while Rock cared nothing for creature comforts, Silence's appetite for same was legendary. I'd find out later that Silence had hired the place for the day to test the allegiance of a disaffected Mafioso whose protection rackets had come unstrung. The carwash was nowhere in particular, unlikely to attract media and safe as long as a spiteful off-duty contract killer didn't perchance use it while we were parked there. By now we'd been washed maybe six times already, the whirring and gushing and mushing a pleasant background to the affairs of the shark being conducted within the Caddy. Now the atmosphere was thinner than Saturn's and hotter than a midsummer picnic on Mars.

Rock continued in much the same voice, arguing for his angle on the Gulf again, but Silence was festering over his godless *faux pas*. Peerless was quiet, too quiet, and I kind of leaned away from Rock in case a stray slug found him, not confident that, as agreed, no guns were present. Silence couldn't settle until the air had been cleaned of Rock's blasphemy. Why did Rock rag on Silence when things had been looking so good? Considering how important the outcome of the summit could be, I examined the question repeatedly but could only draw blanks. Maybe Rock wanted to bug Silence, gain a fresh start on clearcut mutual antagonism, the area in which he excelled. Maybe it was an unconscious blunder – talk is cheat and Rock had rolled himself the wrong way, letting his distaste for all things bright and beautiful surface like sewage.

Rock plowed ahead regardless, making small talk about his deal in Africa, ribbing Silence, now moribund, on his brother-in-law's part in running guns to old Edmund. Rolf Endelbeest, the loveable rogue in question, had come through in the crunch for Rock's side and the war was won. But Silence wasn't having any of it, listening sceptically at best and, at worst, whispering innuendoes to Peerless that were beginning to butt Rock's goat.

Rock, thinking he'd overheard an unfair accusation reflecting on his efficacy as NT major-domo, put his feet a toe from Silence's, planted elbows on knees and said, 'Who *really* wrote the Bible?' Peerless clenched both fists and, jaw set firmly, waited for the order to strike. Silence, recovering from Rock's initial breach of etiquette, produced a slim Good News Bible from an inside pocket, leaned back and said, 'This bestseller has greatly influenced our lives. Who penned and preserved these extraordinary books? Which view is correct?'

Stymied briefly, Rock looked to me for help but, sadly, having never read the Good Book, I couldn't carry the ball for him. I thought of some Dales Jr schtick and laid that on Silence but, fatally, he recognised it and launched into a barrage of invective barbed enough to tick off a Tiger tank. Rock was getting fed up now and, interrupting Silence's sanctified raving, barked: 'Did God walk the Earth?' He was striving to offend and Silence took the bait. A few minutes later a 'debate' was raging out of control and all Peerless and I could practically do was keep our eggheads down and pray for a break in the clouds. Rock had heard tell of Silence meeting Dales Jr about *something* and was dying to wheedle a tip off out of his adversary.

'American Christianity is ripe for revival'. Silence was treating Rock like a recalcitrant Sunday Schoolee and Rock, at the limits of his theological patience, was ribbing hard. There was no way back to the civilised discourses of only fifteen moments ago. Rock and Silence were in a null-man's land of their own making, and only a miracle of the Biblical variety could save the summit. Peerless followed Rock's every move with vacant eyes, their bunny-pink lids deceptively heavy. For my part, I wished I had a stand-in. I was looking for someone to blame and I found a solace in Hell, mentally wreaking revenge on his picayune personality. Meanwhile, Silence was getting righteous, as in a righteous to the jaw, and Rock was verbally ducking and diving to avoid a direct hit. I could see Rock was enjoying himself – a matter for grave concern as Rock only ever enjoyed himself at other people's expense, and I wasn't too sure if he had an expense account with Silence.

Where could I go? The doors were locked, the drivers oblivious, the day young, the story old. 'To find the missing ingredient in your recipe for happiness, read Matthew nine, twenty-nine! To find the missing ingredient in your recipe for friendship read John thirteen, thirty-four,' Silence commanded, his head touching the car roof as he leaned over Rock wagging his ring finger. Rock was hard put to keep a straight face; to him words like 'friendship' and 'happiness' were unrelated and alien, fragments of some hardsell harangue. Having such words hurled at him like Thor's bolts was a Red rag to a Marine and as Silence continued to pile on the pulpit chastisement, Rock became introverted and dangerously restrained. 'In each of these special recipes, you will find that there is one ingredient missing,' Silence went on, with Peerless playing Cheshire cat to his owner's tiger. 'You can find the right answers by reading the Bible verses and then filling yourself with that missing ingredient. All answers are found in the King James Version . . .'

'In nod we trust,' Rock yawned exaggeratedly, grabbing the gold pen he'd dished out to Peerless, breaking it over his briefcase and, with monstrous glee, squirting the refill all over Silence's tie, a gorgeous silk import covered in SKULL logos. Silence, taken aback at Rock's childishness and complete disregard for his hopelessly heartfelt histrionics, collapsed back into his seat, clutching the stain as if to hide it.

Peerless, insulted vicariously, moved like lightning, producing an identical tie from his kitbag and attaching it delicately to Silence's collar – straightening his collar-studs lovingly as an afterthought. Rock elbowed me some more and chuckled uncontrollably at the punchdrunk preacher and his wired ward. I was sitting on my hands and my thoughts, deferring noncommittally to Rock, hoping for a fault line to appear beneath the Caddy and swallow us all up. A few times I even felt tremors. Then, opening my eyes, I realised that Peerless and Silence were outside trying to roll the car, aided by their henchmen. Rock was stoically slicing the back seat with his paltry penknife, sniggering boyishly as the shock absorbers vibrated violently. Water and soap dripped through the slightly open windows as Peerless restarted the wash cycle. I waited for Rock to do something remotely mature and considered to save us from a watery grave.

'Bad sport!' he said instructively, extending a crooked index finger at Peerless, sweating and tousled from his exertions at the door handles. Silence had disappeared. Finally, exhausted and deserted by his helpers, Peerless relented. He walked tall over to the trembling Caddy and, squinting in through the smoked glass to see us, slapped an adhesive SKULL calling card on the windshield. It read "Where's there's smoke there's gunfire!" Underneath the logo were crossed two antique pistols, the tell-tale Jolly Roger peeking from between their barrels.

Rock, never one to miss an opportunity to trawl his trachea, hawked up an obscene orb of bubbly jade phlegm, letting it flatten and slide on the other side of the glass. Peerless pounded the window, cracking it in the bottom corner, then, afraid to overstep his mandate, stomped off like a lumberjack heading for a wild weekend.

I wiped my brow. Rock wiped his nose. The driver wiped the windshield.

I bummed off work next day to glue myself back together with a family pack of those gross Twinkies, two jars of peanut butter and a dose of my favorite TV show: 'Insecurity'. The guys at NTV must have had fun dreaming it up. What a duzy!

'Insecurity' was hosted by a strapping black dude named Lorry LaBonte. He'd been discovered by an NTV talent scout pimping in New Orleans and been shipped north for grooming post haste once six figure incentives had secured a contract. LaBonte was born to bullshit and the ladies loved him, even if their husbands wanted to skin his slick skin off. 'Insecurity' employed that venerable game-show workhorse, the 'sound-proof booth', and with Lorry at the mission controls it was one rocket bound to nosedive. Necrotrivia game shows had one golden rule: No one gets out with pride.

Today's show kicked off with another middle-class couple looking to supplement their passion, Mr and Mrs C. Fink of End-of-the-Tracktown NJ. 'Near Atlantic City?' LaBonte asked as if here were a vice cop about to cuff them. Mr Fink fingered his tight plaid collar, ungritted his molars and attempted to smile. No way.

Mrs F, strapped in the booth, looked out like a test pilot, waving idiotically.

After a few unpleasantries, LaBonte bumped the man of the house into position and turned on the shallow-fry treatment that was his specialty. The audience was hushed, savouring the cruelty to come.

Peering nervously at the overhead spots like Simon of the Desert, Fink waited. LaBonte asked him, quite well-meaningly, 'So, Clyde, you're a travelling salesman I understand?' Clyde: 'Yes, I am.' LaBonte: 'Good.' (You SOB, I laughed.)

'So tell me, Clyde, what does the little Finkwoman get up, or *down* . . . on . . . uh . . . *to* – 'scuse me, hahaha – when you're just *hundreds* of miles away, alone with your samples in some Godforsaken two-horse townlet?'

Clyde looked at LaBonte. He replied tentatively. 'Um . . . I dunno . . . She sees her sister a lot.'

'I suppose she *waits* for you?'

'Well, yeah, of course she does . . . I guess . . . Why?'

'Well, I'm glad you asked Clyde – may I call you Clyde? Thanks. *Well*, Clydesworth, we've been jawing to a few of your wifettes palsy-walsies . . .' Already Clyde is on edge, walking the rough and rocky trail to a deeply private mental precipice. His lifelong suspicions torment him. Mrs Fink *is* a fink! LaBonte, aware that his subject is wavering, goes in.

'Now, steady Clyde,' LaBonte advises paternally, shaming the poor gimp. 'Now, let's be rational here, right? I suppose you and the Mrs, after years of happy, harmonious, model marriage, have complete and unshakable faith in each other, a faith reinforced by a lifetime of love?'

'Well, yes,' Clyde affirms, falling completely for LaBonte's cheap trap. His conviction is tragically palpable.

'Fine. That's fine! Now tell me, do you call the wife when you're on the move?'

'Well, yeah . . . But sometimes, you know how it is . . .'

'Of course we do, Clyde, *we know how it is*,' LaBonte sneers, his insinuation eaten up by the crowd. 'Now tell us about how much you and your Fink trust each other.'

'Completely.' His brusque reply falls on stoney ground.

'Uh-*hunnh*.' LaBonte looks over at Mrs F grooving in the booth and turns back. 'Clyde, has it ever entered your mind that maybe – *just maybe* – Mrs might stray? Just . . . *once?* Loneliness is a crushing burden for a little woman to stand up to!'

'Nope! She wouldn't do it.' Clyde's categorical refutation sounds more hollow than the Liberty Bell in late December.

'You are speaking honestly I take it, Mr Fink?' asks LaBonte imperiously. 'You're that sure?'

'Sure I'm sure,' says Clyde shortly, peripheral snottiness besmirching his dignity.

'Well it's a funny ol' thang, rilly,' LaBonte says in a flatulent *patois* as the audience eases to the edge of their seats. 'Because,' LaBonte continues, drawing a killer bead on his crumbling quarry, 'actually, in point of *fact*, as it happens, the way it is, when the chips are down, the dog is fed and the garbage is out for the night . . .'

'Yes?' Clyde demands, his civility under direct attack.

'The wife *is* a bit of a scalliwag, Mr Fink – a dark *whore*, as it were . . .' Clyde's teeth resume gritting. 'Our private eyes tell us that on three separate, verifiable occasions in the past fourteen days she's slept with a Mr Howie McBatten, of an address not unlike your own bar one digit. Any comment?'

'No.' Clyde is standing still, regarding his wife, who remains oblivious to the bean spillage beyond. Clyde readies himself to attack her at the first opportunity.

'You see, Mr Fink, "Insecurity" always knows! Contestants come on this show sure that they have nothing to hide or to be worried about; their rep is spotless, their closet skeleton-free. We catch them! So I'm afraid you have to forfeit your prize money. Maybe Mrs *Fink* will do better.'

Clyde wilts. Commercial.

'Valhalla', a new SKULL automobile, is blazing across a Nordic landscape, shining in the midnight sun. Thor's behind the wheel, grinning from one vast cheek to the other, his little booties pumping the gas pedal like the dickens. His mighty hammer pounds the dashboard and the sound of a herd of wild stallions in a canyon overwhelms the engine's roar. 'Valhalla' – a Nordic Godmobile with Fleshtone Leatherette and Masthead Hood Ornament Included. The talkover comes on, in a thick Swedish accent: 'Valhalla – a car the gods themselves would drive!'

'Insecurity' returns. Mr Fink, looking chastened, is in the booth. A beaming Mrs Fink rubs up against LaBonte, apparently unaware that her marriage is approaching the rocks in a typhoon.

'Mrs Fink,' begins LaBonte, 'your hubby is a travelling man of sales, is he not?' he asks chivalrously.

'Why yes, he is!' says Mrs Fink graciously, ogling LaBonte's teak skin.

'*Good*. But I guess that means he's away a lot, eh?' asks LaBonte conversationally, all the while sizing up the comely contestant's ample cleavage.

'Uh, yes. But we're so close it's OK.'

'I see. Well, then, if you don't mind me asking you a personal question, if, heaven forbid, anything should happen to Mr F – act of God, murder, abduction, something like that . . . I mean, you'd be taken care of, looked after – financially, that is?'

Mrs Fink looks suddenly uneasy. 'Well, yes . . . Well yes . . .' she stammers.

'OK, let's play ball fairly now, Mrs F. When it comes down to brass tacks, have you seen or signed or otherwise had absolute proof of the existence of an insurance policy of which you are the beneficiary?'

'Of course . . . Well, that's not a very nice question, Lorry, but . . . Well, I haven't actually *signed* . . . or seen . . . but it *does* exist!'

'How, precisely, do you know that, dear?' asks LaBonte in a self-satisfied tone.

'Clyde says so,' Mrs Fink replies frumpishly.

'He does, does he? But, without seeing the thing, I mean, how d'you *know* such a document exists? And are you the beneficiary, pray tell?'

'Well, of course I am!'

'Yes but how can you prove it when you haven't seen it?'

'I guess . . . Well, I don't know . . .' rambles the poor woman distractedly.

'You don't know? And do you know,' LaBonte pauses portentously, about to deliver the death blow-job, 'do you know Mr Fink was previously married, and that you, Mrs Fink, are wife number two?'

Silence. Pale face. Clammy hands. Mr Fink, introspective in the booth, eyes shut tightly, deigns to look at his spouse in her moment of doom.

Applause. LaBonte bows. Commercial.

The clock on the wall said lunch. I said, what a great way to spend twenty-three minutes.


Elaine was playing on my mind again. Not an unpleasant thing to endure, but you'd have to play with her yourself to know why.

We'd had a few more brief-less encounters since our first. None of the relevant parties had yet gotten wind of our wing-ding and we were feeling pretty invincible. Elaine had relented now with the damsel-in-distrust schtick, which had loosened enough of my screws to make me rattle when I walked. I'd never figured myself for a soft touch, but then I'd never touched anything as soft as Elaine. She didn't poke her nose into my working life, which suited me fine since I wanted to forget it every chance I got. We had nothing in common except nothing and we were literally worlds apart, but in the things that matter between man and another man's wife we were getting close for comfort. Elaine's chief attributes were the temperament of a saint and the figure of a sinner and the savvy to know when to use each.

In the groggy aftermath of the summit I was anxious for some undemanding company to thwart the tendency of mind to dwell on the path NT was leading me down. Trying to forget Necrotrivia was as easy as forgetting you have a head when it's aching and

Elaine provided my one reliable refuge. Yes, I was probably trapped, totally, but as long as I could delude myself in idle moments of nubile nirvana I could fend off a final resolution.

We'd taken to meeting at a different motel but the routine remained the same. Whenever Ben made an overnight sensation of his misery, Elaine would get het up enough to disappear the next day for the requisite hours. A coded message on the machine clued me in and I'd take a long, lingering lunch over an *à la carte* menu with specialties my modesty prevents you maundering over.

'Saucy minx not as bad as she thinks,' I was saying to Elaine later that afternoon over a cold coffee. I'd taken on the role of freelance therapist to offset her propensity for self-obsession and often, after a particularly satisfying session, she'd pour out her misgivings about the state of so-called civilisation. 'When you can take the ticket from my hand, Grasshopper, it will be time for you to go,' I jested as she nestled on my chest. Her hair shone in the light of the TV, a washed-out 'Bullwinkle' episode adding comic highlights.

Elaine smiled slightly. There was a half-inch of open space between us, but it was alive with static electricity. She did something interesting with one eyebrow.

'Feelings of stress and tension are eased,' I said, gently touching her face. Necrotrivia was a million miles away and then, unforgivably, Elaine mentioned Ice Hell, that bogus bane of my existence. 'Miracle mouthwash could save your life,' I told her, in no uncertain tones. She was hurt but I was mad and I was damned if I'd have that nerd's name detract from my daydream.

'The promise of freedom was too tempting,' Elaine grumbled and made for the powder room. Our first cross words. At the time I dismissed the episode. Little did I know that in Elaine's mind it wasn't an episode but a whole chapter.


The radio-alarm roused me just past five next morning. Little Joe, the matron's heart-throb-of-the-month, crooned his latest hit, *Hitler Was a Pal O' Mine:*

105

Although South America is home to me
Seems things ain't what they used to be
Israel knows where I'll be
It's up to them to front the speaker's fee

The phone had just finished ringing as I got to it. I picked it up anyways and threw it at the opposite wall. White plaster dust swirled down.

I hated mornings. They always begin with a call. Choices. Or else an urgent assignment like going down to NT to put change in Rock's parking meter because he'd locked himself in his office yet again with some stuff, or women, or both.

I went into the kitchen and threw some coloured goo together. One egg missed the pan, leaving yellow yolk tracks across my matching tiles. The previous night's TV binge had numbed my cortex. The eggs ebbed and flowed whenever I tried to catch some on my plastic cutlery. Eventually I plumped for a jolt of caffeine and cola, half a lemon meringue pie and a new sauce I'd prepared that looked how I felt on top of cold macaroni. Wearily I flopped into the TV chair and flicked on Channel 24's Sports Review.

'Okey, dokey, big rollers, our big tips on the big race at Mollard Circle are in! Ready?'

The odds flashed onto the screen with a disclaimer beneath them in tiny print that said: 'This station and its sponsors take NO responsibility for losses or personal risks resulting from this tip sheet.' Recently a score of suckers had been pressing a joint suit against the station on the shaky ground that the tipsheet had been instrumental in depriving them of their livelihoods.

Then there was the guy who came into Channel 8 with a mixmaster and pushed the newscaster's face down into it on camera because he'd lost his second mortgage on a Derby. He was acquitted. The mixmaster company experienced an eighteen per cent sales boost the following month and the newscaster got a job in medical films, and even did a successful lecture tour on home appliances, organised crime and plastic surgery.

# 11

## The Irresistible Force

Rock being Rock – and let's open-face it, who else would want to be? – he exhibited zero contrition over the summit mangling, ridiculing the whole exercise with one of his practised mini-maxims, 'No crime like the pleasant.' Much doggy-do about nothing was his attitude, and no matter how many irate letters, calls and faxes arrived, he refused to answer Silence. So we never found out what might have happened, only what *did* happen, which in a notoriously imperfect world is what generally transpires.

Although Rock's confidence was frequently infectious, this time I wasn't convinced the soiled summit situation didn't suck bad just because the great patriarch pushed the same old buttons. Call it a hunch, call it paranoia, call it what you like. Rock *was* underestimating Silence's likely reaction, and refusing to rake through the fall-out meant everyone was going to be poisoned in time. I debriefed my colleagues and they couldn't decide if it was the beginning of the end or vice versa. No one wanted to contradict Rock, understandably, but that left me hauling a wagonload of misgivings alone. To make matters worse, no sooner had Rock received a dry cleaning bill from Silence than he sent it back, COD, tied to a rock. Preferring to skip our usual couriers, Rock handed a kid five bucks and told him to throw it through the highest window he could hit. All very well on the schoolground, but rather less realistic behaviour from one of the most powerful businessmen in America.

About a week after the Minute Wash's longest day I began to wish I'd put money on personal bankruptcy. Rock was peeved at my tacit insubordination, and rumours were rife that if I didn't put a sock in it Rock would do it for me with a *real* sock. I put up, shut up and gave up. I should have changed my bet. Rock forgot about my faithless folly but Silence couldn't as easily forgive. In all his life he had never had his shirt besmirched and – this would have been funny if . . . – the baseball cards . . . Well, the damn cards were *fake*. Remember, you read it here first, friends: back a few pages I *told* you Rock's hit charade was too goody-goody to be true. Rock didn't bat an eyelid, or my ear, when I mildly admonished him for such tearing tawdriness, but down inside my qualms were unquenched. Somewhere *out there* where the Great Puppeteer yanks and jerks we were up for a severe jerking off.

'We are looking for a few good boys and girls.'

The voice was crushing velvet, kid gloves bouncing off my defences. I'd been at NT too long not to see a come-on coming. It looked big.

'Have we got a number for you!' Rock was positively jovial and therefore to be not-trusted more than usual.

There was me, Hank Bikinidold, Hell and a few p.a.s, Laurie-anne and a big, ghoulish-looking stiff, all crowded into Rock's tiny roach-haven, shoulder-to-shoulder and not liking it.

'I'm looking for five friends,' Rock said matter-of-factly, eyeing each of his stalwarts with affection, disgust and detached condescension. What *did* Rock see when he looked at me, I wondered, and then declined to take the inquiry any further. I could guess. What does a foot see when it closes in on an ant?

So we're all sitting there, peas in a putrescent pod, waiting for the big squeeze. Rock suddenly leaves the room. We sit, not speaking. The mysterious stranger leans against the wall, six feet and more of human ugliness. His pitted face and soiled company tie rule him out for anything but some horrible scam, undoubtedly the one responsible for our glorious leader's good humour. I catch his eyes for a microsecond and come away with a dry-ice burn. He has his hands in his pocket, his face looks like a biker club sandwich, with the goo dripping out and soddening the crusts. It's pockmarked, as though scored by ballpoint and sandblaster, vestigial acne still in evidence.

Our eyes are about to lock in again when the door is eased open and Rock returns wearing a goddamned chef's outfit! He's pushing in a dusty little silver trolley, a real relic, vintage 1930. Aboard are a small bowl, covered with a pink silk hanky, and a pitcher of milk, also silver and old.

Rock rolls the trolley past us and stops it directly in front of his desk.

'What is the best way to make me a drug addict?'

That rather begs the question, seeing as he's already a five-grama-day man, but we let it slip. The odd man out smiles a thin, twisty smile and licks his lips, at which Rock laughs to himself. Then he yanks away the hanky, revealing some sticky generic breakfast concoction. Everyone cranes their necks and looks at Rock. He curtsies gracefully and says: 'We have this new breakfast cereal we want to sell for our friend here – ' he points to Frankenstein – 'it's called – ' invisible roll of drums, pipe band, etc – 'SMACK.' Rock lets the name go into freefall and each of us fields it in our own way.

Laurieanne snickers in embarrassment; Hell nods approvingly; Bikinidold nudges me; the p.a.s look at each other and shrug; the Incredible Hulk looks lovingly at his creation.

Rock fixes his gaze on me to see how loyal I am going to be. 'When you eat it the sky goes all funny and you *lurve* everybody.' He grimaces ambiguously. Bikinidold and Hell elbow and push each other like little boys.

'Time for a treat!' Rock chortles, scooping some SMACK up and swallowing it dry, hardly chewing. He pours milk over the bowlful and passes it to me, waiting expectantly as I move the spoon to my lips. It goes down easy, marginally bitter but also far too sweet. An aftertaste like battery acid. Texture of soggy cardboard. Ace! I

109

want more! Soon the bowl is empty, everyone dips into the box and chats. Rock and the big slug whisper in a corner.

'Yeah,' says Bug Boy suddenly, turning to address us all, 'you see, it cannot fail. The kids are hooked, they want SMACK every day. All the fuckin' time, right? Anyone can make promises. I need *results!*' He looks at Hell, Bikinidold and myself, especially me. Apparently Rock has given him the impression that I am the pre-eminent lie-perfector.

It is hitting me, finally: the p.a.s are asleep; Hell is gibbering – to himself; Bikinidold is lurvingly fingering a crack in the wall; Laurieanne is taking shorthand; Rock is powdering a few SMACKs, then snorting them, giggling. I feel numbness around my lids, twitching lip, a subtle tinge of nausea. I sit back and murmur. No one notices.

The client walks over to me, crouches by my chair and, his lips forming a half-smile as he speaks, fills in the gaps. SMACK is a new kind of breakfast cereal, coated with a glucose solution of blended narcotics, particularly high-grade coke and . . . smack. The manufacturers of SMACK are looking at the biggest cereal seller ever. Anticipating a landslide victory, they're offering one billion bucks for the best ad campaign. I don't have to be told that only SKULL and Necrotrivia stand any real chance of playing ball with these boys. That war in the Gulf was nothing next to SMACK; this scam has the potential to smash open all the golden gourds and even Rock and Silence, those consummate ringmasters, will have to go neck deep for a shot at the gold star. A billion! And a guaranteed custom-built podium in the advertising hall of infamy! Rock and Silence are gonna need lifebouys just to keep their heads above their own saliva.

I try to visualise how many Twinkies a billion buys when Rock approaches me and says, 'Well, well! Anyone aged over six can get high at breakfast!' He strokes my sweaty palm, licking his finger-tips. I feel windblown, electric, with borders soft and mushy. The mood passes. No concrete memory of the biochemical day-trip remains. Others regain full consciousness and, washed out and wobbling, depart one by one. Rock ushers out the anonymous cereal killer and sits down. Wow, I think, that guy's gonna *swing* for this one!

Rock assures me that the SMACK mothers everywhere take home will be less potent – but nonetheless addictive. He's wangled his sample from an early, rather brutal prototype batch as a special treat. 'What makes other slimes green with envy?' he asks and, with a flourish, pretends to bless SMACK. I am still reeling from the implications of a fight to the finish with SKULL. After meeting Silence and Peerless at the summit the last thing I want is to play quarterback for the coach. But I have to play quarterback for the coach . . . Rock pinches my cheek hard and exclaims 'It even wipes out pimples you don't have. The verdict is coming this July. Just *do* it. But . . . do it *right.*' So I am the chosen one. All I need is a plank, a school of sharks and a blindfold and my day will be made . . .

Rock thrusts my damp hand into his pocket. I feel a slip of paper and withdraw it. It is a cheque, made out to yours truly, five figures long, none under five. As an incentive, it gets full marks. The longer I stare at those odd and even numbers, the easier it all gets. (If you haven't already thought 'Sucker!' then get thinking.)

I have a flash of misgiving, and stuff the cheque in my pants hastily, as if to hide it from myself. 'Offend a fellow human being? *Me?*' Rock looks horrified. 'Few things in life are designed as well as SMACK,' he continues, deadly serious, 'Play billionaire! Break away from the pack!' He thumbs out towards the drones beyond his door. 'The all-stars salute the rookie of the year!' He salutes, brightening up. I cringe, going hot and cold, happy and sad. 'No guts, no glory,' Rock goes on, warming to the subject. 'Run! Meet the greatest challenge of all! *Yourself!* Be all you can be!' He flicks a SMACK over to me. 'These curds are worth a billion.' And then, with reverence, he picks up the piece of SMACK, throws it up and catches it in his mouth, swallowing hard: 'Pure taste, pure pleasure!' His voice levels off and I know it is time to make like a banana. As I get up to leave, Rock swears me to secrecy, shoves some SMACK in my pockets and gives me a pally push out the door.

Hank and Hell beadily observe me stumble out, their bloodshot eyeballs flashing 'jealousy' like little lighthouses. Exe, however, looks at me only with pity. 'The only breakdown you'll get this year,' he sighs, apparently about to embrace me. I shrink back, spit by his foot and go to work. What does that nattering nabob of negativism know for Christ's everlovin' sake? He wouldn't know seersucker from cocksucker, while I – the teacher's pet, arched and starched, groomed for success – am astride the best-kept secret time-bomb in the industry – no, in *two* industries – a billion creamy clams to boot! Exe exhales and I want to belt the bastard. The nerve!

Ha, what do you know, I gloated. If they could see me now, oh, if they could see me now! I hummed to myself, never realising that if *they* could see me now they'd laugh their goddam guts out.

# 12

## How To Play

The abortive summit and SMACK ganged up on me and I was in imminent danger of becoming my own worst enemy. Nowhere did my instability have a worse effect than on my precarious relationship with Elaine. What had begun as your average, sordid affair was developing into an emotional safety net for her that had me twanging like a trampoline. Her heart was in the right place, and so was everything else, but for the first time she was starting to get on top of me in ways I didn't like.

Rock breathing down my neck was putting out the fire under my collar and Ben was sniffing around. Hell had pulled me up and asked, 'Should you still bring home the bacon after he called you a fat pig?' 'Prissy con whines over messy prison,' I'd cockily retorted at the time, but the more I ruminated on this gauche omen the less appetising my unjust desert looked. Problem was: how to deal Elaine out without her whole house of cards collapsing on her? I decided to give myself more rope: I'd always wanted to try bondage.

The next time we met I tried dropping some heavy hints, but they bounced off harmlessly. She wasn't ready for the traitor's kiss and I rued giving it. 'My married beau is running around,' she told me with disgust as I was about to pop the answer. I started uncontrollably, sensing her next mental step. Now she had a revenge motive and I was the murder weapon. Neither of us had forseen the possibility of Ben rebelling and getting a piece of the action for himself. 'Love *is* blind,' I groaned, hiding my discomfiture as best I could. I couldn't dump the poor girl *now*. She didn't only need me more; she needed him less. I was on the horns of a million-dollar dilemma.

'Snail's pace gets faster,' I said, almost to myself.

'Snuggle babies,' Elaine said and began to curl up to me. I couldn't drop an anvil on her! I held her close, wishing I could dematerialise. I was still there a second later when desire replaced caution.

We woke up later than planned but, for the first time, Elaine didn't care. This worried me. I put on a brave two-face and we did it all over again, but my heart and other organs weren't in it and Elaine drew away unhappily from me. 'Do you know this face,' she asked meekly, putting her beautiful beak about an inch from mine. I kissed her but the taste was sour. Time was Elaine'd cough and I'd catch a French kiss. Now all I got was a sting. She was trying to make up for my distance by burrowing up under the covers. There was nowhere for me to go. I drank a cola and petted her, keeping conversation minimal. 'Mystery illness baffles doctors,' Elaine mournfully toyed, trying to fathom my mood. I smiled, stiffly, and drank some more.

Time flew but I couldn't keep up. I'd never told her I loved her. I didn't have to. I *didn't* love her. I didn't even love *me*.

I stepped outside and felt the hot breath of about a thousand cars down my grimy neck. On the corner some guy was standing alone, looking to his left and not saying anything. He walked up to me and shook my hand.

'You got the news?'

'Yeah, why?', I enquired brusquely, not yet certain what exactly was being done to me.

''Cause I got the headline,' he replied and scrutinised my socks.

I demurred and, eyeing his hose right back, recognised with ill-concealed aversion the interlocked S insignia of the ruthless SKULL campaign death squad, or 'Fast Copy Department' as they were affectionately known at headquarters.

I kept my cool, aware that the least indication of perspiration, increased heartbeat or higher blood pressure would be instantly detected by the Micro-Med Bio-Slicer this animal had gotten with his diploma (I mean license to kill, deadheads). Somehow I had a hunch I'd met this sardine somewhere before, under less demanding circumstances. Before I'd had time to slow down my heartbeat sufficiently, my friend pulled out a crumpled paper sack from which protruded a gold double-barrel. Uh-oh, so soon, I thought, jumping over a mental fence like the proverbial bozo sheep when the curtains are calling. I didn't want to seem standoffish, but . . . My last meal passed before my eyes, perfect in every detail except that my flight of fantasy was a lot better cooked.

As I was pondering an epitaph, Mr Friendly quietly popped the big question: 'How would you like to wake up Sunday morning with three hundred thousand dollars?'

'Grunt' is what I really said but it came out as 'Pardon?' as I rejoiced in the reprieve.

'You heard me!'

I did, but pretended I didn't and then realised I was now being propositioned. Slimesworth pulled out a bottle of A1 Scotch from his shiny briefcase, the kind that strips paint off the inside of your stomach when you've swallowed your peeling pride again.

'Can I afford it?' I asked, playing for time and hiding my antipathy for alcohol.

'Of course you can afford it,' he rejoined humourlessly. 'Think of all the money you've spent drinking ordinary scotch.' He paused, then demanded, 'What's a new idea worth?' as he thrust the unwelcome inducement into my limp hand. 'Three hundred K,' I choked, gulping audibly and accidentally blowing my nose in the process. Part of Mars stuck to James Bonded's wolverine trenchcoat like peanut butter on your shoe.

'Sorry.'

'It's only snot, brother. If you want something tasty, hit this baby.' He handed me back the bottle, wiping my mistake on the lip meaningfully. 'The streaming miseries of hayfever,' he smirked.

Yeah, I drank it . . . Let's put it this way, I wanted to live. No reason, see, I'm just like that. The slug just about knocked my intestines through my skin but I held steady, giving ol' playboy puss a winning grimace to show my sincerest depreciation. His power-high revolted me, but his dress sense turned my head – just like the blonde watching us from the opposite corner who kept on mouthing 'No drink can beat it, milk is supreme,' and winking lasciviously, stroking her creamy calf with a copy of *Cosmo*.

'Five minutes that last all morning,' my bartender commented, then chuckled like a real asshole, full of that macho jocularity one experiences when sitting in a car in a car-wash and there's soap on the windshield and you're so bored you tell each other about the last time you scored. By now I was too diverted by Betty Boop's ministrations to pay attention, which annoyed the caveman with breath to match and he stuck the bottle back in my hand.

'No messing around, now,' he said in warning, and I began to wonder where all this outdoor nitpicnicking was going.

'Cut-price chic,' I muttered, glancing at the dame, scarcely a riposte but the best I could do drunk and in fear of my life ending a good forty years early.

'It's fun being a millionaire,' he said opaquely, passing me the stupid bottle back. I grabbed it like the last ticket out of town before they dropped the Big One. Wow, the Fourth of July played in technicolour in the sky as I teetered helplessly under the influence of some exquisite extra-alcoholic ingredient he must've added while I watched the bimbo. 'Internationally acknowledged to be the finest scotch in the world.' He was trying to mislead my frazzled reality control. 'You can take it straight or with a little plain water but do remember that you're tasting no ordinary scotch.' I was by now fully aware that the scotch was about as ordinary as the president passing me in a public urinal. 'Once Arnie brings out the Bacardi half-time can last for hours!' What a hell of a host! Between scanning the traffic for hit-and-runners, scanning

116

the milk-maid for floats and scanning 'Arnie' for fleas I was being brazenly poisoned with something that made Thunderbird just a car again. Seeing double now, counting windows in a skyscraper opposite, I began free-associating, entirely forgetting that my life hung in the balance.

'Arnie, I didn't sacrifice flavour for low tar,' I began, swaying violently into a lamp-post and back. 'The strongest links are forged in gold.'

'The best and newest product ideas from around the world,' I smiled, waving a Necrotrivia business card in his face and coughing drily, not surprisingly considering my throat was now the texture of a Rose Bowl playing field the day after.

'Now! A unique chance to pay more for your next holiday abroad!' Arnie exclaimed, sensing himself surrendering the initiative to my moronic banter. I was interested at that. My last vacation had consisted of sleeping in front of a TV. 'Make the most of this once-in-a-lifetime bonus. Be light years ahead!'

'I already am,' I gloated. 'I'm so human I'm not.'

'What's a new idea worth?' he asked, pressing on me with his obnoxious aura.

'Three hundred thousand,' I replied quickly, now enjoying my last standing. A policeman approached with the look in his blood-shot eyes of the proverbial prick about to.

'I think we understand each other,' Arnie said hastily, sauntering off, but not before casually dropping a dog-eared business card at my feet. I picked it up: 'Nelson Nurse Enterprises. Leaders sing in the rain. Call anytime 234–7766.' They don't come more succinct than that, do they?

The next day I was in the office and recounted my tale of woe. Bikinidold and Barb agreed I'd been the subject of a none-too-subtle come-on-cum-threat; defect or die. But I was alive, and I felt a foolish loyalty to Necrotrivia, Rock and all the people it stood on and walked all over. SKULL could cry wolf at me but I hadn't yet been bitten and, until something or someone tore a chunk out of my physique I was going to stay put. Necrotrivia had taken me in when no one else wanted to know me, they'd fed and clothed and watered me, trained and indoctrinated me, exploited and corrupted me – in a word, made me human. I owed them something. What? Don't ask me, I just work here.

Back at my desk, I picked up the paper and flipped through to a featurette describing a scam whereby our research team had attempted, through a national campaign conducted from a room six floors above, to fob off nuclear test fallout radiation from a recent accidental blast as a new rustproofing technique. 'The acceptable face of technology' ran the byline. Below it was a photo, plain as day, of a car that some gullible sucker had driven into the test zone to save himself a bundle. The car was rustproofed all right, it was a lump of molten steel, plastic and iron about two cubic inches in size.

'Horsepower in a bottle,' commented Exe when I showed it to him. He made a few laconic remarks more and returned to toiling on his current assignment – the creation of flexi-disc campaigns for presidential candidates. Let me make one thing perfectly clear: so few people were actually getting up and going to rallies and meetings and speeches that most candidates had just offed the idea of personal appearances out of frustration. Now Exe was going to pioneer the mail-out campaign comprising a list of 'promises', one three-minute flexi-CD of the candidates' best sound bites, an autographed photo and a free competition for the kids. Market research and NOPs had backed the feasibility of the idea and already Rock had two teams developing software for an on-line election using voters' PCs. This would make voting easier than ordering by catalogue and have the added advantage of freeing party conventions to be completely in thrall to showbusiness interests.

Rock was excited by this prospect and had been to Washington twice to hold top-level talks with various campaign advisers, promoters and lobbyists. You could always tell when he'd had a good trip because he'd be high as a kite on the snow that fell out of the diplomatic bags. He'd parade around balancing a blade and straw on a mirror holding a minor mountain of uncut coke and spiel about 'democracy', picking up a felt-tip to scrawl 'Buy the People' on the walls. Then, ploughing the pile of pure Peruvian with his

118

flared nostrils he'd inhale deeply and, clenching his benumbed molars, slur out: 'Cut out the middleman, become an importer!' A framed picture of the putrescent head of state under his arm, he'd salute his little toy flag and, clicking his worn heels, declare: 'Great things happen when legends come together.'

The latest trip Rock had made to the Capitol had turned up some disquieting rumours about SKULL's parallel SMACK endeavours. 'Merc work!' Rock whispered to me, showing me photographic evidence that SKULL were recruiting killers to mow down our lawn party. Sandy Silence had seen a succession of top survivalists at their hide-outs across the South and come back with a shortlist of hired hands. We didn't know how seriously to take the threat but Rock made provision for all the company insurance policies to name him as beneficiary. He promised solemnly to cut in the aggrieved families, should there by any, but I couldn't really imagine this sultan of sleaze playing Aladdin to a load of wailing widows. To Rock a trust fund meant money no one else can get. It's the thought that, uh..*counts*. He already had more than half his employees' spouses and their children over five stuffing envelopes or transporting over state lines weekends. But for Rock, when opportunity knocks you grab both wrists, 'cuff them and put the chain on the door.

I was, in the midst of this pestilence, stringing together ideas to scotch SKULL's toadies in their web-footed tracks and close the SMACK deal. For the first time since I'd been of Necrotrivia Rock was showing me deference, his natural malignity shelved by his outsize greed. When I got overtired around two or three a.m. he'd gently press pills into my palm – 'New pep, new power!' – and tiptoe back to his office to watch the talk shows. I felt special, I guess, in the way a rabbit feels special when it senses a bird of prey circling high above it. Rock was intent on winning and his expectation of my work was an anvil on my noggin. Hopefully the weight would squeeze the winning combination out of my embattled brain. That was the theory.

Rock insisted that nothing be looked at in depth until I was sure it was ready so I beavered diligently, keeping to myself as much as possible. Hell goaded me once in a while – I think he was hoping I'd blow the campaign and then just blow. His status as teacher's pet was under serious threat and he resorted to juvenile tactics to distract me, break my concentration and bedevil my best efforts. I ignored him the way you ignore a mosquito in your ear. He'd stride over with some tabloid or other, sticking in my face a story 'of interest.' 'Martians found to have credit cards.'

He'd rib me – 'Are you embarrassed by bad credit?' – when I seemed to be getting too much done or he'd watch me, innocently, beaming some 'telecult' rays he'd learned from one of those assinine handbooks he sent for all the time. He'd sit by me and describe how he had to take his girlfriend to an Adult Children of Alcoholics meeting, what was said, who'd been naughty. I came out of charac- ter once and 'accidentally' dropped a huge paperweight on his toes, shaking my head at his transient agony, saying jovially, 'Lucky your toes were separated!' as he massaged the bloodied pinkie through his plaid sock. A few days later he was back on form. Murder was too good for Hell; I lived in the hope that maybe some day he'd look in the mirror and have a heart attack.

One morning I was sitting placidly amidst my office equipment when in stumbled an underling from the second floor huffing and puffing through his big snout and skidding around in his Hush Puppies like an ice skater in deep puddles. Barely able to bother effectively, I fell forward in my seat for the sake of it and pulled up at eye-level to the ungracious slob, our eyes meeting, mine bloodless and white, his red and sore.

'Taking a break? Making a stopover?,' I asked with that custom- ary NT air of malevolent toleration.

'Hummina, hummina, hummina, ahem . . .'

'What the hell are you stuttering about, lardo, what the fuck do you *want?*'

'Well . . .'

His voice dissipated and I became cognisant of a new angle on this cretin: maybe he wasn't merely defective, maybe he was actually in possession of something so hot it was burning his lining and fusing out his free speech. The hair on the back of my neck stood up and saluted the idea.

'An exclusive offer that's music to the world's ears?,' I japed, intending to prompt some intelligible reply. I waited and watched. The little man flinched. No matter what he had to say it was bound to be a humdinger!

'Reports just in . . .' He paused, the gravity of his transmission draining him. 'You know, Bolt's junior has been shot and killed by two guys wearing . . . trenchcoats . . .'

'Trenchcoats . . .' I repeated to myself disconsolately. 'Trenchcoats.'

So, it was tooth and claw now, bodies in bedlam, have gat will travel. What were we to expect now, those of us high enough to feel the first shockwaves? What was Rock going to do? The answer was all too clear: Rock would demand vengeance and see it delivered even if he had to blow his whole wad on a private army. Thoughts swirled around my mind like bats at breeding time.

The messenger was cowering, gripping a gooseneck and bulging out his eyes most distastefully. 'You may go,' I announced curtly. He wobbled off the floor, a wreck of half a man. It left me alone with the possible consequences, most significant of which were the likely turns Rock might take now that he had proof that what the rest of us were willing to dismiss as quaint one-upmanship was in fact murder. Frankly, I considered flying the coop then and there, even picked a place to hide out and a new identity and bank and minor surgery shortlist and . . . Ah, hell, I didn't really want to go. Besides, Rock's offensive could turn on us in no time if we made tracks. I, for one, was unwilling to be the stand-in Trotsky of the lot and get a big fat pickaxe in the pituitary. So I twiddled my thumbs, and tried to feel thrilled by all the chaos I was about to partake of. It was fair rules of play. After all, Rock had made me what I was, including pretty loaded, and at heart I knew I was an inseparable fleck in the NT ectoplasm now. My blinkered devotion was a kind of madness, a driven, insensate urge to be part of the motherlode of crap, nestled safely in the confines of the machine's arms, the everlovin' machine. I sat up and recalled those days not so long ago when I'd wondered where I'd be in a year. I was there now. In the same way that a kitten goes limp when lifted by its mother, I relaxed.

The proofs of my first SMACK effort were in front of me but I wasn't especially interested. An extraordinary poise overtook me and I sat there comfortably for a quarter of an hour, neither asleep nor awake, but cool and steady, a regular human animal at rest. I lucidly appreciated why I loved NT so damn much: I didn't have to play fair or anything resembling fair and it was that perversity about the place and its evil function I adored. No one watched you because everyone was so rotten that the only point in catching you would be so you could civilly compare notes. I was part of an elite of garbagemen of means, crass exploiters. I could hear Rock chewing out someone: a leak had sprung that divulged Rock's plot to frame Dales Jr and Silence for picking up nuns. 'Get a first class return!' You could hear Rock's fist impacting against his prey. I stretched, smiled to myself and went back to work.


I got in next day to find Hank prodding a frog in a shoebox and feeling his pockets. Out came a lighter. Patiently he lit the frog up, cursing as it skittered to a corner. I thought the situation needed some firecrackers and, intending heavy sarcasm, said so.

'Yeah!' Hank enthused. 'Blow up the frog, the little green froggy! Hey, if I give you five bucks will you get me one of those, um, rocket ones? We can launch it clear into Marketing or the cafeteria!'

Face it: when you're at the exploding-frog stage a friendly handshake is not going to deter you. Hank was perfectly normal in every way, but his mind had all the charm of hyenas tap-dancing through a remake of *Anchors Aweigh*.

I went to my desk.

'Compelling proof that people are destructive by nature?'

I cringed noticeably, at least I hoped so. Barb was leaning on my desk rumbling like some godawful tram in need of repairs. 'Caring can involve control,' she purred, drily, like sandpaper against arbrite. I guess it was an off day – I didn't insult her. She sensed my indifference and joined Hank at the frog-baiting finals.

Hank had found a roman candle somewhere, God knows how; when insanity is second nature I guess conjuring can't be far off. 'Hard skin needn't give you a rough time,' he commented, revelling in his co-worker's surfacing sadism. The lid went down tight, they stood back as if Cape Canaveral had just materialised during countdown. A pathetic 'ribbit' and muted explosion followed immediately, the smell of singed saltpeter seeped out and roused us from our caffeinated stupours as both box and carcass caught light and began to burn threateningly. Hank stood up and, chivalrously mind, *pissed* on it. If I hadn't already seen everything I'd say I'd seen everything then. Honestly, pissing on a flaming frog: you tell me???

The long, long trail to SMACK wound ahead so I blocked out the cretinous carousing of my 'peers' and steamrolled on. I had to find something to explode inside the consumer. SMACK wasn't just a narcotic breakfast cereal: it was intended as a thrice-daily ritual, the secret recipe so subtle and superior to your average crackhouse buzz that nobody, but *nobody*, would ever discover they were having a chaw of chemical imbalance.

I entered the dark night of the hard-sell, that spiritual ordeal necessary to purify one's self before producing the goods. The frog-detonators split, their bent energy dissipated, and I was left alone, one overhead gooseneck lighting my path. I felt like a pilgrim, blank billboard waiting for the fickle finger of fate to etch in my inspiration. Hours loitered. Reiner sent up some twenty-four-hour-devour and I chewed on autopilot. Coffee gave me that odd, muscular symptom of mental exhaustion, an odious warmth just below the skin that seemed to move with pernicious sloth about the dermatological undergrowth. I felt like a bottom feeder trying to suck up sensation as dawn broke on me like a raw egg. My finger-drumming became fierce, bush telegraph kettle drums, portentous and booming. My back became numb. I used to have feet, too.

About eleven Laurieanne came in and found me asleep. She shook me awake as Rock was just about to come in and would have kicked my ass air express to another floor. With drained batteries I propped my blob against the chair and then, like a vast coin dropping in a roadhouse juke, three ideas presented themselves: clickclickclick. Well, this simplifies things, I thought, as the ideas crowded down my arms and through my hands onto the paper, escaping finally as three brief slogans.

At that momentous point, verging on discorporation, Rock strode by and, pausing for an instant behind my bowed head, applied force to a pressure point so jerking my block upright. 'To be used for moral purposes only,' he snickered derisively, then went into his windowless shoebox. Laurieanne walked up, massaged my neck so I could move my head around again and, pointing to the already closed door, nodded sympathetically. I lumped my sheets into my portfolio and braced myself. Omaha Beachead flitted through my barnacle-encrusted mind, still smarting and aching from the night's functional phantasia. The door got closer . . .

Rock was seated at his desk, looking, as usual, like a stoned Buddha after a really bitching bender. Lost weekend in Lhasa, etc.

I took my place before him, portfolio tucked conspicuously under my arm, damp from the pit, pregnant with possibilities. Rock, sliding almost imperceptibly into the half-slouch, half-turn position he favoured, glowered at me, expectant. No words were exchanged for some time, it might have been an epoch, I'm not sure. I scratched or shuffled or coughed politely, hoping to trigger the inevitable adjudication. Rock, ever the game sport-fisher, trolled me in with assiduous care. Stalling and stifling yawns or, alternately, dozing in place, he waited for my resolve to disintegrate and, knowing I knew he was watching me through his lids, opened both eyes.

'When art works you don't have to,' he began. 'For years we've been turning American dreams into reality.'

He reached out for my life's work and I was jolted, but only

124

under the skin. While every corpuscle in my bloodstream boiled over, the surface remained relatively still. My weeks of labour were now on the chopping block, to be shredded or exalted, loved or hated. Laugh if you will (and you will), but I wanted to *please* Rock.

He casually rifled the shiny, bound pages, leaving greasy printmarks on the precious presentation. I felt like a clock that was unwinding but, by concentrating on Rock concentrating, I managed to fend off a molecular meltdown. Up'n'atom!

The folio was shut soundlessly and laid at rest like a flier's coffin buffered by breezes on the deck of a Pacific aircraft carrier's flightdeck, draped in flags, wreaths and handwritten commemoratives. Rock stood up as straight as he got, his face contorting, wrinkling awkwardly into a genuine smile. He offered his little hand and, like a granny praising the handicraft of a beloved grandchild, said: 'Satisfaction is your right! The look of a winner!' Then, as relief raked the hot coals of my combusted constitution, he began to chortle. Only digging a trench in my insoles with all ten toes prevented me fainting. Yes, I said he *chortled*. A sort of lead-popcorn-bouncing-on-a-waterbed sound, round and bubbly and . . . wonderful.

He recited my slogans reverently: '*The lower it goes, the higher you get!; You've got to get into it to get out of it!; One bowlful and you're hooked!*' Then he bellowed, air rushing from his lungs like birds fleeing a sonic boom. Again and again he hollered the sacred trio of tacky plugs I'd dreamed up to hard-sell SMACK. I giggled self-consciously.

Then, so help me god, he started to dance! He kicked his chair out, beat it about behind his desk, friskily doing a terribly bad two-step with his antique coatrack. Well, I didn't know what to do! Rock, *happy*? Sure, I'd seen him give an impression of happiness a few times, but this was unnerving in its authenticity. I just sat there, a fixed grin pasted on, fingering the beloved folio, pleased as punch and ready to run like hell at the first opportunity.

Alas, no. Rock set to celebrating, of all things. He ordered two house special greasewheels from Enrico's – 'You ring, we bring! –

and practically gargled the toppings and crust in his glee. I, for my part, consumed no less than sixteen chocolate bars, blood sugar ebbing and flowing, a riptide of depressed lows and hysterical highs carrying me aloft. I was deposited across the chair, intoxicated, as Rock daintily tacked my work on the walls and stood back to regard it with paternal pride.

A day to remember, indeed! I just wish that I could.

Remember it, that is.

My SMACK triumph had me high on life and I'd thrown caution to the wind. A candlelit meal for two at a suave niterie miles from NT, Ben, Hell, SMACK, Rock and all the other gremlins that tailed me was the order of the day.

Elaine looked wonderful in a dogstooth suit and not-too-high heels, with matching handbag and headscarf. If I didn't already know how ravishing she was undressed I might have believed she couldn't get any better. I admired her and she played footsie like a teenager at the prom. It was a fleeting diversion from what we both realised was a doomed relationship. I'd actually explained it all to Elaine and she'd hated me for it but tonight, we'd agreed, would be free of fireworks.

The food was fine, the atmosphere peerless. Nothing of substance was said but we were close again, as close as we ever got, for a few hours. Later on, at the motel, our fourth, she was quieter than usual, and I stupidly took it at face value. Had I pulled off her face the gears moving inside could have taken my finger off. It started coming apart in the wee hours. We'd seen a late show, chatted amicably, done the dirty twice, and were straightening the bedclothes when Elaine looked up at me and said, 'I felt it was OK for me to cheat on him, but it sure as hell wasn't OK for him to cheat on me.' The words hung in the air and I didn't want to pick them out. But she was waiting.

'I jumped at the opportunity to help ease the pain . . . I just wish I could be a doctor,' I finally said, sitting down on the bed and dipping into a bag of chips. Elaine sat beside me, had a chip, and watched me, which bugged me a lot. Friendship is end-ship when the buzz becomes humdrum.

'Let me hand it to you, it was a touching wedding,' Elaine spat, and sashayed into the john, slamming the door. Everybody wants what they can't have? Why can't they learn to behave?

'Heads you lose, tails you lose,' Elaine was shouting behind the bathroom door and the sound of fingernails on glass woke me from my cathode-ray coma. 'King deserves to be crowned,' she yelled, and the mirror was no more. Well, there I was, in a motel room with a psycho on the warpath. I became philosophical, taking refuge in a feeling of superiority. When Elaine appeared she looked chastened but unbowed, and as she dressed she could have been a voodoo doll reanimated and heading out to pin a tail on a flunkey. I ignored her melodramatic outburst, letting the door slam again as she fled. I knew we'd make up – that was in the script, too. What I'd have given for an understudy . . .

# 13

## *A Double Date – With Death*

Sunrise must have been beautiful. Maybe some day I'll read about it and weep. Ol' doughboy didn't rise until the soaps were on. You probably think I'm a prime slime, but really I did my hours the same as anyone else. Rock was fond of saying, 'I call it a bad day if I don't make two hundred and fifty Gs before noon', but I called it bad if I made anything before noon – breakfast, appointments, you name it. On second thoughts, don't.

The clock-radio talked and sang to itself; I deep-sixed the DJ, some ingrate called 'Big Bobby': if they were talking about his brain then they were in 'Big' trouble. Besides, I had other fish to fry, and the way my head was feeling I'd have to use a light oil. The man with the moolah at SMACK still hadn't signed the deal, and knowing that SKULL Systems were at that very moment putting their best twistoes to hard labour on the same scam was giving me a bad case of the wee willie winkies.

I got in so late that Reiner, who I could swear spent 1944 in a black uniform somewhere near Berlin, nearly pissed himself when the buzzer sounded. 'Playing dead just isn't for dogs anymore,' I ribbed him, and he went rigid with disgust. If you couldn't pester a geriatric Nazi, what was the world coming to?

'Fatigue duty!' I snapped, and for a second the old codger looked about to inspect my boots. He caught himself just in time, no

128

doubt afraid that I might wave his forged papers in front of 'the authorities'. 'Victim of the secret sin?' I dropped that one like a feather from twenty thousand feet and you'd have thought Reiner was dragging a piano up an elevator shaft. He didn't sweat as much as liquify. I'd had enough fun, almost, so I goosestepped right on by, quick as you please, Reiner's troubled exhalations, a hair shy of heart trouble, cooling my neck.

The office was empty. I tried a few Matterhorn tricks to rev up the acoustics and found my grubby hole as I'd left it. Shame. The numerous folders stacked there seemed to shuffle themselves, could have been wearing slippers. Anyways, first things first, so I scooped up some freeze-dried coffee and swallowed it. Not something you'd see at the Ritz, but for a highly-paid rascal on top of the Vesuvius of the ad world, with responsibilities enough to break a bear's back, I felt justified in shaving my stomach lining.

Seated, I felt work might be imminent, got scared and bolted for the johns. 'Why are we giving away genuine leather handbags for only ten bucks?' I asked myself idly, thoughts orbiting relentlessly around NT's bland budget lines. I didn't have dick to do with squat at that dead end, but now and then I caught wind of some promotion and it'd stick in my head like gum under a bus seat.

I breezed out of there and walked straight into two of the ugliest pieces of human detritus it has ever been my displeasure and fearsome fate to encounter. They positively screamed SKULL and I knew that if I tried to run I'd have to get to like walking on stumps. No, these men were not for turning and I had no intention of trying.

I grinned at them. They didn't grin back. Well, so much for the dating game. 'Here's proof: bad guys do wear black,' I jested, feeling greener and goner than a trout at the end of two hooks. This is fucking great, thought I, trapped at midnight in the executive toilet with two SKULL agents to whom torture was a hobby and its accessories coffee table conversation pieces.

'It's risky to be frisky,' the short one – a shade over six feet, that is – said in a voice so cut and dried that you could have removed a bunion with it. He looked at me with distaste. Nothing surprising there, I cop to that, but if I was ugly as this drone's gaze made me out to be I'd be lucky to get the broom closet at the zoo.

'Birthday boy squashed by garage door,' the other mountain man said, but his lips seemed to go half-time to the sound. Most disconcerting, especially when I was wishing I'd put on an incontinence bag before I left the apartment. A pregnant pause ensued and, just as I felt about to go into labour, a hairy, wide hand landed on my comparatively quaint shoulder and applied the pressure one usually associates with bending pipes.

Nothing much happened for a few more minutes, as I recall. The louse on the left shoved a big pill in my kisser and pressed my adam's apple to see it went down fast. I thought of the 'birthday boy' – an NT agent who'd been mysteriously offed by his garage door on his way to a birthday party. All he ended up getting was one less arm, a written-off sunroof and a wife with a lot of insurance she ended up spending on pills as big as the one I knew was about to shut me down. I surveyed my towering friends – trenchcoats and brogues, black gloves and company ties, shoulder holsters and brass knuckles. I had a sinking feeling in my stomach. Does the name Titanic mean anything to you? I thought, 'Leisure hour USA,' just as every chemical messenger in my brain hit a brick wall. I think I smiled. About what I have no idea.

Whatever woke me up was wet and not a kiss, unless a lonely-heart haddock was giving me mouth-to-mouth resuscitation. Cool water dripped onto my nose, around my lips and then off my chin; a regular lesson in irrigation. Some seeped into my parched maw, reacting on my tongue like mercury, beading and rolling. I was sick. More sick than a three-day hangover and more hungover than I'd been in three days. If you'd put a mirror in front of me I could've broken it. Ugly – more so than usual, than ever. I've never been *GQ* material anyway, but you could invite me to meet your folks now and all I'd see would be a doormat and even that'd curl up at the edges.

Voices, icy snickers, erupted in my waxy ears like little volcanoes on a walking tour. I glimpsed the back of a clean-shaven neck, the jugular pulsing visibly under hot, unshaded lights, The cheap aluminium card table my cheek was sweating on rubbed me, while my drool pooled placidly beside a stubbled, bruised jowl. If I was dead, heaven owed me one; if I wasn't, I was disappointed as hell.

Now I knew the score. I'd been set up like pins at a championship bowling tournament. My lips had been polished by metal enough to make a pair of Baroque candlestick holders. Sheesh . . . I tasted my blood that had dried in a bilious dome. How I longed to sleep. No such luck: consciousness is not easy to shake when your life is about to hand in its resignation. I smelled the air furtively and got nothing back that I could use. For one deluded moment I believed I was in a hospital, but that was textbook wishful thinking – the operation I was recovering from had little to do with medicine and the nurses all had five o'clock shadows.

Funny, ain't it? I asked myself. I got no reply. I raised my head a full inch and let the throb subside to high tide off Malibu before venturing to open my eyes.

Across the table was a bottle, unlabelled, filled with green, thin liquid topped by a rubber stopper that had seen its share of needles. So had my arm, a pattern of pricks providing a superhighway to my system. I guessed that whoever had administered my injections knew I was awake. They talked lower and stopped altogether when I moaned from one ache or another. I nearly grinned when I imagined my life flashing before me: pan to closing credits ten seconds after opening credits. My life didn't even rate one long commercial. Obviously, someone agreed. A hairy palm pulled me up by some hair, before dropping my head on the tabletop. My chin registered a mild bounce that forced the sharper of my front teeth into my already swollen tongue. Oh dear, more blood . . .

'I'm the Torso-Killer.'

'And I'm the Dixieland Death Machine.'

Please to meet you, fellows. Stillness resumed as I heard heavy footfalls, doors open and shut. I took in a white room, empty but for my table and chair, windowless, rank from used air – underground. A two-way mirror across the opposite side of the room told me that I still had company, even if they *were* shy. I gazed at myself, like a sap at a screen-test does at a lens, aware that I alone had earned that starring role in this little home movie, even if the payoff was, to be kind, a stinker.

I smiled at them, Christ how I smiled! Right at those pigs. I kept on smiling, so hard that tiny flakes of dried blood dropped on to the table every new second. I heard loud voices through the wall.

'Learn the true stories behind twenty-eight of the most sensational murder cases ever!'

I kept right on smiling. In a way I hoped they were actually amused. I could hear laughter. Even a punching hosebag has a bit of Hollywood to spare. I sang a bit, knowing that I was deluded, deranged and deadly serious all at the same time. I relaxed and my head drooped like a burnt-out bulb at the end of a gooseneck. I exercised lamely, to take my mind off things. Escape didn't enter into it. When you're so badly off that just flexing your fingers is reassuring you somehow sense that an escape is out of the question. But I did think of my abduction. Over and over. I recalled it in some detail, savouring my idiocy. If you can't feel at home with your own imbecility, what can you do? This is a buy-one-get-two-free-country after all! I'd buy a hand grenade from a Girl Guide, I'm so dumb. Yeah: with the pin pulled out!

Time marched in chains and I was shackled so tight an ounce of plastic explosive wouldn't budge the links. I was upright on a folding chair, one of those cheap numbers with a plastic seat that, in my case, had stuffing jutting out a good half-dozen holes. Considering the fact that SKULL were netting eight digits they really skimped on office furniture! I stared up at the bulb dangling above me, it glowed and dazzled. A fly adhered to the surface of the socket, fried to a pleasing crisp. It was the first and last time I sympathised with the common house-fly. I felt adhered to a bulb myself . . . or a socket . . . I wish I could have said the same for

132

my tired eyes: They were wired in so tight I thought the capillaries in my pupils were about to split.

I needed to think. I thought of 'Escape From the Planet of the Apes', the last flick I'd seen. I felt for those poor apes . . . I picked my nose and all I got was blackened snot and a sore bridge. Feet shuffled somewhere. My shirtsleeves creased and uncreased. Time crawled on. I stroked my beard, pushing eagerly out through dry pores. Tweaking one minute bristle after the other, I batted my conclusions around and around like beachballs in a vast flat desert.

Noises sounded in the background like kittens walking on glass, but I was now largely oblivious. All I knew was that I wanted no more pain. If pain was on the menu then count me strictly out to lunch, like, cancel my reservation. It was that simple. I planned to knock myself out, should my bloody merrymaking hosts return, and tried a few tentative headbutts against the iron table trim. I shouldn't have worried about it so much . . . Where I was everything was done *for* you. Your car is here, sir. Now lie in front of it.

I looked up to see this bozo with eyeballs and hands big enough to palm Iowa without blinking and just about wet my boxers. I mean, really, what sort of creampuff was I? This guy wasn't homicidal but he'd just as soon waste you as let you into a parking space first. The hair hung lifelessly over his goo-goo eyes and his face, hell, I dunno, saying he looked good on it is like saying The Werewolf needed a shave.

It was about two seconds (long ones) before the needles were out like a tree stripping off on Boxing Day. Take down those lights, take down those lights, Homer, bad luck to leave the tree up, take down the tree, sweep up the needles.

Everything after that point is a memory.


I'm watching TV, from the *inside*, wired to eardrums and eyeballs for sound and vision, extra tubes strapped to my torso for that deep down effect, pummeling my blood. It feels warm, close little lines pulling into a picture, all information to drain your eyes, your temper and temperature and patience, pulp your braincells into cornflakes and pasta. I'm in New Guinea, I'm in Africa, I'm in a deadass watershed feeling so jaded and just waiting for the walls to bend into arcs and open me up – a red-carpet portal to the heavens so I can *be judged again* . . . Pigs are valuable, more to taste, I want pork till the cows come home, an acquired haste, no more time, crawl is on my goosepimples, scaling my ears and into the big dumb SNAP. I feel the full transmission in me: all information, all singing, all dancing.

Things take an aggressive turn as the SKULL baby varies the attack. He turns up the volume and gets a sound that kicks like a mule with all the finesse of a used-up hacksaw blade.

'Try a little aggression!'

He plugs up the walls with his shadow and big boots, the sort of guy who you let feel up your wife because you're worried you're next in line. *Creep*, as in *slug*. He puts on a glove, and then starts grinding his fists into my torso like I'm some big dough recipe he's kneading for a five-star bar mitzvah loaf. I've had more fun, like getting beaten up by six punks who collect switchblades for a hobby. I'm not going to pretend it doesn't hurt, that's like telling you that the Titanic bent its fender. Fuck it, friend, I'm hurting!

My ear for music stinks, but this is definitely white noise. A collage effect is employed to enforce a senseless barrage that is anarchic, barbaric. It puts shivers up your ass faster than a ritual ice bath. Cyclonic, maddened noise that goes nowhere *first*, each moment scant warning of the retribution to follow – Battlestar Galactica crucified by psychedelic bikers from hell. A mind-fry of nauseous guitar scratch and radio jamming. Hogtied tedium, dragged squealing into my future and hotwired to my head. The style is pure annihalation by acceleration, merrie melodies put through a six-speed ice-crusher and rinse cycle to drain off any humanity that slips through and spoils the idiotic din.

'Get your message across,' screams the friendly neighbourhood fascist next to me, watching me writhe with ill-disguised excitement. I think I see a stain in his crotch but it might just be my eyeballs puking. In any case, the term 'bowel movement' attains symphonic intensity. I am drawn and quartered like some Kraft cheese that got left out on the moon too long. A panorama of pestilent NT script juts into my mind, gouging my fear with 'We make it a tradition to be progressive' and 'Innovative thinking, capable technology' – like a warhead is capable.

By this time my whole body feels like running your hand along a clammy log. The other-wordly soundscape shifts like quicksand, sucking in perception and chewing on it like old tyres in a sharp-toothed compactor. All the time the henchmen are fingering consoles. Have you ever overextended your credit cards? Try overextending your sanity. The threshold of pain is nothing to the threshold of sane. They're coming to take me away . . . with a side order. Slice me, dice me, anyway you mice me! I lost all track of I'm.

The last day and night I am captive is indisputably the most extraordinary of them all. At dawn I am awakened by a dialogue run backwards, creating unease and foreboding, the noises resembling recordings purported to be the gabblings of ghosts. At intimidating volume, the churning undertow grinds time desolately forward, waving burning rags in both hands and nailing onto fiery crosses a plethora of contemporary vices and shames, projected inside my skull, reacting with chemicals injected the night before. A succinct parade of observations on the probable fate of the selfish world is related as ethereal voices wearily catalogue a bevy of stark visions. Portentous shibboleths meander darkly, time staggers, percussion and keyboards clash. Were I not of alien conditioning I would crack open like a nut.

One hour plus of this aural nightmare leaves my bones and blood placidly indifferent. Two shapely dames showing the polythene-sheath-cult-worship look administer a new kick, giving a deep and dreamless sleep of approximately six minutes duration. But what a six minutes! My stabilised consciousness nosedives as soon as I aawake, nerves a lump of molten Meccano settling in the fridge, I feel like I'm chewing hard on a bamboo curtain. Eggs beaten with razor blades are my eyes, heartbeat tilting like a crooked pinball machine, hitting high score repeatedly, imagination flooded with discord trifles and ulterior motif. I undulate in self-radiated heat and then, unexpectedly, regain reality control at a higher peg, clinging immoveably to thoughts and ideas via a short-circuit hypnosis common enough where I came from. I restrict my internal transmission to a narrower wavelength than *they* figure on my being able to beam and settle into the diffused antagonism you get for a mediocre movie. You don't necessarily like it, but you watch it anyhow.

I begin reflecting loosely, gingerly letting out some slack. Some substance in my treatment has unleashed powers I'd assumed dead for good. I start thinking about Rock – who else? – and wondering where he lives. In all the time I've spent at NT I've never asked him . . . I suppose he livees in the office, or some part of the building unknown to all but himself and Laurieanne. What use would Rock have for living quarters – he is the original Spartan – and besides, everything he wants comes *to* him: dope, food, people, things . . .

More and more thoughts force themselves into my mind until finally, it's wavering on the brink of chaos. I know, somehow, SKULL observers have me monitored, but these thoughts keep coming - no bone or fat now, just muscle with a jellyfish sting and the reflexes of a cat. A wealth of wacky recollections, of freakish and fanciful occurrences, swamp my beleaguered defences, precipitating a no-holds-barred self-indulgorama of marauding weirdness.

Once the sensorial barrage has lifted, with scant seconds allowed for me to experiment with what vestigial composure I have contrived to piece together, another sonic farce erupts, compulsively mechanical, constructed like a funhouse façade from behind which darts all manner of noise and nuance. This hallucenogenic pantomine integrates amusical sounds and tones into awkward, engagingly bizarre soundscapes, epitomised by a diving-bell resonance of the Hound of the Baskervilles practising coronet over a sci-fi fry-up. Get out your Star Trek models for this one, kiddies!

By now I am utterly, unequivocally lunched out. I am strapped in, stirruped and stoned again, relating to everything, holding to nil. Rainfalls of weed-infested nightmare effects break above me, like breaths from a congested chest, and I recognise the hugely amplified fallings and risings of my own barrel organs. I get the heeby-jeebies, feelings flowing queasily together. Bolting down impressions like pizza, regurgitating them as colourfully, my mind is a callous peeled off layer by layer.

Wallowing pig-happy in diverse forms, isolated and floating like a satisfied amoeba, a feeling of incidental intensity overcomes me. I am alone. They have left me to find my way home, a lonely ragamuffin toughin' it out. Once my mind has come back from the lost and found, no longer splintering and rasping, my internal steering goes back on automatic, albeit rudimentarily. My world turns like an old paddle-wheel: dripping, slapping, sending out pacific ripples. I am happy – damn happy – and blanker than bleached blond. I try to analyse the preceding hours, but rapidly lapse into analysing Elaine's body.

# 14

## *Berserk Bandits*

I was left standing on a streetcorner miles from my neighbourhood, faintly conscious of my identity, studying everything with an alarming, preternatural clarity. I knew only two things for certain: (1) I hadn't divulged anything significant. (2) The contents of my mind had been given a brainwash so thorough that it felt like an enema bag had been hooked up to each ear and attached to a motorised pump. Every sign card had been shuffled and reshuffled – even Cool Hand Luke couldn't have read my deck. It was, in essence, not an unpleasant sensation.

Passers-by touched me or I felt the minor eddies their movement created in space and it seemed to deduct from my aura piecemeal, intangibly. I felt the source of my soul was fading like blood in strong bleach, an outline of my being left in space, filled up with dead air filtered through from another place in time – one I could never inhabit although once I knew it all too well. Put it this way: I didn't know anything of what had happened except that it had; I didn't understand how I could feel so different and yet be visibly, biologically, fundamentally unchanged. I wanted to screen my brain like an aerial photograph and look for the direct hits, the defoliated folds, the empty, stagnant lakes. I was in deep but swimming in six inches of water.

I bore no grudge, felt no shame or defilement, wanted no

revenge. I wanted . . . to sleep and see television that wasn't an infrared, spectroscopic modular reconstitution of my own neurochemical processes. SKULL had a synopsis of my synapses, a record of my zip-cord, a file on every part of me. If a car had hit me I would just have affixed myself to the grille and crawled inside the engine, like a super-fly spread thin against warm metal. My state of mind was seeking autonomy like . . . Look, how many metaphors do you *need*? Just stamp me 'void' and leave me in a deadletter file.

All this lasted rough*ly* forty-five seconds.

At forty-six I woke up like a hot needle had been inserted swiftly into my third eye and with a rush over the grand rapids of Mind I saw the big 5W – who, what, where, when and why – of my predicament. Firstly, Rock was bound to do a Vesuvius, release his skullcap and let his greymatter flow like lava down to his scabby ankles. An athlete's hot-foot! That was one fungus I didn't want to catch . . . What really pissed the old goat off, and I was sure of it despite his vapid, thespian assurances to the ultra-contrary, was that we refused to take it all the way and die for him. No one had the wherewithal to actually resign in writing but, inexorably, as iron filings drawn to a bigger dragnet magnet, the team was being pulled elsewhere. I'd seen him, fuming like a meteor in Alka-Seltzer, picking apart a circuit board with his jewelled nail file, trying to get around the fact that, finally, the lid he sat on that kept the pressure-cooker intact and us prisoners was attaining a critical mass. The slaves were leaving the plantation and the master watched helplessly as they packed their pencil-boxes and pin-ups into portfolios stressed by too many crucial presentations, of which SMACK was the insufferable, implacable and cruellest golden calf. Now the golden calf was on the bar-b-q of our rebellion and sizzling up nice, our ritual sacrifice. Sure, I'd given Rock his dream campaign, I'd liked him liking it and he'd liked me almost like humans do, but his summit stupidity – goading Silence into all-out war – looked like deep-sixing the deal anyway. What was more, and he knew this and it was eating him, none of us – Bikinidold, Workman, Barb, not even Hell – felt much like feeding his furnace

139

any more. Too many corpses, too much sleepless scheming. Living on the edge is fine, you can do it for a long time, but one day your fingernails give out and all the branches on the way down are stunted and you know that there's no everlovin' trampoline at ground zero, just sucking mud enough to turn your intestines into a slot car track and your heart into a flattened salad tomato in less than the time it takes your eyes to blink twice. Half-way to the next blink and blam! Your whole life is a black hole with a 'Do Not Disturb' sign on it.

Yes, SKULL had just about juiced my fruit and I wanted the pips at least for a sovenir necklace of my existence.

In the time it took to think all this distended gibberish I had arrived home, in spite of myself. The answerphone and pager were both buzzing and blinking and having nine-volt orgasms so I let them climax. The room fell silent but I was deafened by the machinations of my own overwrought imagination. It wasn't fear exactly, just piledriving paranoia.

I thought of Elaine – what would she make of all this? I didn't really know what she knew about, or thought about Necrotrivia and SKULL. I'd rarely let slip anything concrete about my work, and SMACK was so top secret that a few times I forgot I knew about it myself. All our fights and fondling seemed equally appealing and appalling as I drifted downstream towards the confluence of fantasy and reality. She must be wondering where I'd gotten to. We'd had a tentative dinner date . . . And I'd ended up being eaten alive by proxy. I could hear her scolding me the last time I stood her up. 'Meet Satan face-to-face?' she asked, as soon as I mentioned Rock by way of an excuse. Not quite, I felt like saying, but instead found myself suddenly interested in the mole on her . . . Well, her mole.

Having exhausted Elaine as an object, I considered what Rock himself was up to. He must know I'd been carted off by SKULL; was he trying to find me? No, no, I doubted it. The only comfort I had was in the knowledge that we'd abducted a few SKULL boobies just before my own untimely disappearance. They'd been tied up in the basement for three days when last I'd been in.

Rock had had them picked up after setting up a fictitious luncheon across town – our lads were supposedly convention promoters. But they'd not coughed up any info worth writing home about. Our interrogators had spared no expense in trying to get the bums to crack, including Rock's 'Body One' method. This involved binding the subject to a waterbed, injecting him with an outrageous dose of Penthropaliminephocol 88 – a designer drug that completely numbs half your body and leaves the other half feeling like a peeled grape on the end of a lit blowtorch – then showing him snuff and splatter flicks around the clock in enhanced simulated quadrophonic sound, followed by salt baths and a chilli massage, all topped off by being hung upside down with a Walkman strapped to the head playing deafening cut-up MOR hits. It had been known to work, but these SKULL fellows were sturdy: after thirty-six hours upside down with only Wayne Newton, Perry Como and The Carpenters for company, all we got out of one hardnosed hack was, 'You lift my spirits!'

The more I thought about it, the better I realised that those SKULL guys and myself were in the same boat. I rolled on my side, picked at the striped upholstery, and asked myself; What's a nice guy like me doing on a planet like this?

I watched the news, full of the SMACK leaks and letdowns that jeopardised the whole project, and recalled Rock's confident assertion once that 'the news isn't really news at all'. Well, OK, but like the guy who boasts he'll never get cancer and then dies of it, once you're on the news, your outlook can vary. SMACK were pulling out the stops now, sensing Rock was sitting on a beaut of a campaign. They'd twisted every arm they held, stirring up a wave of righteous hatred of SMACK, donating enormous sums to every whiter-than-thou lobby in the country, hinting broadly that SMACK wasn't your average morning wake-up call, but more like a long-distance mainline from the scenic hilltop villages of old Siam.

SKULL, ever the sore losers, had decided that the only way to play dirty enough was to play clean and they had every stain devil and Bible-thumping ninny available demanding that SMACK get the thumbs down. Dales Jr, unexpectedly considering Rock was still the joint beneficiary of his merchandising empire, had thrown in his lot with SKULL, playing both sides of the street brilliantly. That burned Rock, too – the only mother in the world he thought was reliably dishonest had defected for who knows, thirty million pieces of silver maybe? When he heard Dales Jr declaiming against SMACK on the six o'clock crock, all the poor chump could summons up was a bit lip. Dales put the cherry on top by sending Rock a huge floral arrangement that read 'Don't hate me because I'm beautiful!' inlaid with poker chips and dime-store jewellery. The cheque for the first quarter of their merchandising was attached, too, with a note in italics reading: 'Need glasses?' Rock just sat there, deflowering the blooms with his penknife.

Meanwhile, SMACK was out in several test markets and selling unprecedented quantities. Dry, wet or damp those little cubes of cupidity were a certified hit, introducing a new generation to drug culture the nice way. 'See a one in a million event!' Rock said of the news report attesting to its ascendancy, taking some consolation from the product's impossible overnight pre-eminence. He knew he was an iota short of Shangri-la and it must have hurt worse than a stubbed Achilles heel. He'd shrug, knowing SMACK's days were already numbered one-to-ten by Dales Jr and Silence, and that in all likelihood he'd only see a percentage of the billion in crisp notes, if that. 'Tales of bitter people,' he'd say of SKULL, contemptuously, but looking and feeling like a man who's lost a winning lottery ticket in a launderette. In principle, technically that is, Rock had won . . . But at what price? After deducting the coupons he was left with a hollow victory.

Sandy Silence was back on the box, too. Rock had tried everything to off the consummate scumbag but his security was too watertight. The night the news had started with a picture of Silence's limo and the headline 'Hit By Plane' Rock had gotten excited alright, but prematurely so. A few minutes later, feeding his would-be assassin a plate of gall, Silence was telling the world: 'If you have questions here are the answers . . . When you're expecting to make a killing everything has to be perfect . . . Carelessness costs lives.' Rock's despair was so total that he hauled off and hit himself so hard he fractured his ribs. Laurieanne was jacking morphine into him until noon the next day. What a mess!

And so there I was in my La-Zee-Boy with the stringy arms and maladjusted footrest, chewing crap and wondering what was going to go on. An hour ago I'd been a nobody on a corner; now I was a somebody around the bend. Accelerate around curves? From where you're sitting I was a blurred blur, friend . . .


Elaine had made two cups of instant coffee, which we drank standing up in my kitchen. Against my better judgement our reconciliation had led us here, fresh from another motel. I wanted to appease Elaine, not let her down sleazily. What was the point in screwing her up; wasn't just screwing her enough? Chivalry's not well . . . but it's not dead.

It was early evening. Elaine rinsed the cups and put them on the draining board which had begun to rust due to my negligence. She slapped my wrist lightly. She ran her hand over my chin – she seemed to be hinting that I needed a shave. Looking at my reflection in the kitchen window, I found this to be true. There was blood on my shirt, and Elaine offered to wash it. I was being mothered. It was dumb, but after having my head used as a throw-cushion, I needed one small anchor to keep me grasping reality. Elaine obliged.

I watched her washing my shirt, rubbing the bloody goo marks out, humming to herself. I wanted someone to either wake me up or let me sleep forever. I went into the living room and, when she'd finished, she sat on the arm of my chair. This brought my face into close proximity with her breasts. She ran her fingers through my hair on the nape of my neck. 'Take me now, Jesus!' I felt like shouting.

'Portrait of a madman,' Elaine said as she held her compact up and I saw my bedraggled face. I laughed with her and tried to remember why I'd been in such a hurry to give her the bum's rush. Her bum deserved better.

'Wacky love life,' I said, mostly to satisfy her unspoken demand for a resumption of the truce in full.

She continued the up and down movement at the back of my head, her breathing forcing kittenish purrs from her flawless neck. She kissed me lightly on the forehead, and as she straightened, the point of one breast grazed my nose. I nuzzled it. Elaine fell into my lap with a delicious thud and started to unbutton my shirt. Then I realised I didn't have one on. Funny thing, though, I didn't ask her to stop . . .

Underwear may change. People don't. The day Rock formed the hit team I saw how deep the mineshaft I was digging in had gotten. His normally constrained psychotic paranoia was redoubled; not only his hands shook mornings – his whole body had the dts. I sized up the situation and decided to be agreeable. I didn't expect any sympathy, but after my ordeal I could do without a hammering from Rock. So I sat there and took it all the way, observing Hell and Bikinidold, men closer to rats than mice and who both smelled like bad cheese in a heatwave. We winced and evinced as a solitary organism, shuffling in a two-step that Astaire and Rogers would have been hard pressed to top. A poor man's Four Tops, we synchro-fidgeted folding and unfolding hands in perfect time, blinking to an unwritten schedule. Rock was placated by this blatant display of chickenshit subservience, scanning our lamebrains like a telepath tripping. He gave no sign of residual sanity these days, always remote and seething, and sure enough he launched straight into a die-a-tribe I'll be replaying upstairs for a long time.

'SKULL on twenty-four-hour call, they're ripping our creative department to pieces, killing *our boys*. OUR BOYS! We have guns, shit, enough guns, enough to start a fuckin' museum: have toys will travel! USE GUNS! KILL THE SCUMBAGS AND LET THE SANITATION BOYS BURY 'EM. Don't let them snuff us out like party candles. KILL THEM, you gotta KILL THEM . . .

I'M NOT GONNA SIT HERE AND FRY LIKE A FUCKIN'
FISH . . . KILL KILL KILL THEM!'

His voice fluctuated between a high-pitched screech and a throaty
baying as he distended his arms and wagged his tongue like a
speeded up film of a rehearsing clown.

'I don't think death is funny, ha ha ha, not mine anyhow. I
don't laugh at funerals!' he resumed in snapping, drooling gurgle,
'And I don't want another fuckin' black wreath. ONE'S PLENTY!
Take guns, get 'em downstairs. Carry as many pieces as your
trunks'll hold and KILL SKULL CRUSH SKULL . . . CONDUCT
BECOMING!' Rock yanked Goebbels off the wall and, after kissing it, spun it like a frisbee over our heads to shatter in a corner
of the ceiling. Fragments of glass filled our collars but no one
moved. Cringing in unison, Hell, Bikinidold and I regarded Rock
with incredulity. Nobody wanted blood on their handguns – good
old-fashioned mud, raked up and piled high, was enough. Rock
saw our reticence and, like a child batterer chastising a son, tore
into us with stinging, toothy epithets.

'YOU USELESS GARBAGE! LEARN THE WORKING
MECHANISM OF A FORTY-FIVE! I DON'T NEED FAIRIES
HERE! KILL OR BE . . . AN EYE FOR AN EYE . . . A
TOOTH FOR A TOOTH . . . a wreath for a goddamn wreath,
a fuckin' kick in the ribs for . . . and like that . . .' Rock tailspun
into a mammoth inhalation that left us windblown and oxygen-
poor. His tepid tremelo that made words wriggle like a corpse
eating slugs ended and I, for three, could feel a grip in my hand
connected to a barrel pointed at a SKULL copywriter.

Rock was becoming dejected, gnawing his bottom lip spasmodi-
cally, hoofing the waste paper basket and thereby spilling a bottle
full of stale urine across the sticky floor. While I watched Rock's
full-bodied piss soak into the cracks I speculated on exactly how
far his latest brain thunderstorm was going to blow me. All right,
we had to fight back, but why couldn't he just use the cops or
some hired guns, why lean on us flatfooted bozos? I'd seen it
coming, understanding how Rock's laissez-faire attitude to SKULL
had been eroded by the summit fiasco and now this sour grapes

campaign to sink SMACK before a buck changed hands. Rock's veneer of tolerance had been stripped away by what in normal men was called fear, but which in Rock went through an alchemical process that transmuted all emotions of vulnerability into pure venom. Either way, there was going to be plenty of ad men down the morgue by month's end and I hoped I wasn't going to be a slabmate. For some reason, the phrase 'lucky stiff' seemed decidedly unfunny for the first time.

Dawn broke around the usual time,
It's going to be a beautiful day.
I got out of bed, I felt dead,
I usually feel that way.

The redneck refrain slapped my attention upright until all the energy in my body was turning on one pop chorus like a spinning top with a bite taken out of it. Fourteen days and nights without sleep, but who's counting? The windows shut tight to keep out the rainless, cloudless, resolute sky. How is it that just when everything is figured out to the last minutiae the puzzle dissembles, more meaningless than ever. The doorbell went and I slugged it with an ashtray from fifteen feet. Finally I answered.

'Would you be interested in a set of encyclopaedias?' a painted collegiate piece of ass enquired solicitously, with enough suction to invert a straw.

'About as interested as you'd be in reading them to me non-stop on my lap, baby,' I retorted curtly. The ennui hung low in the air like stale cigarette smoke.

'May I come in?' she asked prettily, as if I'd just handed her the keys to the goddamn city.

Lost in a welter of cliché, I said, 'Sure, you can do whatever you like, as long as I can watch it for free.' I leered generously. Leering.

'Well, maybe I'll leave a brochure, then.' She backed off just enough to extend one arm and screw down a shiny booklet into my scaly palm. 'If you need further information, just call the number inside.'

I was about to make a play on words that would scare her off for good but instead smiled and said, 'If I needed any more info I'd reach into your head and fondle your folds, honey.' Politely I eased the door shut.

Turning on my heel, I returned to ogle the box, eyeing the door spitefully, daring life to come in and draw me out. So, is this loneliness, I wondered, not able to come to grips with something so fundamentally idiotic. The radio droned on:

Since my baby left me I don't get cooked for no more.
No, since she left me there ain't no decent food no mo'.
Reckon I's gwine t'steal me a pizza and eat it off the floor.
I get them blues in the mornin' tho' I wake up after noon.

I sort of leaned over from the neck and saw some dishes putrefying in the sink. I liked the thought of the stale food, the grease hardened with no dissolution in sight. Nope, it was *not* a day for dishwashing. Not given much to self-pity and disinclined to act or think, I resigned myself to remembering useless things. There's always plenty of useless junk to remember. People are so weird, I reflected, just the damndest blob of scum this side of a portable toilet on Mars. They're so fond of being shunted from one disappointment to the next. How often do you have to be rejected before it sticks? Still, the radio kept me company, serenading my mock-autumnal self-indulgence. Well, I could have done some homework, eased into a routine and hoped to sleep at nightfall. Who was I kidding? The bums were out to kill me! Pop my cork! Lay my rug! Insulate my attic! KILL *ME*!

Rock was well-lunched back at HQ, don't you know? No hope of deliverance there at all. The last time I saw the guy he was putting the wings back on to a fly, f'r Chrissakes, and that is serious for a man not unused to eating the things. Compared to him I was OK, really. Just about to be killed is better than about

147

to wake up from the sleep of the undead in time to have your head and hands fed into a shredder. Sure, the guy was a hateful little twisto . . . But if you listened to the sociologists he could still be rehabilitated into a regular guy providing he could be made to say I'm sorry enough to some palefaced understander of mankind. Haha, well, that bill would take some paying!

The phone rang just as I was imagining that no one remembered I existed.

'Come to the office. Boy's night out,' breathed Hell, with an obsessive urgency.

'Why *moi*?' I enquired.

'*Are* you coming in?' he asked testily. 'Well, are you?'

'Yes. I am . . . *not*.'

I went to get my coat.

# 15

## *Verdict In A Crystal Ball*

Workman had contrived to drag Rock from his downhill slalom, a just-like-old-times exercise, anything to boost the boss's crashing personal stock. So there was just me, Workman, Exe and two guys from graphics, Wally Hinkle and Bob Gruberman; they spent their days gift-wrapping an atrocious array of junky furniture and fittings. Hell, typically, had decided to work late to hoard Brownie points. We encamped, inevitably at Enrico's, an intimate niterie but for the fact that the express subway lines it was parallel to made it feel like an A-bomb was going off next door. Rock, patriarch incarnate, sat at one end of a long table, the rest of us strung out down both sides making talk so small you'd need a microscope to see the point of it.

Rock had offered to treat us to supper, which was fine, except that when the bill came he was bound to be in the john. Then he'd nab the receipt – he paid no taxes. To keep the peace we let ourselves be fleeced.

Orders were placed, cutlery fumbled and senselessly rearranged, legs crossed and uncrossed, jokes told and laughter extracted. That was about two minutes after we were seated. It wasn't that we had nothing in common. *Au contraire:* we had *too much,* so damn full of intersecting lines and interfacing facts that it was painful and redundant to revel in it all off hours. But Rock had to be placated.

The inconsequential MOR drifting from the ceiling intercepted our laboured repartee, submerging it in parts, accentuating it in others. We became animated involuntarily, ultimately entwined again in the gristle and fat of business.

While Rock looked on approvingly we parried and jockeyed, discussing (what else?) SMACK. Rumours about SKULL's progress on a killer campaign that would torpedo ours with one hand amputated were rife.

'The challenge of the century,' Workman sighed, pulling his mozarella off his slice like bubblegum. 'Makes it hard to get away from it all.'

'Using only these objects try and win the Nobel Prize for Physics,' Rock cajoled, taking pleasure in our discomfiture. 'The beauty is . . . it's beautiful,' he added, as if he were describing a Van Gogh canvas and not a product poised to make everyone under twelve a narcotics fiend.

'Try a little wishful drinking,' Workman said, proffering the vino with one hand and juggling yet another broad wedge of sculpted grease with the other.

Conversation turned, as it often did in these casual conflabs, to Hell. 'It's raining supermen,' Exe sneered with disgust, but you could almost see his blood go green in his veins as the envy drove his pressure up.

'Big enough to fill your shoes and your fantasies,' admonished Rock with measured disdain. Rock didn't like Exe and the feeling was mutual, cubed and quadrupled. But Exe was a real *drone*, conscientious and scared as hell of getting dumped. By now he was pretty sloshed, dangling his tie in the wine, doing finger painting on his pizza, generally disporting himself like the slob he was. Rock watched him out of a corner of his eye, indifferent. He might have been looking at an inefficient dairy cow.

'Do you dream?' a voice asked. It was Rock.

'Slip in your salary!' I rejoined, not missing a step, although I felt like I was tripping at the top of an escalator. He liked that. He left me alone some more. Conversation entombed my attention.

150

Then I heard the front door open, slam against the doorstop, the window smash, glass fall. I looked up.

Holy Roman Empire, Batman!!

What I report to you next was recorded from under the table. I couldn't see much because I had to shield my eyes. The couple across from us were trying to traverse a floor wet with spilt water and soggy with wilting flowers. Enrico was a-shrieko in the kitchen, plea-bargaining with the Gods not to level his hole-in-the-wall into a pinhole-in-the-wall. Workman, Exe and I were huddled together for moral support while Rock, ever the loner, had darted under his end and was swearing torrentially as the fragments of wood and glass tumbled by in a slipstream of gunfire and smoke. 'This is where the fun is,' shouted one of the submachine-gun-toting interlopers, perforating the menu. I looked at Exe. He looked back. We were looking! Gruberman was bleeding. Hinkle was crying. Rock was gnawing his chair-leg and slamming his fists into the floor in an impotent rage.

Time did elapse. I know because you can't just discharge thousands of Uzi rounds in a microsecond. I asked, just like I felt brave, 'The answer to all the world's problems?' but no one was buying. Meanwhile, Groberman was buying: *it*. He may not have been dead yet but he certainly wasn't alive in the normal sense. Two holes above his heart were red and he clutched them like winning lottery tickets. 'Gunfighter bites the dust and doesn't get up!' called out the guest gunmen in turn, laughing hysterically as they finally emptied the last of their ammo on a plaster bust of the Venus de Milo. Well, she didn't have *any* arms now. Gruberman was out for the count, on his way to the big pizzeria in the sky. We weren't phased, the guy was never the life of the party with breath in him, now he just seemed about right. But he was dead.

The noise subsided and Rock peeked out from under his chair about the same time as Enrico, wailing at various saints for a refund, came from the kitchen, ashen and all but dead himself. The couple crept out, holding onto each other. This was one romantic evening they wouldn't forget.

A card lay on the middle of our table. It read: 'Hey, Wake Up!'

and had the entwined double s of the SKULL logo monogrammed beneath the legend. Rock plucked it up and read it over and over. 'Crooks recycle highway aluminium,' he pondered, picking up a misshapen slug from the floor. 'Chicken loaded with gunpowder blows up chophouse,' he added, then leaned back against the nearest wall and began mumbling incoherently. Usually he mumbled coherently, so we were rather concerned. Exe dutifully called an ambulance for our late co-worker and we straggled out the door. SMACK was right across our mouth now. Tasted bad. Fat lips.

In the car, silence reigned. I didn't know what to say and even Rock, our fearless leader, was strangely mute. We dropped off Workman, Exe and Hinkle at their respective homes and continued on to the office. Rock wanted some company while he mulled over our next move.

Reiner let us in and tried not to flinch at our dishevelment. Dust and plaster was all over our clothes, I was bruised and Rock even dirtier than usual. He pressed the elevator button, and I know he was satisfied seeing us a little out of synch. I made a mental note to put the Third Reich rodent through the maze as soon as possible.

'Who will care for my child?' Rock chided himself as we both detoured to the little executive's room. 'Facing reality,' he said, and it must have been abhorrent to him. He'd have to bury Gruberman but, more importantly, bury the importance of it. We'd traded shots, figuratively, with SKULL for months now, but literal murder was another story and a hard one to hide. The last thing Rock wanted, still in with a chance of scoring a billion clams, was some hack uncovering the secret war.

We pushed the john door open, tired and fed-up. Just as we were both starting to piss we heard two cubicle doors open gently behind us. I flashed on the situation instantly, primed by our restaurant shooting gallery fun. We turned as a man and regarded two SKULL boobies, each armed with a magnum. They wore scarves over the lower part of their faces, Western style. They wore trench-coats, brogues, gloves – *very* stylish. Rock just looked at them. 'Quit while you are behind,' he said, icily.

'Where's Mummy?' said one of them, and snickered.

They lifted their barrels and I was trying to invent a rosary when they gestured for us to enter the cubicles. You could say I was flushed, but it might be a bit premature. We walked the plank into the claustrophobic rectangles and were induced to kneel down and stare into the bowl. 'Remember when the ocean was beautiful? We do?' said one of our new friends. We were crouched there for a few minutes, then they let us stand up. Nothing too unpleasant, although I've spent happier times. They didn't have to *say* anything: looking into a toilet bowl at close range does things to you.

Then the implausible happened. We walked out of the cubicles and who should be standing there but Reiner, bless him, with a big shooter pointing in their ugly faces. 'Be active in a passive way,' he commanded, summoning an authoritarian inflection defrosted from glory days of yore. The light was falling on his shoulders and a halo seemed about to break through like a rainbow after a storm. Rock gleamed with pride and vengeance and, wresting the gun from his underling, shoved it hard into one of the pig's snouts. 'Freak accident kills bad guy in a mock street shoot-up,' he hissed, referring no doubt to our recently deceased graphic artist. The SKULL twins stayed stock still, pouting and embarrassed. Reiner was eating it up; me, I was just watching. Rock probably wanted to kill them, in fact I know he did, but he wanted to keep the gunplay to a minimum, to buy himself a pardon. He must be a prime target – twice in one night, after all - and two senseless killings would come back to him like a boomerang.

'Am I in your way?' he mocked, rustling in their crotches with the gun, his finger sliding up and down the trigger excitedly. They stood their ground and waited. Rock asked Reiner to escort the SKULL men out and he did, holding the piece up to them as they moved ever so slowly down the corridors and into the elevator. We watched on the security system while Reiner poked and punched them out. A moment later he was at his station again, fondling their weapons, which Rock had awarded him for bravery.

Back in our slots, we moped around and tried to put two and two together, but after the night we'd just had we couldn't make them meet. 'Some are ground down by the nature of their employment. They're overworked to the point of exhaustion,' Rock said, in a rare moment of self-pity. Then he called a cab and left.

I went back to my desk and started looking over my work for the next day. The harder I looked the less there was to see. Already the first cracks were beginning to show, cracks that would shortly become chasms and canyons. And here I was feeling like the Coyote in the Roadrunner cartoons, a huge rock poised inches above my head.


A week after Rock's celebrated cameo, a nothing guy named Ernie Parks pulled up a chair to the desk once occupied by one Pandora Worlds, a temp recruited at short-tempered notice by Laurieanne when a girl Rock favoured for party-training turned out to be a wet security blanket. Worlds had gone back to the Kansas backwater that spurned her and Ernie Parks showed up with his own pencil set, a toothbrush and monogrammed towel. Parks had a centre parting gracing his unblemished pate and a nice line in mauve Nehru jackets he told us he got wholesale from an East Side ivory merchant. He wore owlish glasses and his thin, long ears couldn't help but be compared to Mr Spock's. A shapely schnozz offset his curly cupid's bow. Parks, in the immortal words of Bikinidold that first day, 'looked like a wooden workhorse.' How right he was. Bikinidold may have been as essentially repellent as most of the NT lifers but at least his IQ bettered his shoe size.

Parks fitted right in, by which I mean he was as out-of-place as the rest of us. Curiously he had no vices, bad habits or pernicious personal history. More curious still, Rock thought nothing of it; I did momentarily, but made no mental note. Unlike Bikinidold, the amateur private third-eye, who meticulously collated all our new workmate's attributes on his WPC, using a flexi-scrambler to frustrate any peeping toms or tomatoes. Days passed with Ernie making conversation and his agency fee and passes at a few of the girls.

One morning, though, Bikinidold collared me inconspicuously as I came out of the john and, leading to a concealed vantage point behind some boxes of stationery, had me watch Parks for a while. I swore softly at first, then louder, till Hank shushed me. Parks, Mr Nobody, was sure a somebody now, but he didn't know we knew why. He was tinkering with his teak ioniser but, after watching him a while, you noticed he was doing more than tinkering. Unless he was readying himself to audition for a part in 'Harvey', Parks was talking to somebody, very quietly and very carefully. When I whispered to Hank that I was impressed by his detection work, he just tapped his noggin, mouthing 'We never close,' and smiling self-satisfiedly. Hank produced a wrinkled news cutting next. It described how a carpool had been ambushed on the same morning Parks landed and it didn't take free lessons to make the crucial connection. What we were spying on was a *spy*! Hot damn!

I was ready to pounce but Bikinidold restrained my impulsive lust for vengeance. We returned to our places and winked at each other cheerily before attacking our work. But we both were thinking about how to rumble the rat as soon as possible. On a pre-arranged signal, just as Parks got up to go to the little boy's room, Hank calmly tailed him and I, understanding fully, stayed put. We went on like this for a few days. Hank would circumspectly pump the bum by the hand dryers and report to me every day at lunch. Parks was good, very good, but Hank managed to piece together a convincing profile of our undercover operative. Seems SKULL, not content with smearing SMACK and kidnapping me, had sent in Parks to find and filch my frankly incredibly ingenious campaign plans. As all the major components were safely in a vault miles from the office, we enjoyed virtual impunity as we investigated.

Three days of diligent observation later, Bikinidold, passing my desk, dropped a ball of paper on my blotter. Unrolled it simply said: 'Showdown at the KO corral.' I knew what to do. Parks was hard at 'work' on proofreading some minor copy. I ambled over, friendly-like, said, 'Thai break,' and handed him a jaunty joint. Parks' weakness, we had learned, was good grass. He appreciated the gesture but was spooked and, pocketing the doobie, merely nodded and then returned to his allotted task.

Parks left for the john shortly thereafter and one look at his

155

rheumy eyes as he resumed work indicated he was now totally vulnerable. Glazed and dazed, he skittered from one job to the next. Hank nodded at me and we both wandered over to his desk, unfriendly-like. Hank, intoning clearly, said 'Tough street talking,' and then politely asked Parks, whose hackles were raised but slightly inhibited by his mental muzz, to join us by the water cooler for a 'chat'. Parks couldn't escape and we savoured the turning of our worm as he attempted to slur his way out of the inevitable. Eventually, through a combination of coercion and double entendre, he was wheedled into position.

By the cooler we told Parks we were onto his game and that, ultimately, he had to lose. He was petrified, literally – I thought we'd need a blowtorch to loosen his joints. But when Hank yanked him to the window and asked him to think about skydiving, he suddenly sprang to life, thrashing like a chicken six inches from the axe. Pitiful, just pitiful, but I have to admit I enjoyed it. What I couldn't have predicted was a homicidal streak in Hank, who I'd taken to be mean but not *that* mean. I was planning on scaring Ernie into submission and then cutting him loose to squawk to his superiors back at SKULL. But, oh no, Hank was out for blood and wouldn't take slow for an answer. Before I could say or do a thing, Ernie Parks was halfway out the window and trying to black out. Hank was laughing maniacally, naming off the NT guys pushing up daisies so far thanks to SKULL and poking Parks in the ribs with a long black stapler. I tried to pull him off, honest, but Hank was experiencing one of those peak moments of adrenalin one hears tell that mothers are infused by when their children's lives are endangered. Parks was exhausted now by his futile efforts and lay limply over the ledge like a rag doll left out in the rain. Hank was really giving him a hard time, slapping his face and shouting 'Tribal genocide claimed,' each time his victim peeped feebly, terror overwhelming him. Hank was into free-association, too, and the oddest stuff was coming out.

I thought better of hanging around for the finale despite Hank's invite, 'See the whole show from the best seats.' I left, but thoughtfully sent Reiner up for the fireworks, figuring it was the sort of thing he might get off on. How right I was!

According to Hell's eyewitness report, he'd just come back from lunch when Hank was on the verge of tossing Parks out. But Reiner wasn't satisfied playing passive onlooker and fielded numerous suggestions as to what could become of our pigeon. Others arrived, full stomachs somersaulting as they found yet one more extreme breached. The girls split, leaving Hell and Exe rooted to the spot as Reiner and Bikinidold manoeuvred Parks over to the roll-top that sat forlornly in one corner, relic of a bygone era. Reiner held down Parks while Hank bound and gagged him with yard upon yard of twine, his feeble grunts pathetically muffled by the swatch of correction ribbon crammed in his quaking maw. Incidentally, all through this quite surreal mayhem Rock was indoors and only once opened his door a crack, surveyed the chaos and said, 'The heavens dictate,' thereupon sneezing and farting as he tiptoed back to his monastic reverie within. Anyhow, no one even noticed Rock, which goes a long way to telling you just how inverted and insane life at NT had become.

Where was I? Oh, yeah, – I was at home. But Hell said that next Hank began reeling off some markedly heretical last rites concocted on the spur of the moment. Reiner, ecstatic, was dancing about in his surplus jodhpurs giving an impromptu display of call-and-response Nuremberg crowd-pleasers. In the midst of this was Laurieanne, reading a women's mag and crocheting a flowerpot, indifferent on her special chair. Parks was now being pushed to almost certain death on the roll-top. Hank and Reiner, shirtsleeves raised to reveal knotted, straining muscles, shoved the unwieldy antique across the floor with much disfiguring of the lino and deep pile.

Finally, the desk dropped anchor against the windowledge. Hank ran off at a gallop to enlist some boys from downstairs. They all returned a minute later and, as though raising a sunken wreck, managed to lift the desk and Parks up high enough to clear him for take-off. Floors below, between incinerator stacks and big garbage bins, was the chosen target area, entirely hidden from the street and soundproofed by discarded styrofoam and torn cushions.

The Yale rowing team couldn't have been more spirited and disciplined than those fellows in their moment of gory as they shouldered their flameless pyre skywards, and, with a profound composite 'Unmph!' slipped it over the edge. Hell described the resulting impact in terms too vivid to be quoted in full in a family novel such as this, but if I were to tell you that 'flat as a pancake', 'wood everywhere' and 'ricocheted off a bin before settling against an incinerator' were included you'll get the idea! Hank, in the aftermath of his orgasmic feat, collapsed in a corner while Reiner rubbed his hands in a workmanlike way and spryly returned to his station. Everyone else left or went back to work, too, forgetting the inhuman drama instantly. Hell revived Hank, stroking his arms, and carried him to the spare room where an army cot let nightshift addicts catch forty winks. Rock conveyed Hank a message via Laurieanne, written in his own childlike hand on a defaced 'Congratulations' card: 'See how he loved him!' it read.

The next day we sent a Tarzan-o-Gram to Silence: 'Skydiver disappears into thin air,' with a Polaroid of the remains and a piece of Parks' hair stapled to it. It was the only time I ever liked oneupmanship.

# 16

## *Big Misfire*

Laurieanne tapped my shoulder gently. Without thinking I went for my piece. If I'd been thinking I'd have gone for it sooner, that's how bad the waking nightmare had become. When I realised, sheepishly, that no big bad SKULL mug was going to use for me an ashtray, I reached over and touched Laurieanne back, just to let her know I knew. Knew what was another question. Knowledge may be power, but I felt terminally disconnected.

The inner sanctum stank worse than a gym. Rock was sweating so much that I wondered how he didn't look like a dried leaf. But there he was, eyes closed, hands folded, a corpse with mileage left. Exe and Hell looked at me; I looked back. Looked hard. Workman, as always now, wore a sad, little grin that seemed to say, 'Just let me know, is it over yet?' I looked back as though to say, also sadly, 'It isn't.'

Rock, who obviously wasn't long off a big crank, suddenly sat up violently and, his hands clasped so hard I honestly thought his knuckles would snap, began an extraordinarily jumbled monlogue.

'Whip, dribble, spin, rescue, duck, hurdle, bombard, screen, roll, dive, evade, pass attack, jump, swerve, sprint. Raid, dunk, hurl, loop, capture, lead, defend, stab. Shoot, invade, blast!' he howled, like a coyote with a stubbed paw. Jesus, the four of us just about fell over ourselves keeping our temperatures normal.

Laurieanne shrugged like a dismissive den mother.

But we were getting worried. Rock's bottoming out was going into double-overtime. To say the atmosphere was strained is like saying Good Friday in the Bunker could've been better. Rock sat down again, sprawled over a pizza box and some pens, and just made strange, gagging noises. If he was about to die I wasn't about to try and stop him, but I'd rather have heard about it second hand. But, no, the old trooper gradually regained his composure and, smiling at us as genuinely as his years as a hardcore huckster would permit, said, 'No more under-eye puffiness. Under-eye puffiness minimiser!' thereupon gesturing for each of us to hold out our hands and receive his chosen anointment: about six grams of uncut coke. What the hell do you do with a pile of loose coke? I put mine in a top pocket and grunted ambiguously. Hell scoffed the lot while Exe dropped a bit, apologised, and returned the balance to Rock's heap. Workman and Hell had already gone – you could almost hear them sharpening blades and shining up a mirror.

'He's been awake since birth,' whispered Exe.

'Introducing the new rascal,' grumbled Rock, marking the return to his pale features of his standard, miserable, intimidating demeanour.

I didn't know whether to leave, laugh or batten down the hatches and freeze until dismissed. No hint was forthcoming so I let go a modest, unpresupposing sort of chuckle.

Rock looked up with a savage, contemptuous storm gathering on the retinas and, in a clipped and gutteral fashion, said: 'Amazing worms are six-feet long.' Even by his exacting standards this was a pretty good put-down. I resumed my sombre vigil. Exe was breathing heavily.

'Are you the guy who didn't marry the boss's daughter?' Rock asked him. The poor slob just shook his head glumly, hands upturned in the sign of resignation characteristic of self-made losers everywhere. That seemed to placate Rock.

'This certainly can happen to you!' he said, brightly, and crushed an already dead fly. 'Learn karate – the deadly defence,' he advised further. 'Beat Bond at his own game.'

'Shock and surprise greets plans,' Exe croaked tentatively, and I blanched uncontrollably at his incalculable recklessness.

Rock twiddled his thumbs and, fondling a paperweight, smiled at Exe magnanimously. 'The time *has* come to defend yourself,' he said. Exe started wriggling.

'No.' Exe's stubborn syllable died in the air between him and Rock, shot down savagely by the latter's outraged expression. I'd never actually heard anyone say 'No' to Rock other than in a purely conversational manner. The novelty of the situation deflected any immediate appreciation of what risk Exe was taking.

Rock looked at me. 'This man went to hospital,' he said, pointing at Exe, who was clearly taking in the view from a private precipice. 'And this man,' he said, pointing at me, 'walked home.'

Exe was looking at me, now, but much as I would have liked to rescue him I couldn't bring myself to return his desperate stare. I've never been the sort of person to hang around the scene of an accident.

'Rape. Robbery. Murder!' Rock began anew. *'Defend yourself!'* A command.

'Enemies attack his style as based on constant swings of the axe,' Exe said to me. I nodded, much as one would to a lunatic on the subway, and folded my hands.

'Play Russian roulette with Igor the Bullet. It'll blow your mind,' Rock said, baiting Exe maliciously. 'SKULL: is its real motive . . . *money*?' Exe didn't answer. He said something under his breath. Rock asked him again.

'He was a good and trusted worker until something inside him seemed to snap . . .' Exe said, his voice distant.

'Read the fine print with magnifying reading glasses,' Rock said very slowly, in a way that you couldn't mistake as other than terribly threatening. He wasn't getting through. Exe had retreated into himself. Like, totally.

'Your big misfire,' Rock said. 'Our area has more maniacs than

161

any other. You need only one tool to reach them.' He threw Exe a derringer from out of his pants pocket.

Rock was telling us, in his own inimitable way, that it was every man for himself now. SKULL were loose in the neighbourhood and from here on in we had to fight our own private, dirty little wars, but still answer to Necrotrivia like lucky puppies on a short lead.

'Thanks to you my life's a wreck,' Exe exploded. I never suspected the guy had so much guts in him but, now that they were revealed, I knew Rock would want them for paté.

Standing up and glaring like an irradiated owl, Rock unhunched himself and belted Exe so hard that I thought for a minute I'd be carrying him out of there. Exe, curiously, didn't even move. He was unconscious so fast he just sort of eased back in his chair, exhaled once, and then, uh, *died*. Rock had obviously brained the guy! I sat there, dumbfounded and a little queasy, waiting for a signal.

'Boss gets brush-off and goes beserk,' Rock shrugged boyishly, as though he'd put a baseball through mean old Mr Smith's window. Yeesh, I thought, this man is *so* fucked up . . . *whew*! Well, I patted his arm agreeably and then got the fuck out of there like a lion with a thumbtack in its hind paw. Laurieanne, unphased, was on the blower to the mortuary. Rock would handle the cops, ha ha. As I closed the door behind me I distinctly heard him say, 'Dad cheats son out of thirty-five grand.' And then he kissed the stiff, by God, like a matron at her baby's funeral!

I walked back to my hole and seated myself limply on the dirty cushion. Workman, high as a rocket-fuelled kite after a few dozen toots, looked over out of curiosity, obviously innocent, as were the others toiling there, of the spontaneous homicide only feet from his desk.

I looked at him, speechless, and then, gathering my withered wits, said very softly, 'Jump start your ad career.'

He understood in an instant. He went back to work. So did I. What was I supposed to do, deliver a goddamn *eulogy*? Exe had finally earned his name. In spades. The way the rumours had it next day, though, it was more like a royal flush.

My salad days were getting limper by the minute, but I'd not lost my appetite for tomatoes. After our breaking up and subsequent making up, Elaine and I had drifted into a careless liaison.

Ben knew the score now, Hell had seen to that. The fact that it didn't matter any more was frankly depressing. There'd been no confrontations or recriminations, no knocks at the door, no abusive messages. Ben was glad to be rid of his runaround screw, now that he was cheating himself. Fortunately the office at large hadn't got wind of my covert operation, and Hell restricted his gloating to an occasional 'Crocodile in trial marriage' doodled on my blotter, already overpopulated by gargoyle caricatures of Rock and Laurieanne.

'Burns twice the calories of an exercise bicycle,' Elaine giggled in the wake of another bedspring-tester, 'as it firms and tones your entire body.' I giggled back emptily, wondering how much I could tell her without having to make an appointment to have my mouth widened to accommodate both feet. Elaine knew I'd been in some big trouble; I stopped short of supplying measurements.

'I battled sharks, raging storms, searing heat and thirst for eighteen brutal days,' I said humorously when Elaine politely pried into my obvious melancholy. Exe's demise had been a bitter kill to swallow and I felt that time was running out – with each swing of fate's pendulum I got a swift uppercut to the jaw. Habit of force, which NT ran on, was wearing me down. I was never Mr Nice Guy, of course, but even bad guys like to feel good. No, there was no way I could let Elaine in on my secrets. We went window-shopping at the mall, watching the mall rats scurrying for pop and popcorn.

'Time's up, chowhound!' Elaine laughed, dragging me off for a hot fudge sundae. The walk back to the motel was endless; I said nothing. Elaine felt duty bound to add a commentary on my misery, and that didn't help. She pointed to the full moon and the pinpricks of light surrounding it: 'Reach for the sky. Your lucky stars!' I made a wish. I wished some big bastard white dwarf would fall on me.

Entering the motel room, I went straight to the easy chair and pulled Elaine to me. Her plaid cardigan fell into my hands. I swung the light garment on my thumb, sending it off to land against the far wall. Elaine lay on my lap and I massaged her immaculate shoulders and back. 'Make anyone do anything you mentally command,' she panted, a rosy glow on her cheeks. We stayed that way for a long time, drinking in the dregs of our mutual intoxication. 'We did everything very quickly,' Elaine lamented with an air of finality, and I could see this was nearly the end of the road.

'What people are wearing,' I said in a scholarly fashion, running a finger under her brassiere strap. 'A closer look reveals who's lowest.' She laughed at that.

'Now is lowest,' she said, and straddled my legs, turning to kiss me, her torso a comely corkscrew, her libido about to pop its cork. She fixed me with a stare that dared me to say a word. I didn't say a word. My fingers did all the talking.


He had been holed up in his office for days, seeing no one. Take-out delivery boys went up and down the elevators like clockwork yo-yos, dumping pies. Every few hours Laurieanne got up and propped the carton in his doorway. The smell would perforce waft under the door and Rock would pick his nose enough to notice. Eventually a scabby hand slithered out and fingered the latest offering, easing open the lid at the threshold to satisfy itself that the contents weren't going to explode, then snatched the prized package and disappeared before any of a dozen onlookers could interfere. He wouldn't even creep away to throw up when, as often happened, an injection turned on him. Some promotion-hungry coolie had spirited a Jumbo's worth of airline sickbags off a business flight and presented them to our ailing boss as a gift. The guy never did get his promotion, but he sure got to carry lots of puke to the Gents.

Brooding with ominous concentration, Rock's festering soon had the whole floor eating downers like overprescribed housewives. Typists started hitting the keys with their noses after a cap or two.

Even I, having smugly deemed myself above the fracas, wound up more than once on the receiving end of a self-administered syringe, an eventuality that I would have abhorred only weeks before. The office was more tomblike than ever. At the speed we were living you had to hold a mirror up to your mouth to check you were alive.

Nothing would drag Rock out. A doctor went in on day four. I don't know what he gave the old salty hot dog but a few hours after his examination he trundled out fuller of beans than a Mexican with gas. 'Things aren't as bad as they look. No!' he exalted flatulently. 'Life is a contact sport. It's tough to feel rough but we'll give them a pain in the neck for Xmas.' You could have inflated an airship with the combined exhalation of relief in that room. Then Rock appeared in the doorway, paused to wipe some bilious drool from the corner of his sagging mouth, and smiled that wacky Death-to-the-Infidels smile he saved for the morale rallies. 'It's come to the crunchie. Let's open this one now: Mitchum was a hustler, Elvis was a bisexual, there are no more great men.' I was aghast, and judging by the score of open mouths around me, I wasn't alone.

Rock had never been this casual. He was either cracking up or he was so chock full of bonhomie that a truckload of killer ants couldn't put the bite on his gladhandling. It wasn't over yet: 'A lot of people have been using our name. Let them reap what they sow.' Well, Dales Jr would have enjoyed that one, but to see a man as suited to theology as Attila the Hun start talking in parables put goosebumps up my hoosegow. He paused, his eloquence deftly suspending our incredulity on a wafer-thin slice of awe. 'Yes we want blood. *Now!*' The tension swept back, freezing his foul features into a mask of sheer willpower broken only by the mucus precipitating steadily from his inflamed and flaring left nostril. 'Rag the bums!' This last edict he screamed as jaggedly as split crystal and harsher than a sportscaster with the grippe. Several of the more frail workers recoiled spinelessly at the generalised harangue, disoriented by Rock's timing and thespian ad libs. He had our trust and now he wanted to make it squirm like the disembowelled roach he would flick across his desktop when an odd mellowness overtook him at a briefing. Like his little insect friends, he had us all on pins, writhing to the occasion.

My dream lover was becoming a nightmare – even my customarily untroubled sleep pattern had fallen prey to subconscious subversions too hot to handle without tongs and an asbestos container. And those were the nice ones! I had one real duzy that decided me against pursuing my sprung chicken any further. This little chickenhawk wanted out, a grappling hook over the henhouse before some dumb cluck broke every tooth on his comb.

It went like this: I'm in my room, its numerous aesthetic defects grossly exaggerated. I've just attempted to lure out a rat by aiming toxic spray into his hole. I give up on this idea and then see a puddle of fresh urine flowing out from under a table and across the room, spreading along the worn, peeling painted edges of the wooden floor. Two small birds that have been nesting in the walls have broken through and are walking confusedly beneath the table. I open a window to let them out but I have to be careful since the windowpane is broken in several places, sharp edges exposed. I'm struggling to open the window when I look down and on the street Hell, Elaine and Rock have just gotten out of a cab. Hell is telling Elaine the cabbie has overcharged. I call to him and he and Rock acknowledge me cursorily. Elaine scowls up a moment later. The three of them come in and lie on my bed. Hell isn't in the room for some reason. Elaine immediately and quite maliciously begins to criticise some friends of hers I've never heard of. Rock is quiet but obviously enjoying it all. Elaine insults me for saying something in her absent friends' defence and then, her face wrenching into an expression of mock anguish, she asks me if I'll do her a favour: go away with her for a few years. All the while she is quite unreasonably hysterical, her face ugly and grotesque as she implores me. Finally she says, 'You can change in just a few hours, first we take your head and put it . . .' She is obviously referring to some drastic

166

form of reconditioning – mental and/or physical . . . I recoil across the bed and awaken.

And you think you got problems!

I came here with nothing except high hopes and low expectations. Now I've got no hopes and no expectations and I can't even leave. That was what was playing tag in my head, bumping against my cranium, reverberating and rolling. My life had compacted into one little ball of dirt so densely packed that if it exploded it could knock the planet out of its orbit no problem.

The morning's mail contained a letter, composed blackmail-style with flowers and fairies in the borders, that read 'Frightful friends. She'll live three months as a cavewoman. Join the hunt for America's most wanted.' The answerphone too was bumper-to-bumper with Elaine's shamelessly beseeching one-liners: 'Mystery illness forces soap star out of guiding light.' 'Burial expense.' 'I can help you get a yes when it counts!' I wasn't counting any more . . .

It was understood that our days of whine, neuroses and miscellaneous Kama Sutra contests were over. But she couldn't call it a night, much less a day. I finally returned her calls, said, 'Be a success with people just by knowing *when* to talk to them,' and closed off softly just as her voice sounded.

A bouquet of rotted rose stems arrived several hours later. 'Your daddy and mommy don't love you' was all the message card said. I folded it six times and burned it. Elaine didn't contact me again.

I saw her once more, though, from the backseat of a sluggish rush-hour cab navigating the downtown. Crossing the street with a few bags of designer sale items, Elaine was too busy dodging traffic and leers to notice a morose figure lying diagonally across the back seat of a passing cab, munching a candy bar and lazily trying to see up her dress.

# 17

## The End Is Here

I decided to check on Rock. Fact was, if he declined to keep fronting the circus and blew town overnight, we'd be picking up the pieces, and I didn't really want to be my own thousand-piece jigsaw.

Greeting me as I entered the lion's dump was a tableau destined to be indelibly etched on my neurons. Laurieanne had tied a big bib on Rock – I think it said something like 'Food: Overrated'. She was holding a small funnel, upended to Rock's open mouth. Pouring down the mis-shapen throat was a freshly liquidised portion of some hopped-up, highly concentrated health elixir. Rock had taken a sudden and surprising interest in his health when he happened on the notion that it might end soon, along with rest of his vital functions.

In the days that followed, he would surround me with his grimy, ectoplasmic aura and say 'Garlic beats arthritis!' or 'Flatten your stomach in four and a half minutes', producing the relevant product with a flourish. He spent a small fortune on toll-free calls culling the health racket warehouses of America for their tawdry wares. Three times a day now Laurieanne had to gorge the jerk with enough high octane nutrition to keep a decathalon team cooking till Doomsday. Interestingly enough, however, these attempts at immortality never made the blindest bit of difference, probably because Rock was simultaneously indulging in a parallel binge of drug abuse that easily eclipsed his previous, stupendous excesses.

Anyhow, there was Big Chief Vitamin-Breath guzzling the soda fountain of youth. I could have laughed – loudly – but I valued my furry tongue too much. Soon, Laurieanne detached the foul device and Rock looked at me with slight reproach, like a coach checking out an unrepentantly out-of-shape quarterback. He was about to spout some ludicrous platitude, for which I was braced psychologically for once, when the door opened a shade and a temp slipped nervously in with a brown-wrapper parcel.

Rock dug into the seal like a kid at Christmas, no doubt expecting a fresh stack of Danish filth. It wasn't until I heard his screech that my reverie derailed. What made Rock squawk was a photocopy of one of the fellows he'd sent off to avenge SKULL's incursion at Enrico's. It looked like – no, it definitely *was* like – those SKULL jokers had held this poor schmuck's head under the copier cover and put the squeeze on his noggin. As you flipped through the multiple copies you could see the guy's initial brave bemusement gradually metamorphose into horror and then sheer terror as two or three brawny terminators slowly crushed his skull on top of the blinking glass.

'When reproduction goes wrong . . .' Rock said, leafing through the grim evidence. For once he didn't know what to do. The instinct for revenge seemed temporarily suspended; instead of a hot wind there was only an eerie silence. He sighed, for him a very difficult concession, then meticulously stapled the pages together at the top left-hand corner and put them on top of his in-tray. He lit up a cigarette top-loaded with Produce of Columbia, the tell-tale fumes of flaming cocaine filling the office – just by incidental inhalation I felt myself becoming enervated and restless. Rock looked around his little box, the grey walls closer than ever, apparently nostalgic for something he'd foresworn. 'Close your eyes when you try this cigarette,' he said, handing me the rest of his escape hatch. I'd never seen Rock look tired before but suddenly bags under his eyes appeared that would cost you a small fortune to put on a plane. He sagged like a sodden J-Cloth. I'd been to

169

the marshmallow mountaintop with this ruthless tycoon and now, just as surely, I was in the venal valley, a mule and marching boots my only comforts.

The phone rang. Rock lifted off the receiver, stuck it in a bottom drawer and shut it. And I asked myself what could happen now.

Dumb question. 'Coming soon to an arm near you,' Rock said softly, 'just when you thought it was safe to roll up your sleeve . . .' He reached for his works, kept spotlessly clean and antiseptic in a locked, silver footlocker, the type used by small children to keep bubblegum cards and favourite socks or T-shirts. I got up and he didn't even notice, already measuring out a sizeable crank from the many vials at his disposal. The door closed behind me. I looked over at my spot, curious and cool, as if I'd seen it in a catalogue or museum. Everything seemed musty and stale, my workmates frozen in time. I had a minor headache, a sore leg and lower backache. I wanted to sleep. Workman looked over quizzically. I tried not to return his stare but, on impulse, decided to throw my Exacto at his head. He ducked, chuckled and went on tunnelling. I came up for air, closed a few deals on the blower and then left. The sky was deep blue and I felt drawn to it like rain to the sea. Oh well, I thought, it could be worse. But *how*?

Rock warned us a week or two beforehand that one fine day he'd spring a religious instruction on us. This was like Hitler telling the Poles to expect rain . . . Anyhow, sure as The Vatican is bulging with Dutch skin rags, one morning we were shepherded to the auditorium to see a corpulent preacher, straight off the six a.m. Sunday cable slot, holy-roll up and start bashing Bible and podium alike to stir our devotion. We were, as Rock realised, devoid of devotion, and I couldn't understand why the chief was wasting everyone's time with such crap. Maybe Dales Jr's canoodlings with SKULL had given him a chill; maybe he just liked to watch us yawn. Either way, Rock wasn't about to throw away years of sordid soul-sullying on one pop – the logical longshot. To him a chastity belt was hitting a hooker, and the only wafers that had passed his cracked lips had three shades of sugar sandwiched between them.

The preacher we were presented with was a great deceiver – obviously hooked up to a big tithe-in-the-sky tabloid scam – who looked like a vainglorious factory-farmed hog in a thousand-dollar black three-piece. The size of his nose gave his bourbon habit away as we sunken treasures sidled up to his I'm-OK-you're-not cant. Ten words strung together from this conniving granny-fleecer made you feel like flexing your fist on his Adam's apple, then giving it to Eve to make a pie.

Some cheapo churchy organ music faded ignominiously and Rock contritely took the podium, coughing as he explained how Rev. Gabe was a friend of his from 'back home' (wherever *that* was!) who had 'found God' – the way Rock said that you'd think God's own Gabe had picked up a hundred in the street. Rock continued to reel off some vaguely theological fluff, grasping for manger straws. 'No witchcraft, no amulet, no mere magic charm can compare to the power of Jesus,' he said, reading off notes on his cuffs, badly under-rehearsed.

Donning a velveteen cassock inlaid with gothic crosses, Rev. Gabe unrolled some scrolls that were projected behind him immediately: 'Love and Affection'; 'A Money Blessing'; 'A Divine Healing'; 'A Happy Family Life'; 'Protection From Evil'; 'Being a Winner in Life'. Rev. Gabe made obeisance to his sacred concepts and then, slowly turning towards his captives, began broadcasting *au naturel* in a redneck-dawn backwater brogue.

'We are living in a death culture. We're our own best sacrifices. But what does God think of it? What does God *do*?

'Does God wear a three-piece suit? Does God read the daily paper? Where does he eat when he goes out? People who don't like Necrotrivia tell you all the time how you're . . . well, *scum*. But what does *He* think of you and of Necrotrivia? And what do you hardboiled eggs tell your kith and kin when they ask you what in tarnation y'all do for an honest living? D'you say, Uh, baby, I'm . . . *scum*? Hell no! Y'all can't say *that*! You got to bring home ye olde bacon. Put food on the table regular and love your lady and little skedaddlers like Jesus Hisself. Je-sus loves you so why shouldn't we love 'em? Don't let big business put the bite on your big happiness.

'Well, here's what I reckon – and you know, I've been God's faithful servant for close on thirty years now and twenty-eight of those I waited and waited to even get one goddamned cable slot, not even prime time – I'd say to you with the Holy Spirit sitting in my heart like a cattle car full o' fresh sod, go forth and do unto your neighbours like they done to you. The old gold rule: love it, live it, give it. God knows we modern men suffer lots. Shee-*it*, didn't he let his own flesh and blood get hammered to a bit of wood just so's you, me'n the corner grocer'd get to Heaven in the express lane? Don't tell me that a God who'd do that to get your soul will shortchange you now on a love transaction.

'*No one* – not me, not you, not the Pope, the Rockefellers, not the President – knows the real score. Only God and Jesus alone know that score. Only they know why birds fly, fish fry, pigs sty – yuk-yuk – or a little child drops dead of starvation while you're cuttin' into one o' them big, juicy sirloins. Think of it – starvin' black babies in the tropical hell of a rainforest thousand of miles away eating their own diapers for food: shee-*it*, thin as chicken-wire – goddamned *Jee-suss* . . . AAAAWOARHGHH!'

He broke off, foaming at the mouth. Rock and Hell led him off, suppressing cynical smiles.


'A healthier way to sleep,' Laurieanne said, sleepy herself, taking in another tray of ground-up Sominex '2' to the boss. The blue powdery swirl was just one more ingestible escape route for our besieged leader.

Without Laurieanne I think Rock would have rolled over and dried up like a dead insect that week. I've not said much about Laurieanne because she was so much a function of Rock's life that she had little personal identity to spare. She was a slit-eyed, very thin and pallid girl, a lost soul chasing its ratty tail, hungry for

172

some good times baby. Unfortunately the only good times around Rock were the ones when he wasn't around. I don't think Laurie-anne loved Rock but she suffered from some tortured Catholic redemption-transference syndrome and had targeted Rock for saving. You tell *me*! In fact, she may once have planned on being a nun but, according to Bikinidold, who made it his moonlight to excavate the dirt on every piece of tail wagging in our section, they'd rejected her because of her track record – and, possibly more to the point, because of her track marks. Despite the fact that she looked like a beaten dog on its last hind leg there wasn't a red-blooded specimen in the section who didn't want a part interest in her most privates. But any temptation to trysting by nightlight was severely curtailed by the idea of Rock discovering you sleeping with her. Imagine a fold-up bed with a pickaxe handle sticking out one end and you've surmised our reasons for restraint.

The details of SKULL's masterful table-turning of the SMACK sitch were seeping out and I was party-pooper to a few juicy tidbits reported back by Bikinidold, who would be leaning against Rock's door with a glass six times a day while Laurieanne commiserated with her maudlin master. It seemed that it was the Dales-Silence part that really got to Rock. Although he had happily involved himself in Dales' merchandising it was only on the unwritten pro-viso that he need not sully his calloused meathooks with Godgrime. Then Dales had exploited Silence's desperation to sink SMACK if he couldn't take the billion-dollar payoff himself, and pulled off the coup that had set Rock on the rack – exporting the whole of his game to SKULL. Rock and Silence were supposed to have agreed to keep out of the God racket and Rock was outraged at being triple-crossed by his arch-nemesis. You had to admire the symmetry off it all – Silence had killed SMACK and used Rock's best account to do it.

Silence had embarked on imitating countless gurus-in-waiting before him by taking a cynical and puerile journey to the heart of panto profundity, stopping at consumerism, sham transcendental-ism and sundry other pilgrimage points along the Holy Billfold Path to Montezuma – and hitting Rock squarely below the Bible-

Belt in the process. For Silence it meant muddying the crystal waters of his Founding-Fathers-filled soul with a lot of oriental ballyhoo, but he had his priorities, too. Swarms of proto-priests, trained by Dales Jr, had toppled SMACK with a deft blow administered to the heart centre from the head centre via the shopping centre. Dales and Silence had found Rock's weak point: he was resolutely against devil-may-care worship.

Silence and fellow mendicant Peerless were now indulging in televised flights of theological delirium, a drama-class collage more than palatable to people raised on 'Peyton Place'. They peddled their freeze-dried platitudes so convincingly that I almost confessed over lunch watching their new weekly three-hour 'service'. Looking like Dalai Lama dress-up dollies included with a 3-D pop-up monastery, you could see them exhorting the plebs to dump cheques and valuables in the plastic begging bowls circulated around the chosen stadium. Their raps were hilarious, facile chants linked up with self-congratulatory positive-thinking slop distilled by Dales, full of insipid advice for those seeking self-realisation.

Then the icing: recordings made at Jonestown, Guyana, in simulated stereo no less, of a Dante's Inferno-a-go-go of lost souls in choral harmony, a gripping representation of true netherworld perversion. As an experiment in establishing a self-important society of deluded airheads I'd say it was a *bona fide* success, a brilliant promotional exercise in piercing pancultural plagiarism.

According to Hank, Rock nearly did a Sodom and Gomorrah as he watched videos of Dales' latest SKULL satellite crusade linkup, and sure enough after a lengthy session with the effervescent evangelicals Laurieanne would slope out like Olive Oil on the verge of a nerveless breakdown to fetch more drugs from the safe, the fridge, or wherever else Rock climbed to hide his stashes. Shit, I found enough Ecstasy to deliver Brooklyn floating in ziploc bags in the toilet tank one morning!

After one particularly repellent report from Hank I walked in on him to discuss the downers dazzling his bloodshot eyes and he just shot me a brief he'd had Exe draw up – his last assignment – on Crypto Peerless, the mysterious henchman Silence had kept by

174

his paediatrically straight side all his working life. After flicking through it – and confirming to myself that when it came to hooligans Peerless was in a class of his own – I handed it back to Rock. He threw the lot against the far wall and shouted: 'Apache! Here . . . There . . . Everywhere . . . The taste the world is turning to!' and lapsed into a catatonia only Laurieanne's medical stash-bag could counteract. I left respectfully, tapped *her* shoulder for a change where she sat by the door reading Harlequin Romances and knitting mags – she never did have her own place – and watched her trek the ten paces to his door. A daughter was never more devoted, a slave never more pussywhipped. If I'd wanted kids I might have adopted her . . . Ah, what the hell am I talking about..

Let me tell you about last Friday, the day it ended. I got there and nothing worked. The security didn't work. The escalator didn't work. The phone was disconnected, the lights out. I felt my life had been liquidated like so much old stock, cheap. Punked out, flunked out, funked out, junked out. Words failed me, but then so had most of my teachers. I thought I knew the score but really I didn't even know how to keep it.

The top of my desk was clear but I sat behind it, eating a prune Danish I'd picked up at the Juice. At street level, in the launderette across the road, an old Chicano woman paid to watch the rinse cycle over and over. She was either very lonely or she loved laundry, I never figured out which.

Secretaries were burning files, just to feel they were contributing to the Wellesian melodrama cooking on our rack like a cake that's just had the oven door slammed in its face. One girl was removing polish from her fingernails with the solemnity of a mortuary guide. My guts curdled, food boiling in acid that swam into my gullet and caused severe hiccups. I leafed through an old issue of *TIME*, finding an article on some guy who had brought a case against Necrotrivia for offing his son in a lab experiment. Of course he'd lost, and NT wouldn't even give him his son back. 'Suffering builds consumerism' was one of Rock's favorite aphorisms, and now the ethic was worming through him relentlessly. The customers would always keep coming, buy whatever they were meant to, but poor Rock couldn't see the humour or glory in it any more. He was in his office hammering nails into his palms, spurred on by a sense of self-persecution which demanded the highest sacrifices. Laurie-anne was running back and forth with J-Cloths, mopping up blood and generally tending to his delusions. Hell was at home: confidentially he'd told me he'd decided to defect and was taking treatments from a private plastic surgeon. He would have a whole new face in three days: it's an ill wind that blows no one good! Meanwhile Workman was living up to his name despite the fact that SKULL had his wife and child in the trunk of a vintage Buick suspended over the river, waiting for Rock to pay up. Not much to be added there! Bikinidold, oblivious for the most part, was reviewing old accounts and checking on NT stock abroad – the SMACK pap hadn't yet smeared much in the farflung corners of the empire and Hank felt duty bound to exercise some discreet damage control. Rock came out and, patting his shoulder, said 'Beauty comes from within.' So ludicrous it worked.

Barb was already packing for the coast where she'd been offered too much to model designer latex for the over-fifties. She came in for her last paycheque only to find Rock shredding it absentmindedly while listening to the golden oldies station, an expression of stricken nostalgia etched in his features as though a woodburning set had followed the lines in his face.

I started clearing out my drawers, wondering how it all went so bad so fast, feeling like some two-bit character in one of those interminable, awful pulps I sought on the shelves of the chintziest used book stores in my neighbourhood. I thought of one at length, a pathetic piece of collegiate trash that consisted almost solely of plays-on-words meant to savagely cannibalise contemporary culture . . . I don't know why, but it seemed uncomfortably familiar. Anyways, I piled up the throw-outs and dumped the keeps in my crummy briefcase with the broken lock and mock-alligator-hide finish. That damn briefcase and I had been through a lot together. Big fucking deal!

I was trying to chip my name off my plaque, just for something to do while my world fell apart, when Laurieanne, a grave look in her pretty sky-blues, implored me to see Rock. I had no excuse so I followed her sheepishly to the playpen and peeked in at a man no longer worthy of the term.

Rock looked up, through me, the laser-beam eyes cutting clean, revealing untold dimensions of mental unhealthiness. I seated myself unobtrusively, having to remove most of a pizza from one pant-leg before settling. I saw the bandages on Rock's hands and the bloodied nails and a pair of new pliers. He was calm, remote and resigned. A noise issued from his throat, a kind of time-lapse backward gargle filtered by black phlegm, and he pulled open the bottom drawer of his desk, grabbed a handful of stuff, and let it fall haphazardly onto the desktop.

It was two feet of occult/New Age mail-order detritus, postmarks recent!! Some packages were empty, some full, others in disarray. Like some po' white trash from 'gator country desperate to raise a car payment, he started running his hands through the paper, charms, plastic amulets, incense, crystals, stars, charts, crosses, spells, dolls, book, leaflets, posters and miscellaneous form letters requesting tithes, donations and cold hard cash. Worse, he then began stroking an amulet here, a charm there, chanting quietly. Had Dales Jr finally got to him? No, this was LCD trash, not Dales' glossy portfolio style. This *was* depressing, to see a once indomitable cynic, atheist and general crooked bastard reduced to the level of some lousy spiritualist's mark. I sat there, incredulous, as Rock sold me on the merits of each one. Waving about a little garish plastic cross with a 'mustard seed of faith' embedded within, Rock cooed and caterwauled about beating on SKULL with a psychic-stormtrooping offensive incorporating voodoo, witchcraft and creative visualisation. Gee, I didn't know what to do – should I draw the five of pentacles on my chest and start in with gospel? Should I fill a tub and walk across it? Should I just pooh-pooh the whole thing in case, please God, it was a gag?

Rock opened his mouth and about three seconds later the sound started trailing the motion of his parched, cracked lips. 'When you're not in love you're not alive. Silent law of God: time will not end until every human wish is fulfilled. Dream state . . . cold room . . . asleep . . . bodymind quiet . . . inspiration can come through because bodymind still . . .'

I was embarrassed for both of us. Like a man sleepwalking on a ledge, Rock started pacing, his pockets stuffed with conjurer's trinkets, his head moving turtle-like in and out of his black polo-neck which he had pulled up to his small ears. He turned to me, paused, then pointed to a stack of unopened metered mail and said: 'Since we've been offering the lowest rates in the business we've been getting lots of letters . . . If the television is a medium, ours is well done.'

It was all too creepy to be a well-rehearsed snow-job, unfortunately. I longed for Rock to hit, tweak, rebuke or scare me like he used to, not stalk around like a hopped-up maiden aunt at a séance. I sat on my hands until the heat became unbearable, then laid the reddened digits in my lap. I inspected my fingernails and knuckles, anything not to see Rock degrade himself.

I could hear people leaving for the night . . . Forever, I guess. I remained unmoved but Rock ran over and pressed his ear to the door, gritting his pointy teeth and pounding one foot against the book that he used as a doorstop when he still had a reason to open it. Fuck this, I thought. If Rome's burning, why do I have to be the damn fireman? I'm out of here, *now*!

But of course I wasn't. I watched and waited. Rock returned to his desk, leaned on it and lit up a big joint. He started laughing to himself – I thought he'd forgotten about me. I crept back to the door and, hands shaking, turned the knob like it was the tumbler at Fort Knox. Rock's giggles sounded like far-off mountain water on smooth pebbles. I opened the door.

Thwack! A leatherette-bound copy of *The Theory of Intellectual Violence* – Rock's own contribution to consumerist philosophy – rebounded off the doorframe just by my left eye. I turned, panicked but steady, to take him – *it* – all in. Rock was standing, legs astride, implacable, hateful, strong again for a moment. 'America: the paperback version,' he said in a flat, deep tone. I half-smiled, looked as casual as possible and split.

It was the last time I saw him.

I left the office and locked the back door behind me, throwing the key in the gutter. I went down the steps and left the building behind me, a huge mirrored reflection of a cloudless baby-blue skyscape. Mirthlessly preoccupied, I paused at the corner but didn't go back. It was finished. I had clothes on my back and cash enough in two accounts to waste money. I felt like a worm cut in half.

As I crossed the street I heard a scuffle by me and saw a punk mugging an old woman. I walked on. It was the way I felt.

# 18

## *Nice When It Stops*

I awoke at dawn. I don't usually. Usually I'm damn lucky to wake up period. My eyes were open but my brain wasn't, and I knew if I blinked my eyelids would stick together, little sandy tendrils entwining across the jungle floor of my corneas. I was dreaming around spasms of consciousness . . . dreaming of a dog floating downstream, its mottled coat worn away like an old rug, water flowing through the pale, discoloured torso and out the red stump that used to be a neck when it still had a mouth to go to. Four fleshy lumps served as reminders of limbs. No tail. I paused by the corpse, then got out a knife and fork and commenced eating. I was nauseous but compelled to bite the soggy, spongy meat, bitterly chewing twenty times. The dream was so vivid that I woke up dribbling from the corners of my tightly-closed mouth, white thick drops, rabid drops, foamy. You have a disease, something was trying to warn me. Pulling the covers up I felt my face, savouring the pockmarks. It gave me some comfort, but when I relaxed I tasted dogmeat again, smelled it, touched it. I was awake now. The sun, high in the window, burned with an oblivious intensity. No, strike that: it *was* intense, but I provided all the oblivion.

My mind began turning, stoked to red-hot coals of total consciousness. How much is that doggy-bag in the window? Put the sign in the window: CLOSED. I can't put the sign in the window, it's open, always infernally open. I grappled with my wakefulness, thoughts rampaging. It was tearing me, the dulling complexity of my plight. Yes, I'm rational! Yes, I'm irrational! UGH! Let's not glorify the absolute inanities of my existence, they're here for all to read . . . I mean, why doesn't somebody publish this exquisite swampland of reconnected logic and obscure messages. Stranglehold . . . All my strength is gone, the air is heavy and fragrant. I want to walk long tonight and see each star in the firmament blinking at me, some shooting, some falling, some dying. Brings out the romantic in me – if there is any, and I doubt it. Lying on the bed, my clothes rustled. Even they sensed that their wearer was not a normal human animal. What an unfortunate way to be carrying on.

I peeled the corner of the curtain back and fitted my mug into the gap, a mummy with the bandages off. I'd gone underground, which, since no one in their right mind would want to enter my flyblown keep, merely entailed changing locks and my number, growing a beard and getting my geeky provisions only at night. I was that scared of walking into another counter-espionage cowpat.

Occasionally the phone next door would ring and the nerves in my mouth would send pucker messages to my lips. Not a pretty sight, but I wasn't expecting Cosmo to surround the place and threaten me with Model of the Year, either.

As the days passed I started digging my urban hermit number. I'd never been a social animal, so now I could entirely subtract 'social', leave 'animal' and go nocturnal. Hell, I could piss in the sink and not even rinse it. My piss was answerable to no one and that, friends, is freedom.

The papers were full of the unholy trinity: SKULL, SMACK, Necrotrivia. Why's it always that those who are with syndication cast the first stones? It was a landslide now, the presses were burying SMACK – you couldn't even see the trees because they'd pulped all the wood.

The only NT castaway I'd run into since fleeing was Reiner. We collided at the corner deli. I was checking out the weekend specials and there he was, buying a boil-in-the-bag schnitzel! I was over-come by affliction! We exchanged greetings, asked each other how we were and what we were doing. I invented a story on the spot about my mother's illness and how I was waiting on her hand and foot. As for Reiner, he was investing his life savings in a small yacht and kitting her out to sail to Bolivia. Seeing him away from Necrotrivia was fun: we reminisced about the day Ernie Parks met his matchsticks, how Rock's feet smelled so bad at day's end that you literally had to have air freshener handy the second he was gone; Laurieanne, that thin waif of a mother-figure – where did she get those thigh-high boots?

We shook on old times and parted friends.

Our gab about Laurieanne made me think again about Elaine. What did she ever do to hurt me – that I didn't want her to do, I mean. She was like all of you inferior Earthbound specimens. And I was so mean to her . . . I was beginning to sound like a soap opera!

Rock! What a crazy, loveable heap of thick-sliced mortal hideousness. Rock: cantankerous, indulgent, primal, fecal, slimy, plastered, enraged, engorged, disengaged. A big soggy woollen glove of a man, hairy and itchy, the real superhuman fly. Rock may have taken a big pratfall but I knew he'd bounce back . . . and I was glad. His was never a mechanism lubricated by pity – for himself or anyone else. On the contrary, he was raw and strong, a T-bone walk-up with enough stairs to wear you out and leave you hanging. Rock: a succession of games, one rapidly dismantled to make way for the next. For now the candles were going out – pissed on in our time – but all he'd get in the end would be a slight burn to the fingertips, a puff of smoke, a nasty smell and some melted black wax.

I secretly hoped that Rock might try and contact me. What shape was the mad bastard in by now? It would be some weeks before I'd see a small box in the society pages of my daily announcing the engagement of Rock and Laurieanne, with a shoddily retouched photo that made them both look practically loveable. Win a cupie doll for guessing the identity of the 'best' man?!?

So now I know how the dust feels as it gets sucked up the vacuum cleaner! Whooosh! Meanwhile, countless light years away my mail remains unopened and it doesn't matter. My destination is again obscure, a blank cheque: these are withdrawal symptoms . . . ha ha ha. I'm just another great schlepp for humanoidkind.

Let's not kid each other: you've suffered this bilge in good faith. I'm an idea whose time has come and gone. One more cosmic anticlimax. The big hose sucks me in, brushes my hair. Why does the wild card always get played? Because the Big Player has them all marked. (I sound just like Dales Jr!) The world's a burn and I'm a cinder. I'm too *deep*. What was my percentage for a heap of fused days and nights? Pity the poor illegal immigrant!

To sleep, perchance to sleep in. I dream and dream. Every night Sad Sack goes AWOL.

Thank God for television! When the dreams get too scary I shove the antennae up my spinal column, adjust the vertical hold, and follow the bouncing ball that spells R-E-S-I-G-N-A-T-I-O-N. It's heartbreaking, breathtaking, utterly pathetic. Munching on an overripe taco chip and guzzling root beer I can begin to fathom the elephantine neuroticism of this Garden of Eden gone to seed.

Funny, but the desire to kill has disappeared. I used to be so keen on murder, too. Tupperware-party homicide could have been my forte. If I went home now I'd be considered handicapped. Not that everyone there murders each other, no, that's an Earthling thing - people here live until someone comes along and shoots them. The damage to my internals is irreversible anyway. I can't go home so I may as well go out and find the meanest junk food imaginable.

*The Theory of Intellectual Violence* – now that's a great bedtime read. I went out and bought a copy – don't ask me why. But there's some heavy-duty craziness on those pages. Try this . . .

*I woke up and it flashed in my mind, a big neon sign, and it says: 'Don't do something you won't regret.'*

*I tried to love mankind. Honest! I need to be loved like I need another hole in my dick. All the fairy tales are anathema to me, just rustling hulks. I'll never be one of those clods who kill themselves because they haven't any hope. What idiot has hope in a world like this?*

*I fear nothing: love, death, life. I stand by and steal money from a beggar's tin. The customer is always wrong. If you want free kicks, now you know where to begin.*

Rock: what a *way-out* guy!

# The Getting Started in Series